"I've waited a long time for you."

Amanda's mouth dropped open. "Why?"

"What kind of question is that?" Choice asked sharply.

"It's a perfectly logical question. Why have you waited for me?" His was the most startling confession she had ever heard. He had *waited* for her?

Choice slowly came closer, moving with that pantherlike grace she had always admired. When he stood before her, his hand rose to the back of her neck. Her system sparked from the prickles his touch evoked, and she saw the same feeling erupt in his gray eyes.

"Picking things apart makes little sense to me, Amanda. I'm not much of a talker," he muttered. "I'm more of a doer. Can you deal with a doer?" His dark gaze washed over her face. "Think about it."

Abruptly, he released her and swung away.

Dear Reader,

Hot off the presses, the February titles at Harlequin Historicals are full of adventure and romance.

Highland Heart by Ruth Langan, another title in her popular Highland Series, is the story of Jamie MacDonald, a continuing character in the author's tales of sixteenth-century Scotland. And from Donna Anders comes *Paradise Moon.* Hawaii during the turbulent days following the end of the monarchy is the setting for this fast-paced romance between star-crossed lovers.

For those of you who enjoyed Sally Cheney's first historical, *Game of Hearts,* don't miss her second. *Thief in the Night* is a humorous tale of a British detective and a pretty young housemaid who may or may not be a thief. The author's quick wit and delightful secondary characters make her a wonderful storyteller. And readers of Westerns should be sure to pick up a copy of Jackie Merritt's *Wyoming Territory.* This well-known writer's first historical is a sensual romance between two headstrong neighboring ranchers.

From your cherished favorites to our newest arrivals, take a look at what our writers have to offer you this month. We appreciate your support, and happy reading.

Sincerely,

The Editors

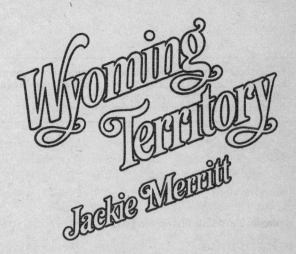

Wyoming Territory

Jackie Merritt

Harlequin Books

TORONTO • NEW YORK • LONDON
AMSTERDAM • PARIS • SYDNEY • HAMBURG
STOCKHOLM • ATHENS • TOKYO • MILAN
MADRID • WARSAW • BUDAPEST • AUCKLAND

Harlequin Historicals first edition February 1992

ISBN 0-373-28714-3

WYOMING TERRITORY

JACKIE MERRITT

was born in Michigan, but has lived in the western states for most of her life. Writing is a passion for Jackie, and she feels that stories set in Wyoming, Montana, Idaho and Nevada are especially appealing, due to the rich and exciting history of these states.

An early retirement from the accounting world gave Jackie a lot of free time, which she has enjoyably filled with writing. Always an avid reader, she now creates her own characters and romantic plots.

To my husband, Bill, my biggest fan,
whose encouragement and support never falter

Prologue

⟨ornament⟩

Choice Brenton rode his favorite horse, Bolo, from his place to the Spencers'. Brenton ranch land abutted Spencer ranch land, but the houses, barns and bunkhouses were miles apart. Choice was all slicked up. Beneath his best hat, his thick dark hair lay almost flat to his head in unaccustomed submission. His dark gray shirt was buttoned to the collar, where a narrow black string tie formed a knotted bow. His trousers were black and practically new, and his feet were shod in shiny black boots, a pair of handmade calfskins that hugged his feet like a soft, silk glove fit a lady's hand.

Even Bolo was brushed and gleaming, prancing in a spirited high step, as though he sensed his master's excitement.

Len Spencer had gotten married. Choice's good friend had found himself a bride, and Choice was on his way to meet the new missus. An invitation had been delivered to the Brenton ranch by one of the Spencer hands. *Come by for Sunday dinner and meet Amanda.*

Amanda. The name sounded special to Choice, maybe because he was so sure that Len's bride would be a special lady.

Len must have been keeping an eye out for him, Choice thought, seeing his friend come out of the house and wave at him from the front porch while he was still a quarter of a mile off. With a faint grin, Choice raised his arm and waved back.

A figure in blue came through the door…Len's new wife. She was no taller than Len's shoulder, slender, with rich, dark auburn hair.

As Bolo's steady gait quickly closed the gap, details became visible. Amanda's hair was loosely knotted at the top of her head, with a few straying wisps drifting around her face. Her full-skirted blue dress draped from a tiny waistline. Its fitted bodice was adorned with something white, probably lace.

The wide brim of his hat shaded Choice's eyes, and he used the concealment to study Len and his bride as he got closer. Len was grinning from ear to ear, and a soft smile played across Amanda's lips.

Len bounded off the porch and came out to meet him. "Glad you came."

"Glad you asked me." Choice dismounted and shook his friend's hand. "How'd you find someone dim-witted enough to marry you, Spencer?"

They laughed and slapped each other on the back. Amanda was waiting on the porch, and Len turned. "Amanda? Come and meet Choice."

The man in black gave Amanda a funny feeling. In spite of the blatantly masculine laugh he had just shared with Len, he appeared a disturbingly somber man.

He was wearing a gun belt low on his hips, a gleaming black leather belt with a holster containing a long pistol, a six-shooter, Amanda noted. Many men wore side arms— Len did at times—but she sensed that Choice Brenton was a little more dangerous than most men.

Choice watched her step off the porch, and an unexpected ripple of awareness traveled up his spine. It wasn't because of her pretty face and striking auburn hair. Lots of women had pretty faces and hair. Lots of women had softly curving bosoms and small waistlines, too.

But not too many women radiated what Amanda Spencer did—a pure and electric femaleness. Choice couldn't smile at her, although he tried. He took the hand she offered and looked into her beautiful green eyes, and all he could manage was a rather gruff, "Nice meeting you."

Amanda drew her hand back quickly. The handshake was like she had touched something hot, something better left alone. He had the most inscrutable eyes she had ever seen. She couldn't tell if he liked or despised her, found her pretty or plain.

She glanced at her sunny, sandy-haired husband. Len had pronounced Choice Brenton a longtime friend, and she wondered about friendship between two such opposite men.

Len's arm looped around her shoulders, and she smiled up at him while he proudly told Choice that she had been a schoolteacher.

Amanda wanted to elaborate. She hadn't been a legally qualified teacher, and she had attempted several times to explain the difference to Len. But it didn't seem to taint his pride in her, and she could see by Choice's disinterested expression that it would matter even less to him, so she said nothing.

They walked to the porch, where Len had placed chairs earlier, and sat down. Immediately, it seemed, the conversation turned to ranching.

Amanda listened because she was genuinely interested in her wonderful new home. She was happier than she'd ever been in her life. She loved her husband and the Spencer ranch and vowed with nearly every breath to be a good wife, to learn from Len, to be his helpmeet. The beauty of Wyoming and the valley in which the ranch resided warmed her heart. There were many people to meet, a small town to explore, customs and traditions and routines to uncover and absorb.

Perhaps the only disturbing factor in the wonder of her new life was Choice Brenton. Amanda's gaze moved to the man and lingered when she saw that he was intent on something Len was saying. Choice's pose was no less casual than anyone else's, yet beneath his loose slouch, he seemed coiled to spring.

She recalled the few facts Len had told her about his friend. Choice had worked as some sort of lawman for two or three years, which might explain that long gun on his thigh.

In truth, she had never met anyone like him, and Amanda inwardly admitted a strange fascination. He was startlingly handsome, with his heavy dark mustache and guarded gray eyes. There wasn't an ounce of fat on his sinewy body. He had long, slender fingers and feet, broad, angular shoulders, a hard, unyielding jawline, thick eyebrows and sun-weathered, dark skin.

Amanda shivered and forced herself to look elsewhere. She should not be staring, nor thinking about anything but the conversation.

But throughout the afternoon, Amanda found herself scrutinizing Choice Brenton. A couple of times he caught her, but when her blush passed, she did it again. She couldn't seem to extinguish her curiosity, although she repeatedly chided herself for too much boldness with Len's friend. She served a good dinner and was complimented by both men, but seldom did Choice address her with a direct remark.

That night, when the house was dark and she was lying beside her husband, Len yawned and commented on the pleasant day.

Amanda's eyes were wide open. "Does . . . Choice come over very often?"

"Choice? Nah, not much. He's got his ranch to run, same as me."

Len's reply was comforting, and Amanda closed her eyes. She couldn't visualize ever being close to Choice Brenton, and she didn't want to hurt Len's feelings by saying so.

Chapter One

1886

The wild grass, so lush and verdant during the springtime, had gradually browned and crisped throughout the unusually hot, dry summer. Overhead, the sky was cerulean, vivid, cloudless, as it had been for months. Dust rose from the old wagon trail as Amanda's horse's hooves struck the ground with a plodding rhythm. It was a Sunday afternoon in late August. The Spencer hands had left the ranch for the day, and Amanda had donned trousers, boots and floppy-brimmed hat for a ride.

The intermittent Sundays in which her hired hands were gone sometimes dragged for Amanda. She had puttered for a time today, then whistled Ginger from the pasture and saddled the pretty roan mare.

Amanda was riding without direction, haste or purpose, following a trail that branched to other trails. The Spencer ranch had numerous such wagon-rutted and hoof-worn paths cut through its grassland. Amanda knew where each one led, although it had taken her a while to learn the layout of the immense ranch. She was glad she had been so adamantly curious about every phase of the ranch's operation. If she had not been so questioning, the tragedy of sudden and premature widowhood would have been compounded by ignorance.

Amanda noticed everything as she rode past. There were occasional irregular, arid spots in the normally grass-covered landscape, thrusts of sage and Russian thistle, clumps of low, flat cactus, then, without warning, bursts of wildflowers. With the latening summer season, the sunflowers were beginning to open their golden heads, and rabbitbrush, also gold in color, fringed the dry creek beds along with willow and cottonwood trees. The foothills, far from where Amanda was riding, boasted canyons with red and yellow wild currant and rosebushes, and aspens that were just beginning to evidence autumn's encroachment.

There were birds, huge crows that cawed and flapped their wings at Amanda's obtrusion, tiny sparrows that swooped and dove and twittered, and far off, the regal splendor of an eagle gliding on a high, soundless wind.

Amanda loved this place. She loved the clean, brilliant air that seemed to bring the majesty of the distant mountain peaks within reach. She loved the freedom of riding on her own land, the sense of accomplishment she felt at the end of every day, the respect she was beginning to receive from some of her neighbors. A woman running a large ranch alone in these parts was doubted and judged, Amanda had learned. But she wasn't above asking advice from her ranch hands, and they were experienced men, lifelong cowhands, a little uncertain at first about working for a woman but gradually receptive to her determination.

Some straying cattle came into Amanda's view, but she couldn't tell at that distance whose brand the animals wore. Everyone's main herd was still in the foothills, where the animals were driven each spring. The lower pastures were traditionally saved for the long, hard winter months, and at present, the discolored grass was knee-deep and dense.

The animals' coats were beginning to thicken, Amanda noted. The annual fall roundup was already underway, if rather lackadaisically. The abundant grass in the foothills was utilized as long as possible, and the Spencer cowboys spent most of their workdays in the routine end-of-summer task of looking for strays, the maverick cattle who wandered far away from the main herd.

There were at least a dozen brands among the thousands of cattle roaming the hills. The valley contained eight large ranches and several small operations, and everyone followed virtually the same practice. Roundup consisted of several steps: gathering the strays, sorting by brand, then driving the herds to their home ground. Once the cattle were rounded up, each rancher determined which animals would be sold, then another drive was necessary, the drive to the railhead. The nearest site was about sixty miles away. There, the cattle buyers congregated for one week at the end of September.

It was probably the most crucial stage of the breeding process, for the herds had to be decreased for winter feeding, and the annual sale produced cash for the upcoming year's operation.

Amanda knew she was getting the hang of it, even after only one year of running the ranch on her own. She had picked Len's brain, thank God, pestering him with countless questions. And Len, bless him, had answered patiently, although Amanda knew that he had found her insatiable curiosity bothersome at times.

She was holding the reins loosely, allowing Ginger to walk at her own pace. The hint of a wistful smile touched Amanda's lips as memories of Len filled her mind. She was over the shock of losing him and could remember him without unbearable torment now.

But sometimes she was so very, very lonely. A day like today made her feel especially isolated. Her closest neighbor was Choice Brenton, hardly a man to drop in on for some simple conversation. The valley was immense. It took hours of travel to reach any of the other ranches, and even longer to reach Leavitt, the closest town.

The trail was forking again, and on impulse, Amanda directed Ginger to follow the right fork. In a few minutes, she pulled the horse to a stop and slid to the ground. There was a small huddle of trees here, three very old and gnarled cottonwoods and a cluster of tenacious saplings. A pole fence guarded the Spencer family cemetery, and Amanda unhooked the gate and entered the enclosure.

There were half a dozen headstones and markers. Len had identified each of them for her. His parents were buried here, as well as two uncles and a brother who had died in infancy. Amanda went to the newest headstone and sank to her knees to remove a few weeds that had sprung up since her last visit. The inscription on the headstone read, *Leonard Spencer, October 4, 1852–June 21, 1885. Beloved Husband.*

At thirty-three years of age, a month before celebrating his first wedding anniversary, Len had died in a buggy accident. It was one of those rare, sad events that make a person ponder providence. His buggy had lost a wheel, which happened to everyone at one time or another. Only the buggy had flipped, and something struck Len's head in the tumble. He shouldn't even have been injured and he had been killed. The shock of it had nearly killed Amanda, too. The ensuing days and the funeral were still only a blur to her.

It was Choice Brenton coming around, strange as it seemed to her now, that had snapped her out of it. He had stood just inside the kitchen door.

"What can I do to help?"

"Help?"

"You can't run this ranch."

"I can't?" It took several moments to grasp the meaning in Choice's blunt observation. *"Why can't I?"*

"For several reasons. First, you're a woman. Second, you don't know what has to be done. Third..."

"Stop! I do know what has to be done, and my sex is not the deterrent you think it is."

He stood there staring at her, obviously uneasy with her attitude. "Amanda, I can direct your men along with my own. Len would have done it for me if I had a wife."

She drew up her shoulders. "Thank you for the offer, but I will take care of the ranch myself."

Choice came around very seldom after that. His calls were brief and studiously polite, merely neighborly gestures out of respect for Len's memory, Amanda suspected. The two of them, she and Choice, had not been friends before Len's death and could not pretend friendship after he was gone.

Amanda removed her hat and laid it on the ground. Her hair was mussed, and she poked some straying wisps into the coiled and pinned knot at her nape just above her shirt collar. Then she sat against a tree trunk and admitted her melancholy. A year and two months had gone by since Len's death. She was over the trauma of the fatal accident, but there were moments, like this, when she wondered what fate had in store for her.

There was nowhere else she wanted to be. The ranch was her home, her life. There was an indelible sense of security here that she had never experienced before marrying Len and coming to his ranch. She would trade that for nothing, not for all the wealth in all the cities of the world.

But there was no ignoring the void she lived with. If she had only been blessed with a child, she thought with a long sigh. How she had yearned for a baby! Every month she had prayed and waited, and every month she had been disappointed. Len had told her there was plenty of time and not to fret.

But time had run out, and there was no child to love and care for. Perhaps that was the most profound of all the heartaches connected to Len's untimely death.

Amanda drew up her knees, wrapped her arms around them and looked off absently, strangely drawn into her own past.

She had never been on a ranch before marrying Len. Her early life had consisted of dusty, dirty mining towns and settlements, and she had never known security. Why should she find loneliness so distressing now? Hadn't loneliness been part and parcel of her youth?

Her mother died when she was ten. Her father worked the western silver mines, mostly in Nevada, drank too much and dragged his sad little daughter from one filthy hovel to the next. Amanda remembered scrubbing the shacks with lye soap, trying very hard to make some sort of home out of little or nothing.

How she had managed to learn to read and write was a mystery, because without any warning, she would be taken out of school and moved to a different town. Sometimes there wasn't any town or school at all, only a narrow, gaunt canyon with shacks perched on arid hillsides around ugly holes and bracing, where men dug for silver.

There was one common thread in Amanda's memory of those years, the women who trooped from one mining area to the next with the same tenacity as the miners, the prostitutes. Amanda was only fourteen when a man asked her to sleep with him for money. The terrible part of that memory was that she had considered it. She had been so desperate for something nice, and her mind had leaped to what she might buy with two dollars.

No one had intervened. No one had magically appeared and talked about right and wrong, or told her to refuse, but that's what she had done, refused the man and told him to stay away from her. That was a turning point, she later realized. She would not sell herself for a few dollars or something nice, and she would somehow manage to get away from the mining camps.

The decision had been final but not easily executed. They were in a horrible place, an ugly, isolated camp connected to the rest of the world by a narrow-gauge, spur railway. That track was the only way into the canyon and the only way out. Her father was drinking up his wages and giving her very little money, barely enough for food, never mind for saving. She looked for work and learned that the miners' laundry business was closely held and guarded by two nasty hags who told her they would slice off her nose if she dared to steal even one of their customers.

There were numerous bawdy houses where a man could drink, eat and gamble, but no decent restaurants. A Chinese couple served hot meals right out in the open for an exorbitant price, and they chased Amanda off, babbling excitedly in Chinese when she asked if they needed a serving girl. The place had been dreadful, a nightmare, and there wasn't one thing she could do to earn enough money to buy a train ticket out of there, other than what the prostitutes were doing.

Amanda was so relieved when her father came home one night and announced that they were moving again, she had nearly collapsed. And when they got off the train in Alma, Nevada, a place that looked like a normal town, she knew her chance had come. She was sixteen years old.

Within a week she located a job in a boardinghouse. It wasn't great, but she was able to leave the shack her father had moved her into. Working under the watchful eye of the heavy woman, Mrs. Milwikee, who owned the boardinghouse, Amanda helped with the cooking and did most of the cleaning and laundry. She toiled seven days a week and fell into bed every night exhausted. But room and board were part of her wages, and she saved nearly every penny of the cash she received each Friday.

One day, quite by accident, she learned that her father had moved on. Without even saying goodbye, he had gone to another mine. She wept that night, feeling completely alone in a cold and frightening world.

She refused any and all male attention. The boarders at Mrs. Milwikee's changed almost weekly, but they were all men. Her figure was developing, and she often caught hot, glittering eyes on her breasts as she carried bowls and platters to the dining table.

She had been working at the boardinghouse for a year when someone tried to get into her room one night. She raised such a ruckus with her screams that the intruder scurried away, but a minute later Mrs. Milwikee pounded on the door and shouted, "What's going on in there?"

Trembling, Amanda opened the door and gasped out that someone had been trying to break into her room.

"You're fired," the stout woman declared, stunning Amanda to speechlessness. "You can stay until morning, then I want you out."

"But...why?"

Mrs. Milwikee threw up her hands and walked away, muttering something about troublesome girls. She tossed over her shoulder, as though she needed to reinforce her harsh decision, "First thing you wake up, Amanda. Not a minute later."

She had packed her few possessions to the accompaniment of confused sniffles. Her little horde of money, a year's wages, amounted to almost a hundred dollars. It would have been more if she hadn't had to buy shoes and a new winter coat.

She had hardly explored Alma, she realized as she left Mrs. Milwikee's boardinghouse the next morning at first light. Carrying her bundle of clothing and the heavy coat that had been so necessary only a few months before, Amanda walked along, wondering what she would do. She stopped at the Union Pacific depot and read the itinerary posted beside the entrance door. Tickets could be purchased to travel west, to Reno, to San Francisco, or east, to Salt Lake City and points beyond.

"Points beyond" held her interest for a long time. Where was points beyond? Peering through a window, she saw a man wearing a green eyeshade and garters on his sleeves working behind the counter.

Working up her nerve, she finally pushed the door open and crept into the depot. The man looked up. The building smelled musty, Amanda noticed, as though it had been closed up for too long.

"Something I can do for you, young woman?"

She took a breath and walked to the counter. "How much for a ticket?"

"A ticket to where?"

"Uh . . . points beyond."

The man seemed to get a kick out of that. "Young lady, that takes in a powerful lot of country."

"It does?"

"Do you have a destination in mind?"

A destination. No, she did not have a destination in mind. She only knew that she wanted to leave Nevada, to get away from dust and miners and men who leered at serving girls, from women like Mrs. Milwikee who fired a girl for shrieking because someone was trying to get into her room in the middle of the night.

Amanda cleared her throat. "How far can I travel on..." She hesitated, then decided to hold some of her cash in reserve. "On eighty dollars?"

"Eighty dollars, hmm? Which direction, east or west?"

"East."

The man opened a thick book and flipped a few pages. "Well, young woman, you can travel clear to Chicago on seventy-nine dollars and fifty cents. Is that where you want to go? 'Course, that's just the price of the ticket, mind you. You'd have to provide your own eats on top of that."

"Chicago?" Mercy, did she want to go clear to Chicago? Amanda frowned. Where, precisely, was Chicago? But then she remembered Kentucky. One of her father's drinking cronies used to talk about Lexington, Kentucky, and the man had gone on and on about how green and beautiful the Kentucky countryside was. "Could I go to Lexington, Kentucky on eighty dollars?"

"Well, let's see now. There would be transfers. . . ." The man turned to the book again, mumbled to himself and jotted numbers on a small pad. He finally looked up. "Eighty-three seventy-five."

"I'll buy a ticket."

The moment she plunked down the money, Amanda began to worry. But mingled with the worry was excitement. She would leave this place. She would make a new life among green, growing things. She would never come back to Nevada, never! A moment later, while the man worked on her ticket, she thought of her father and how he would never find her if he returned to Alma.

She sighed. If he had cared about her in the least, he would not have gone off without a word. It had been a year, and she had to look out for herself.

"The next train east leaves this evening. Five-thirty, on the nose," the man told her as he took her money and handed her the ticket. "Lexington, Kentucky, hmm? You got kin there?"

Amanda silently shook her head, then managed a shy thank-you. She felt the man's questioning gaze on her back as she hurried out of the depot.

Two days later she was still on the train, exhausted, dirty and bewildered. The train seemed to go backward as much as it went forward. She had lost track of the number of times it switched cars at some isolated, woebegone settlement or stopped to take on water and fuel with nothing in sight but sagebrush, a water tank and a hillock of coal. There was a conductor, a black man, on the train, and he showed her a map. After two days and nights of misery, she wasn't even halfway to Kentucky. The conductor pointed out where they would be stopping next, and she saw the name *Cheyenne*. "We're in Wyoming Territory, miss," the kindly man told her.

She was so stiff from trying to sleep sitting up that when a two-hour stopover was announced at the outskirts of Cheyenne, she gladly gathered up her possessions and got off the train to stretch her legs and find something to eat. There was no food for sale on the train, and most of the passengers ate from picnic baskets. Amanda had to buy her food during stopovers.

"Miss," the black conductor said as she prepared to leave the car, "go to the Red Wing Café in the next block. They are accustomed to serving ladies."

She sent the man a grateful look. "Thank you."

And it was there, at the Red Wing Café, that she made the decision that changed the course of her life. A sign in the window announced a need for a cook's helper. She didn't want to go to Lexington, Kentucky at all. Cheyenne was buzzing with activity, with drays and draft horses, with construction, with corrals crowded with cattle and horses and sheep. She had marveled at the beauty of the plains country for miles and miles now, ever since daybreak. The train had chugged across vast prairies and barren deserts during the past two days, but Wyoming Territory was kinder to the senses than those places. She had a sense of crispness, of fresh, clean air between herself and the far-off mountains. Today she had caught glimpses of rushing streams, herds of animals in seemingly endless green fields that she heard someone say were antelope, and funny-looking birds that stood on one leg, which someone else said were heron. From the window of the train, she had admired wildflowers and greenery and a boundless blue sky.

Her heart beat with a strange rhythm; she had reached her destination. It was 1880 and she was seventeen years old.

Amanda obtained the cook's helper position at the Red Wing Café. She located an affordable room to rent and looked to her future. She read the newspaper, the *Daily Leader,* and avidly soaked up stories and articles. James Garfield was elected president of the United States. Electricity was becoming practical; New York streets were being lit by the mysterious—to Amanda—power. Louis Pasteur discovered a vaccine for chicken cholera. Railroads were expanding everywhere. "The world is becoming smaller," one columnist wrote.

But to Amanda, the world was becoming larger, not smaller. Cheyenne was a rip-roaring frontier town. She quickly learned which streets to avoid and where it was safe to stroll. There were people of every description, cowboys, dudes, Indians, farmers, ranchers, politicians, shopkeepers. The women, as in every place else she had ever lived, fell into two categories—the painted, bawdy ladies of the night and the respectable women.

There was a sense of freedom in the very air. The town was growing by leaps and bounds, and with it, Amanda felt the expansion of her own spirit. She made some friends, although she was still very cautious with men, especially those who were young and full of vinegar.

One day she read an article in the *Daily Leader* that made her blood race. Settlements in the territory were advertising for schoolteachers. *Teaching credentials are desirable, but not absolutely necessary. Our youngsters need to learn the basics of reading, writing and simple arithmetic. Anyone with those skills may apply.*

She wondered if she dared be so bold. She could read well, write with a pretty but disciplined hand and add, subtract, multiply and divide. Her knowledge of history and geography was greatly limited, but she could learn right along with her students. The towns in the article were unfamiliar—Colby, Seldon, Hopperstown—all three, apparently, located within the territory. The wages were cited as twenty dollars a month, with room and board at a local home.

When she investigated further and learned that Colby and Seldon were mining settlements, she chose Hopperstown, which was a farming community a hundred miles north and slightly east of Cheyenne, nearly on the Nebraska border. To her surprise and delight, her letter received favorable response.

Before winter truly set in, she was situated within the farming community, residing with a widow lady who took in sewing and boarders to earn a living. The school was constructed of lime grout, a local cement, and consisted of only one room. Amanda had six very young students, and she had never been happier in her life.

Four years passed. Instead of summer closures, the school took a three-month winter break because of the almost intolerable weather. During those long spells of idleness, Amanda read and read. Much of her monthly wage was spent on books, which she ordered from catalogues. Her landlady, Mrs. McCardy, was a pleasant woman, and she taught Amanda the game of dominoes and how to knit. With the freezing winter wind blowing up terrible blizzards outside, Mrs. McCardy would tell long, rambling stories of her and Mr. McCardy's early years in the territory, when Indian raids had been an almost constant threat.

Often Mrs. McCardy would comment, "It's time a pretty, young woman like yourself found a husband."

During clement weather there were occasions to meet young men—barbecues, dances in the various barns and church meetings. But not until Amanda met Len Spencer was she the least bit interested in finding a husband.

One of the farmers in the area raised magnificent bulls. Cattle people came from far and wide to inspect and purchase the excellent breeding stock, and that is what brought Len Spencer to Hopperstown. Something wonderful happened when Amanda and Len were introduced, and she knew when he stayed beyond the time for him to leave that the delay was because of her.

They were married in Hopperstown's small church, with Mrs. McCardy and other friends in the community attending the ceremony. There was no honeymoon, such as Amanda had read of in some of her books. Instead, Len brought her to his ranch.

She had fallen in love with it on sight and felt that she had truly come home. There were times in the almost giddy happiness of the ensuing year when she wondered about her father, if he was still living and where. But she thought more often of her mother and wished that Molly Dolan had lived to see how happy her daughter was, what a good marriage she had made, how good and kind and decent her husband was.

Beneath the cottonwoods, Amanda stirred as if coming out of a dream. The past *was* a dream; *this* was reality, the ranch and this beautiful, bountiful land.

So was the cemetery.

Sighing, Amanda got to her feet and dusted off the seat of her britches. She didn't often go so far into her past, for the old memories always left her with a strangely vulnerable feeling. She wasn't vulnerable now, not like she had been as a girl. Any vulnerability now lay within herself, invisible to others. She would never be homeless again, never again have to endure the kind of hardship and deprivation she had grown up with. The Spencer ranch was legally hers, and no one could ever take it away from her, no one.

Maneuvering through the gate, Amanda picked up Ginger's reins and swung up into the saddle. She urged the mare forward and followed the trail to the fork. Stopping there for a moment, she decided she wasn't yet ready to return to the house, and she turned Ginger's head in the opposite direction.

Chapter Two

There was something on the breeze, an unfamiliar sound, occasional, erratic. Amanda strained to identify the distant mewl, but it came and went so fast that its origin escaped her. A cat? Lynx, as wary as they were, were sighted every so often, and even more rarely, cougar. Animal life abounded in these parts, grizzly bears and wolves right along with the more docile creatures, deer, elk and antelope. Few people, male or female, rode without a weapon, and Amanda carried a Winchester repeating rifle in a saddle scabbard. Len had taught her how to use it, and she had also done some shooting with a pistol, a Colt .45. Her interest in guns, however, was limited to self-protection.

There it was again! Amanda reined in Ginger to eliminate the thudding of the mare's hooves and listened intently. The sound was far off, coming with the wind's whimsy from somewhere within the gently rolling terrain ahead. It wasn't the cry of a cat, nor of any animal she had ever heard in her two years on the ranch. It sounded like—was it possible?—the bleating of sheep.

Frowning, Amanda clicked her tongue and moved Ginger forward again. She followed the sound, telling herself that it couldn't possibly be sheep. Sheep on Spencer land? Sheep in this valley? Not that she had any great hatred of sheep, but the other ranchers certainly did. Len had belonged to the Wyoming Stock Growers Association, along with nearly everyone else in the valley, and Amanda, too, had taken care of her financial obligation to the group after last fall's cattle sale.

Founded in 1871 to protect the cattle interests in Wyoming territory, the Stock Growers Association was a force to reckon with. Cattle rustling was a never-ending threat, and rustlers caught red-handed were hung on the spot. Incidents of violence toward sheepherders were not unheard of, either. Some two hundred miles west, around the Rawlins area, sheep were accepted, but not here, not in this deepgrass valley. Anyone daring to bring in sheep was risking life and limb.

She had attended a rather impassioned meeting of association members with Len one time, and had heard several of the ranchers—one of whom had been particularly loud and unnerving, a man by the name of Wes Schuyler—state in no uncertain terms that the association would not tolerate three things in this valley: barbed wire, cattle rustlers and sheep.

She had questioned Len during the long buggy ride from Leavitt to the ranch, as she hadn't understood Schuyler's blatantly nasty attitude toward sheep. Barbed wire was neither here nor there to her, and anyone with half a brain despised rustlers, but sheep? Why on earth would Wes Schulyer be so red in the face and puffed up about sheep?

Len had calmly explained, "Cattle crop the grass off, sheep rip it up by its roots."

Len's reply had made sense to Amanda, at least giving her a logical reason for so much emotion at that meeting. People had a right to protect something they had worked so feverishly hard to get. Ranching in this vast, untamed country, with its long, grueling winters, was a demanding way of life. It created hard people, or at least it drew hard people. The weak or lazy did not survive here. Schuyler might be a hard case, but he had every right to protect the grass in the valley and foothills from animals that destroyed it.

That was the bind, of course. Although consisting of almost entirely deeded land, the whole valley was considered open grazing, which gave big mouths like Wes Schuyler an awful lot to say about its usage. There were no fences, except to protect ponds or other fragile sources of water and buildings and places like the Spencer cemetery. Schuyler cattle might turn up on Spencer land, or Brenton cattle on Schuyler ground. Legally, specific sections were owned by specific people; practically, each rancher used the entire valley.

As Ginger progressed along the trail, Amanda's heart began beating faster. She was definitely hearing the bleating of sheep, quite a few by the sound of it.

At the crest of a hill Amanda pulled Ginger up and stared at the scene below with her heart in her throat. Sheep—at least two hundred—were milling around one of the few creeks still running at this time of year. There was a shabby wood wagon with a rusty stovepipe protruding from its roof, a scrubby-looking horse and a man, who was sitting on something, maybe an overturned bucket. He appeared to be working with a leather harness, probably the same harness he'd used on that spindly old horse to pull that disreputable wagon onto Spencer land.

Amanda sucked in a slow, uneven breath. The man was a squatter, a sheepherder, the bane of the valley's cattlemen. She certainly didn't mind a traveler camping for a night or two at the valuable creek the sheepherder seemed to have adopted for his and his animals' use, but he had no right to squat on Spencer land, no one did. Two hundred sheep were gnawing away at grass she would need herself this winter and muddying an important water supply. Yet those problems would be trivial compared to what might happen if someone else caught wind of that herd's presence.

The man should be warned. If he was a stranger to the territory, he might not have any idea how determined some of the cattlemen were to keep his kind away from particular areas. This was one of them, this valley she loved and felt bonded to as surely as if she had been born within its boundaries. She didn't completely object to the idea of sheep, although she didn't favor sheep, either, but she did object to the almost certain trouble to come should that herd linger too long.

The shepherd was unaware of being watched, Amanda realized, no doubt because of the incessant bleating of his animals. She didn't like the idea of riding into anyone's camp unannounced, but there was little way of getting the man's attention short of firing a shot into the air, which she was also reluctant to do.

Her reluctance went deeper than that, Amanda finally admitted. She wasn't all that sure of her own gumption, when it came right down to it.

Maybe it wasn't necessary to do anything today. Maybe the herd was merely passing through the valley. When had she been out here last? Two days ago? Three? The sheep hadn't been here then, and they probably wouldn't be here tomorrow.

Amanda slowly turned Ginger's head, pointing the mare away from the encampment at the foot of the hill. It didn't feel right to just ride away from that herd, but she wasn't emotionally prepared to deal with it today. She would return tomorrow, and if the animals were still there, she would go down and speak to their owner.

Very early the next morning, with the sun just barely peeking over the horizon, Amanda talked to her men. Jess Lang was the oldest and usually the spokesman of the trio.

All three were lean and lanky. Buck Conners was the youngest and the first to laugh about something. Woody Samuels was the only one who was married. His wife lived in Leavitt, which was where he spent his free time.

They were down by the main corral, discussing roundup. "Lots of strays this year," Jess declared. "The hot weather sent 'em deeper into the hills than they usually go. We should probably take campin' gear and stay out for a couple of days, leastways."

The men normally stayed in the ranch's bunkhouse. Amanda provided a hot evening meal, a pot of stew or beans or soup, but the men lived in, cared for and ate in their own quarters. It was the routine Len's parents had initiated years ago, when they first bought the ranch land from the government at two dollars an acre and moved onto it. They had erected the bunkhouse as one of the first buildings, as they needed hired help and had to have a place for them to stay. Len had been a mere lad and had worked with his father. The Spencers' first house on the ranch had been a soddy, a one-room structure made from chunks of sod cut and dried like bricks.

But the Spencers had not arrived in Wyoming Territory penniless, as so many of the hopeful pioneers did. Buying their land rather than homesteading the government's allotment of one hundred and sixty acres was proof of their affluence, especially when they had purchased nearly two thousand acres.

The reason for the sod house was time and the scarcity of nearby trees. Winter had been coming on, and shelter was a dire necessity. The following summer, however, Len's father and the family's hired men had gone into the mountains and cut enough timbers to build a second house.

And that's what Amanda lived in now, a pleasant log house with two bedrooms, a parlor, a large kitchen, a pantry and a wide front porch. She truly adored the house. It had varnished plank floors and handwoven rag rugs, splendid furniture in the parlor, including a spinet piano, several cast-iron heating stoves, and a marvelous cooking stove in the kitchen.

Behind the house was a huge woodshed, which was packed to the rafters with fuel for winter. A chicken coop was attached to the back of the woodshed, and the coop, too, had a stove, so fires could be built in the worst weather to save the poor hens from freezing to death in mid-cackle. A sizable building had been constructed around the ranch's drinking water supply, which consisted of a well with a strong, sturdy hand pump. But the exterior of the building was deceiving, as it had thick walls to maintain an even temperature so that it could be used to store meat and eggs and other perishable items even in the most extreme weather.

There was garden space on one side of the house and a privy on the other. The Spencers had planted trees, Russian olives, poplars, cottonwoods, and the homestead was nicely protected from the sun in summer and the worst snowdrifts in winter. Some distance away, there were the corrals, the bunkhouse, a barn, a hay shed, a toolshed and a forge. It was quite the most efficient setup Amanda ever could have imagined, and she wasn't about to suggest changes in years-old procedures.

She truly hated to see the men ride off for days at a time. It had to be done, of course. The Spencer cattle were scattered over thousands of acres, and the only way to bring them to lower ground was to go after them.

"Yes," she murmured, thinking suddenly of the sheep in the south pasture. Maybe it was best for the men to be gone a few days. They were as stoically steeped in the cattleman's philosophy as anyone else she had met in the valley. As staunch cowmen, they might take it upon themselves to roust the sheepherder.

On the other hand, without Jess, Woody and Buck to fall back upon, she would have to rely completely on herself in dealing with the man.

That was probably best, too. She had to learn how to stand up to people when the occasion demanded it.

"The weather's holdin' real good," Jess observed in his Texas drawl. "There's no rush yet to get the herd in."

"There's a tang in the air at night now," Amanda remarked.

"Freshenin' up a mite," Woody agreed. "There's time, though. We'll all know when it starts turnin'."

Amanda's two years were enough time in this part of the world to make her agree with Woody. When the weather changed, it changed quickly. One didn't have to guess and wonder when fall was coming. When it came, it came with very little fooling around.

Woody spit a stream of tobacco juice. He and Buck chewed, and Jess smoked cigars. All three men wore heavy beards. Actually, they looked like a trio of outlaws to Amanda, but they had worked on the ranch before she came along, and Len had trusted all three. And they certainly looked no worse than the miners in her memory. Better, in fact.

They were respectful of her. She had never heard a cuss word come out of their mouths, nor even the slightest innuendo that they noticed her gender on a personal level. She appreciated their courtesy, for there had been too many times in her life when she had received none.

"You'll be taking your blankets with you then," she said.

"Yup, reckon so," Jess replied.

Amanda's gaze rose to the distant hills. They were miles away, a long, hard ride. She looked at the men again. "I'll see you in a few days, then."

It was the sort of meeting Amanda was accustomed to having with the men. They knew what had to be done on the place. She knew, too, but it was rare when she had a different chore in mind for the day than what Jess, in particular, specified. There were days when Amanda joined the men and worked beside them. The first few times she had done so, she had perceived some startled expressions, but now no one batted an eyelash when she showed up.

They did a good job, these three men, and there was little chance of Amanda or anyone else running a spread the size of the Spencer place without them, or men like them.

They set to work, first saddling then packing their horses for a stay in the hills. Amanda saw them off, and when they were gone, she walked to the house and went to her bedroom. Thoughtfully, she belted the holstered Colt around her waist. She slipped on a jacket that lapped down over the weapon, went to the kitchen and made sure the fire she had kindled in the stove for coffee and breakfast earlier was banked, and left the house.

She began saddling Ginger. The morning air was cool and clean, the sky clear. The final days of summer were always very precious. A flock of geese passed overhead, honking their way south, and Amanda stood for a moment to enjoy the sight. Smaller birds flitted and trilled various melodies. One of the barn cats stretched lazily in the sun. There was hardly a breeze.

Peace suddenly filled Amanda's soul. Unlike yesterday, the quiet didn't feel like loneliness. She drew a deep breath, glad that she again felt capable of facing life's challenges.

If the sheepherder was still camping at the creek, she would deal with him the way Len would have, courteously but firmly. For his own safety, the man and his sheep could not remain in the valley.

Amanda was about to mount her horse when a distant movement caught her eye. Someone was coming, a horse and rider. She narrowed her gaze to squint at the visitor for a few moments, then led Ginger into the corral and let her go. A strange sensation tightened Amanda's chest as she closed the corral gate, the same feeling she always experienced around Choice Brenton. She never knew what to say to him, never felt comfortable with him.

At least he never stayed long. His calls were seldom and brief—duty calls, Amanda was certain. And this was the way he always arrived, too, just popping up at the strangest times. But wasn't early morning a strange time to pay a duty call?

She would never understand him, so there was little point in trying. During the long stretches between his visits she rarely thought of him. Absent, he was merely another rancher in the valley, albeit her nearest neighbor.

But when he was on Spencer land, standing before her with that eternally inscrutable expression he wore, she did wonder what went on behind his guarded gray eyes, just as she had at their first meeting. She was a naturally curious person, she knew without question, and she couldn't fault the very trait that had allowed her to take over the ranch with some degree of confidence after Len's death.

Curiosity about Choice was no more than wasted energy, however, sure to do her little good. Len had told her a few things about the man. He ran his ranch with an iron hand, kept to himself most of the time and took no sass from anyone, although he asked nothing of his hired help that he himself could not do. He had been a U.S. marshal for several years, wandering the western territories and states, Len had related with unmistakable pride in his friend. That was before Choice's father, Riker Brenton, died, when Choice had been free to leave the ranch.

When Riker became gravely ill, Choice returned. He had been back in the valley only a short time before Amanda arrived. He had never married, and Amanda sometimes wondered if he even liked women.

It wasn't that she felt anything so obvious as dislike from Choice. Perhaps that was what bothered her; she wasn't sure of what she *did* feel from him. Whatever it was, it was disturbing.

She waited near the corral, her hand at her throat. Her reactions to Choice were not controllable. There was always an odd flutter within her when he was near. She couldn't deduce its meaning, not when it was completely alien to anything she had felt before.

She watched him getting closer. He rode a large black horse, a strikingly handsome stallion that she had always admired. Concentrating on the long, rippling muscles beneath the glossy black hide of the horse, rather than on its rider, Amanda strove for composure. She would not behave like a schoolgirl with Choice, fluttering pulse or not.

He rode his horse up to the corral fence. Ginger had pricked up her ears long before, and she nickered softly and came to the fence to greet Bolo.

"Hello, Amanda."

"Choice," she acknowledged quietly. His black hair was longer than it had been the last time she had seen him, well below his shirt collar. His thick, black mustache concealed his upper lip, although his granite-hard jaw was clean-shaven. She didn't like thinking of him as handsome, but he was, and she did.

He leaned on the saddle horn and looked around almost lazily. "See you're keeping everything in good shape."

"With the help of my men, yes."

Choice narrowed his eyes on Amanda Spencer, taking in the uncommon sight of a woman in men's trousers. Male attire could not disguise the female beneath, he noted with masculine satisfaction. Even in shapeless, ill-fitting clothing, Amanda had the kind of beauty that could bring an ache to a man's body very quickly, and Choice sat there and recalled the several attempts he'd heard of on the part of would-be swains in the past year to court her.

Those men had been too hasty, too eager to gain an advantage over the other single men in the area. Amanda hadn't yet been ready for another man's attentions.

A strange silence stretched while he looked...and frowned...and thought about it. Under that silly-looking old hat on her head lay a wealth of auburn hair, and an urge Choice had felt before and stifled, a desire to wind his hands through that hair, broiled and mingled with the admiration he had for this woman. Only an old and important friendship with Len had prevented him from joining those foolish men who had unwisely presented themselves as interested suitors before she was through with grieving. A year and some months had passed. Amanda wouldn't live alone indefinitely, not when women, especially beautiful women, were at a premium in the territory. Men would line up at her door at the slightest indication from her.

But her expression invited no familiarity. Choice cooled his thoughts. "Mind if I get down?"

Amanda started, then shook her head. "Of course not. Would you like a cool drink? There's some lemonade in the well house." She felt pink and warm all over from Choice's much too intent study and had fallen back on common courtesy, the only attitude that made any sense around a man who caused incomprehensible flutters and scared the stuffing out of her, both at the same time.

"Sure would. Thanks." Choice threw one long leg over the front of the saddle and slid to the ground. He looped the reins over a corral rail. The two horses were gently rubbing noses over the fence. Animal instincts were as sure as sunsets, he thought, noticing the camaraderie. Male and female, stallion and mare. The time might not be right for mating, but Ginger and Bolo understood one another very well.

A heck of a lot better than he and Amanda did. With a wry expression, he followed along as she started for the house.

As they walked along, Amanda concentrated on mundane things, like the trees and the birds and the ground squirrel that suddenly darted in front of them and disappeared, although the tall man at her side was an almost unbelievable intrusion. They passed the chicken coop, with its string of mesh fencing to keep the poultry in, and the two plump turkeys within the enclosure imperiously ignoring the chickens, who clucked and pecked at the grain Amanda had strewn earlier.

Amanda veered to the well house and pushed the door open. Its interior was dark and cool and smelled of the several hams that hung from a rafter. Sides of bacon wrapped in heavily waxed paper added to the aroma. There were bins of potatoes and onions, bounty from her own garden. The butternut and acorn squash were still ripening on their vines, but would soon be harvested and stored for winter.

The jar of lemonade resided on a shelf. Lemons were like pure gold and purchased, when available, along with the hams and bacon and items such as coffee, sugar and flour, at the mercantile in Leavitt. Fresh milk, butter and cream were expensive and delivered by one of the ranchers who raised some dairy cows along with his beef herd, and who made the tiresome trip to some of the other ranches about once a week. When the weather got really bad, however, there were sometimes very long periods between deliveries.

There was always plenty to eat, though, more than enough. Buck loved to hunt and fish and often brought Amanda a nice venison roast or a string of speckled trout. And there was always beef, lots and lots of beef.

Plucking up the jar of lemonade, Amanda stepped out of the well house and closed the door firmly. Choice was waiting, and they proceeded to the house.

Amanda invited him to sit down, but he remained standing while she washed her hands and filled two glasses with lemonade. She left her jacket on, not wishing him to see the handgun she was carrying. She didn't wear a gun like an extension of her own body as he did, and he was bound to wonder why she was wearing one today. Replying would be difficult, because she had no intention of mentioning the sheep to him or anyone else.

She brought the glasses to the table. Choice removed his hat and sat down when she did. She left her hat on her head and saw him place his on the table to his right. She drank. He drank.

"Good lemonade," he said.

"Thank you."

"I've been meaning to come by for some time now."

"It's . . . nice of you to call."

"I came for a reason today."

"Oh?" His eyes were boring into her, the same way he always looked at her, and she fought a blush and wished to God she knew what there was about the man that bothered her to blushes.

"You probably don't know, but there's a herd of sheep on your land."

If he had suddenly jumped up and kicked her Amanda could not have been more stunned. She felt herself blanching. There were few secrets in the valley, but how on earth had he discovered those sheep almost as quickly as she had? His ranch was north of hers. The sheep were in her south pasture.

She cleared her throat. "I do know. I saw them yesterday."

"I thought I should talk to you before taking any action, seeing as how they're on Spencer land."

"Action? What sort of action?"

Choice sat back, although one eyebrow rose slightly. "Talk to the herder, urge him to be on his way."

"Urge him how? At the point of a gun?"

Choice's voice softened, taking on a threatening undercurrent that Amanda had always suspected was a critical part of his dark and guarded personality. "That would be his decision, Amanda."

The gun belt around her waist mocked her negative judgment of Choice's method of handling troublesome issues. Hadn't she thought it necessary to be armed, just in case? What had been in the back of her mind, yanking the Colt from its holster and threatening the sheepherder with it if he hadn't readily agreed to moving on?

No, of course not. She could never turn a gun on another human being. She had merely felt a little more secure with it strapped under her jacket.

Chagrined, she lifted her chin a notch, attempting bravery. "I would like to deal with the sheepherder myself."

"You would. And how do you plan to go about it?"

The vague hint of amusement in his gray eyes increased her courage. She was not a fool and didn't like being treated as a silly woman with ideas she couldn't possibly implement.

"I can talk to the herder as well as you can," she said with remarkable calmness, considering the turmoil in her system.

"And you think he'll listen to you?"

"Once I explain how things are around here, yes."

Choice raised his glass and took a long swallow of lemonade, his eyes never straying from her face. Where and when had she gotten so much grit? Had she been so gutsy before she married Len? Before she became a widow? When he'd seen the two of them together, Amanda had always deferred to her husband's opinion.

Choice had been set back on his heels by Amanda's decision to run the place on her own. Not that she didn't have capable help. But Buck, Woody and Jess were only hired hands, and who knew when a cowboy would get the urge to wander?

There were other lady ranchers in the territory; Amanda was not completely unique. But the ones Choice had met didn't have soft skin and small pretty hands. It took tough people to operate a ranch year in, year out, and he hadn't seen Amanda Spencer as tough.

Until now. Maybe there was a streak of toughness beneath that smooth, silken skin, after all.

Amanda wondered what was going through his mind. His opinion was important to her, she realized. Very important. Maybe because this was the first real test of her abilities, of her determination to do as well as Len had with the Spencer ranch. There was no logical reason, to her way of thinking, that a woman couldn't operate a cattle ranch as well as a man. Choice had hired help, the same as her, and so did the other ranchers in the valley. If it was a matter of brute strength, then she couldn't begin to compete, but it wasn't only brawn that brought success to a venture. Intelligence was every bit as crucial, and she was far from stupid.

A need to prove herself arose without conscious intent, and she suddenly leaned across the table and placed her hand on Choice's, which was lying loosely on the table beside his glass. "Please let me handle it. Those sheep are on Spencer land. Please don't interfere."

Choice stared at the small hand on his and felt a surge of desire rip through his body. How many times had he thought of Amanda touching him? Of him touching her? Slowly he turned his hand over and let his fingers curl around hers. Then he raised his eyes and saw Amanda's sudden, sharp knowledge of what she had just incited.

"I . . . I'm sorry," she whispered, her eyes big with dismay. She had never touched Choice after their first brief handshake. Now, in the blink of an eye, all the caution she had practiced around him was wasted. She felt heat and life in his big rough hand, and she had a frightening sense of what he was feeling. Though still guarded, there was a new light in his eyes, one that sent alarm skittering up her spine. She tugged against his hold on her hand.

Choice studied the small fingers he held, the ovals of her shortly pared nails, and desire curled within him like a swirling dark cloud. He looked into her face.

Amanda's eyes darted, and she was aware of the heavy beat of her heart. The intensity of his gaze struck her with overwhelming force, causing a deluge of emotions. His eyes moved down from her face, and she felt them on her throat, then on the front of her shirt and jacket. Her cheeks flamed. "Please . . ." she whispered huskily, and pulled against his grasp again.

He wasn't a man to flatter women. When internal pressures raised havoc with his system, he went to Leavitt and spent an hour or so with one of the ladies who lived above Foxy's Saloon. But what he was feeling for Amanda went back to the first time he'd seen her with Len's arm around her shoulders as he proudly presented his bride.

Choice couldn't stop looking at her. She had to be lonely. She must need a man. It was his nature to think pramatically, so it was only logical to him that a year and two months was a long enough mourning period for anyone. He'd deliberately brought Len to mind whenever admiration of Amanda had crowded him, but Len would not have wanted his young widow to live alone for the rest of her life.

Slowly uncoiling his six-foot-two-inch frame from the chair, Choice reached his full height, still holding onto Amanda's hand.

She could barely breathe. Nothing like this had ever happened to her before. She wasn't even sure she liked Choice Brenton, and he was making her body lurch and quicken in a very questionable manner.

"Amanda," he said softly, coming around the table to stand before her. He tugged on her hand, urging her up.

She managed to shake her head, to deny her own impulses as well as his. "Don't. You have no right."

He stood there, weighing her resistance against his desire. But he had never pushed a woman into anything and he couldn't start now. Especially not with Amanda.

He let go of her hand. "There's something between us."

Her lips were so dry it was difficult to speak, but she managed a shaky, "We're...neighbors."

"There's more."

She got up and ducked around him. Her legs were unsteady, her heart racing.

"Maybe there's always been more."

She whirled, shock and outrage on her face. "No! How dare you suggest such a thing!"

He'd gone too far, too fast, and he cursed his unthinking haste, likening himself to the other men who had tried to rush Amanda in the past year.

Moving to the table, he picked up his hat. "I'll be going now."

She was so glad he was leaving she felt dizzy. From occasionally dutiful neighbor to ardent suitor was too enormous a step for her to digest quickly, if at all.

He stopped at the door. "You'd better let me see to those sheep."

"Stay out of it," she said, low and hoarse, wishing for the courage to add, "and don't come back here, not ever again!" That he would even think there had been something between them, let alone say it, was appalling.

Choice hesitated. Amanda's sense of propriety had been offended by his remark. But it was true, dammit, true!

He slammed his hat on his head. "I'll stay out of it for one day. If that herd is still there tomorrow, that sheepherder and I'll have a little talk."

Then he was gone.

Amanda sank to a chair, her eyes on the door. Minutes ticked by, and she seemed unable to move. She felt caught in the grip of something large and overwhelming, and outrage that Choice would dare to suggest something between them during Len's lifetime couldn't seem to dispel the sensation.

He wasn't right, he wasn't! He was crude and cold and...

But that was the crux of the problem. When his hand had been clasping hers, he'd felt anything but cold.

Chapter Three

It took about half an hour for Amanda to pull herself together enough to proceed with the day's plans. Before she left the house for the ride to the south pasture, however, she took off the jacket and gun belt and carried both to her bedroom. She needed neither, certainly not the jacket when the sun was warming so nicely, and wearing a handgun would be an open invitation to violence, should the sheepherder be so inclined. Talking to Choice had influenced her attitude. There were some things she could do as well as a man and some she couldn't, and bravado with a pistol was one thing she shouldn't even attempt.

Riding Ginger wasn't quite as pleasant as it usually was. Even yesterday, as blue and lonely as she had felt, she had derived satisfaction from riding on her own land. After this morning's episode with Choice, there wasn't much satisfaction anywhere in Amanda. She kept going over it, the way his hand had closed around hers, her reactions to the heat and solidity of his rough palm. Choice was nothing like Len had been, and Len was the only man she had any personal experience with, the only man she had ever let get near her, the only man she had ever made love with.

Was that what Choice wanted, to make love to her? The question gave her a shiver. Not because the idea of making love with Choice was repellent, but because it wasn't. That's what was so scary about the ripples in her body when she remembered Choice holding her hand; she hadn't been at all repelled. Shocked, yes, but not repelled.

Had he known that would be the case? Was that what he'd meant about something between them? Had he been thinking of her as someone other than Len's wife—Len's widow—all along?

The conjecture made Amanda's mouth go dry, and she opened her canteen of water and took a long drink. Ginger plodded along, and Amanda tried to think about the confrontation she could be facing with the sheepherder. But Choice's image intruded even on that worry.

She deliberately brought her gaze to the countryside, to the dry creek bed wending through the ripening grass at her right, then to a clump of juniper, an outcropping of shale, a lonely cottonwood. Usually she thrived on nature's symmetry, but not today. Today Choice Brenton blocked her enjoyment of simple pleasures.

She couldn't deny that he had always disturbed her. But she hadn't thought of him romantically, she couldn't have. No one believed in the sanctity of marriage more than she did. Even as a girl she had known the difference between good and bad women, and a good woman, a good *married* woman, especially, did not fantasize about her husband's longtime friend.

Besides, she wasted precious little time on fantasy. Life's realities had always come in strong doses for her. She was consistently hopeful, but not a dreamer.

And Choice would not convince her that something had been going on between them while Len was alive. Nothing was going on now, either, except in Choice Brenton's mind.

Amanda became aware that she was holding the reins too tightly. She was wearing leather gloves, but she still felt the bite of the straps and relaxed her grip. She was deeply aggravated about this morning, and she didn't know how she would behave the next time Choice came around. Rationally, she disapproved of his forwardness and yet she still quaked internally at the memory of sensations she should not have felt.

Was she weak? Or was the loneliness she had been trying so desperately to ignore getting the better of her?

She would not turn to Choice Brenton or any other man out of loneliness. If and when she married again it would be for love, just as she had married Len for love. Choice probably didn't know the meaning of the word. Had she ever witnessed a truly kind expression on his face? Heard compassion in his voice? Felt any hint of sensitivity?

Of course, she thought with a rather forlorn sigh, she had spent very little time in Choice's company. When he and Len had gotten together, it was to discuss some aspect of ranching or to go hunting. She and Choice had never talked, except to say hello, goodbye or please pass the salt.

It was all too unsettling to dwell on. Choice had tried...well, he'd tried something and she had refused, that's all there was to the episode. He would probably not try again, which was the way she preferred it.

Noticing that she was passing the fork that led to the cemetery, Amanda straightened her shoulders. If the sheep were still down by the creek, she should be hearing them very soon now. She told herself that she would ride boldly into the encampment—if it was still there. If Choice was aware of that herd, others could be, too, and she did not want trouble on Spencer land. This incident was going to be handled diplomatically, peaceably. Choice was not a man of peace, she felt, and neither were some of the other ranchers in the valley, Wes Schuyler in particular.

Still, at the first evidence of sheep on the breeze, Amanda shuddered. She chewed on her bottom lip and listened, frowning when she heard more bleats. The herd was exactly where she had seen it yesterday, and there was no time for another bout of reluctance. She had refused Choice's intervention when he had been perfectly willing—*eager*—to handle this unpleasantness for her, and she must see it through.

At the crest of the hill, the same spot she had studied the encampment from yesterday, Amanda pulled Ginger up. Her heart thudded with foreboding. Everything looked the same down by the creek, the sheep, the wagon, the horse and the man. Except the man was near the wagon today, apparently checking one of its wheels.

He squatted and put his hands on the wheel, as though testing its roundness.

Breathing deeply, Amanda nudged Ginger into a walk and started down the gentle incline. This had to be done, she told herself, squaring her shoulders and erasing emotion from her expression. For the sheepherder's own safety, if for nothing else.

The man did not notice her until she was nearly at the creek. Then he looked up, obviously startled, and lunged for the rifle leaning against the wagon.

"There's no need for that," Amanda called.

She received a puzzled look. "A woman?"

Her clothing had been deceiving, which Amanda understood. She had seen a few other women in trousers in her lifetime, but britches instead of skirts were uncommon enough to rate a second glance. Amanda urged Ginger across the creek, scattering sheep in the process. "I'm Amanda Spencer," she yelled over the animals' protesting bleats.

The man eyed her cautiously. He was still holding the rifle, but it was pointed earthward, lying in the crook of his arm. Amanda saw him looking behind her, checking to see if she was alone. Then he stood very still and watched her until she was about twenty feet away. "That's far 'nuff," he said flatly.

Amanda tugged on the reins, and Ginger stopped instantly. She studied the sheepherder and registered him studying her with the same degree of intensity. He was at some indistinct age between twenty-five and thirty-five years, she decided, a plain-looking man with weathered skin and a dark beard that needed trimming. He wore heavy dark trousers and shirt, a shapeless jacket and a wide-brimmed hat. His boots were work boots, thick-soled and graceless, vastly different than the boots she and most cowmen preferred.

He was not wearing a handgun, and Amanda was glad she had left hers at home. She spoke, putting authority in her voice. "You're camping on Spencer land."

He did nothing for a moment, then turned his head and spat. "Don't see no fence lines 'round here."

"We don't use fences in this valley." Amanda looked at the herd of sheep. "This is cattle country. Sheep are not welcome."

"There's 'nuff grass for everyone," the man sneered. "My animals—"

"Are eating my grass and drinking my water! This land has been in the Spencer family for thirty years. You can't stay here. Your animals can't stay here."

"I don't take orders from females."

His disdain for her sex put a little starch in Amanda's spine. "You will in this instance. You're camping on deeded land, *my* deeded land. Your sheep are muddying my creek. You could at least have kept them away from the creek." His expression was so insolent and sullen, Amanda felt anger rising within her. "I want you to move on. Immediately!"

The wagon door opened, and startled by the movement, Amanda watched a weary-looking woman come out. She was carrying an infant, and a toddler clung to her skirt. "What's the matter, Jed?" she asked fearfully.

Jed turned angrily, barking, "Git back inside! Din't I tell you to stay in if anyone came 'round?"

Amanda felt suddenly deflated. The woman and children made an enormous difference. She didn't stop to question her reactions as she inquired of the man in a kindlier tone, "How long were you planning to camp here?"

Jed's head jerked around. "As long as we damned well wanna! What makes you cattle people so high and mighty?" He swept a big hand outward. "Look at all that grass! Why're you so stingy with it? Well, lemme tell you somethin'. Me and the family are all done takin' orders from cattle people. We're stayin' right here."

Amanda's stomach turned over. Her gaze flicked from the angry man to the visibly cringing woman. The child, which Amanda could see was a boy of no more than three years, was hanging onto his mother's skirt as if his little life depended on it, and the baby in the woman's arms was only a tiny bundle, scarcely more than a newborn. The whole family reached something maternal and protective in Amanda's nature. It was obvious they had little. Their clothing was poor and not overly clean, and Amanda strongly suspected they all could use a square meal.

She sighed woefully and looked away from the foursome for a moment. Then she brought back softer eyes to the group. "Don't you realize you're in danger?" she asked quietly.

The man scoffed. "Lady, we been in danger ever since we crossed the Missouri River!"

Amanda's back stiffened. "I'm not talking about the ordinary dangers of traveling through unfamiliar country. The cattlemen in this valley dislike sheepherders to the point of violence. You have a wife and children to think of."

"Lucy can handle a gun good as me," Jed mumbled, shooting his wife a fretful look.

He wasn't going to listen, and his stubbornness sparked impatience in Amanda. "Do you think that only one or two men would come out here if they decided to run you off? There would be dozens!" She saw pigheaded inflexibility on the man's face, and still that note of disdain because she was a woman. He would not be so contemptuous if it was Choice giving him advice, Amanda thought.

But Choice was one of the people she felt would deal too harshly with the situation. "Think of your family," she pleaded.

"Jed?" the woman croaked, so obviously terrified Amanda's heart went out to her.

"She's only tryin' to scare us off," Jed growled. "She wants all this grass for herself!"

"Stop being a fool!" Amanda snapped, then saw the barrel of the rifle rise a few inches. "And don't threaten me. Whether you want to believe it or not, you *are* on deeded land. Even without anyone else's help I could have my men roust you!"

She turned Ginger's head. "I hope when I ride this way tomorrow morning you won't be here. Believe me, leaving on your own is the most sensible thing for you to do."

Crossing the creek again, Amanda felt the man's hatred right between her shoulder blades. She understood his anger. It was a simple matter to drive a herd of animals into the valley, and the lush grass had to be a powerful draw. Being ordered to move on, especially by a woman, when he so obviously had little respect for women, had to be hard for Jed to swallow.

He probably wouldn't swallow it, Amanda thought with a mournful sigh. What on earth would she do tomorrow if the sheep were still at the creek? There was little she could do on her own. The man was careless with his family, but could she be so heartless as to risk violence for those people by asking for help from someone? And who was there to ask? Buck, Woody and Jess would be gone for several days. Going to any of the other ranchers, Choice included, maybe Choice *especially*, was bound to cause that family more trouble than they deserved.

If Jed wanted to risk his own tough hide on bluster and denial of the truth, that was his prerogative. But Lucy and those babies were a different matter. Did Jed think Amanda had lied about the cattleman's attitude?

At the crest of the hill, Amanda noticed the tremble in her body. Now that the heat of confrontation was behind her, she felt shaky. This was no way to prove her worth. There was more to owning and operating a cattle ranch than tending the animals or amassing food and fuel for winter. She must deal with whatever problems might arise, however unpleasant. She had faced problems before coming to the ranch, hurdles that had seemed insurmountable at the time, and she had overcome them and survived.

She would survive Jed and his sheep, too. Tomorrow morning she would return to the encampment, and if the family and the herd were still there, she would...she would...

Amanda brushed away a tear with renewed anger. Damn the man for putting her in such an untenable position! If he was still there in the morning she would have no other option but to turn to a neighbor. To Choice, more than likely, because he already knew about the sheep. Involving the other ranchers could blow the whole thing out of proportion.

But she didn't want to turn to Choice, not after this morning. Could she even talk to him without remembering the intensity of his touch? The hot light in his eyes? Her own extraordinary reactions?

A strange thrill spiked through her body, and Amanda chided her wayward thoughts. She shouldn't dwell on this morning, and she must never give Choice any reason to think another such advance would be welcome. He was not a man to toy with, not for a woman like her. Oh, she remembered how some women could bat their eyelashes and lead a man on. But she never had, and if a woman did that with Choice, she suspected the outcome would be his decision, not hers.

The family at the wagon haunted Amanda during the ride home—that poor sad woman Lucy, her small son, the infant in her arms. Was the baby a boy or a girl? She would have liked to gather up a load of food and take it to the wagon, to speak to Lucy, to hold the baby, to talk to the lad.

It was impossible. She could not actively seek friendship with a family of sheepherders.

Finally reaching the buildings, Amanda wearily dismounted and unsaddled Ginger. After turning the mare into the horse pasture, Amanda stood near the corral and let her gaze sweep the compound. There were always chores to do, but her heart was heavy and mundane tasks were unappealing.

Slowly, she worked the leather gloves from her hands, then took off her hat and lifted her face to the sun. Soon, very soon, the sun would lose its warmth. The air would become crisp, then cold, then bitter. There would be long stretches of rain, then longer stretches of snow. Some blizzards took weeks to blow out. Days would be short, nights long. She would seldom leave the house, and then only for the most necessary duties. The men would spend most of their time in the bunkhouse. Their work would consist of hauling hay to the cattle when the snow was too frozen for the animals to paw through it to find the grass beneath, and making sure there were holes in the ice at the watering holes so the animals could drink. Winter seemed to last forever, and in fact did last for months and months.

The family at the wagon returned to her mind, the children in particular. At least Lucy was blessed with children, if little else. Imagine children here on this beautiful, bountiful land, Amanda thought sadly. Imagine that small boy running and playing, whooping as only a small child can. Imagine herself caring for the infant, bathing it, feeding it.

Her arms ached with emptiness. Winters would not be long and lonely with children in the house. She would teach them their letters and numbers during the bad months, make them good things to eat, build roaring fires in the stoves and keep them warm and safe.

Amanda gave her head a shake to clear it, then started for the house. She would water the vegetables remaining in the garden and go on from there. Daydreaming about children was a futile and painful exercise.

With the garden watered and the final crop of green beans picked and carried to the house, Amanda bathed and put on a dress. She brushed her hair, which reached almost to her waist, and knotted and pinned it again, settling the fat coil at her nape.

In the kitchen, she built a small fire in the cookstove and warmed some soup for an early supper. After eating and washing the few dishes she had used, she set to work on the beans. It was a spindly picking, and some of the beans were tough and stringy. Discarding those, she tossed the good ones into a pot. She had canned two dozen quarts of green beans during the summer, but this batch wasn't worth the bother. When the hands returned in a few days, she would make up a ham and green bean stew, which was a favorite.

Amanda carried the pot to the well house, then returned to the kitchen to sweep up the bits of beans she had dropped on the floor. In the utter silence and waning sunlight, the swish of the straw broom was a comforting sound. She had so much, she thought with another burst of compassion for the family at the wagon, and there were people who had so little. How well she remembered the days, the years when she had been rootless and penniless. She thought of her father and wondered again if he was still alive, and if so where he might be.

Another sound penetrated the silence, the sound of hooves. Amanda scurried to the front of the house and peered through a parlor window. Her heart nearly stopped beating when she saw Choice riding in.

Quickly she fled to the kitchen, picked up the litter of beans with dustpan and broom, then put the implements away in the pantry. She couldn't assume that Choice was here only because of the sheep, not after this morning, but surely he hadn't decided to make another attempt at familiarity so soon!

So soon, so soon. The words echoed in her mind. Maybe that's what felt so wrong about this morning. Maybe it was too soon after Len's death to consider another man.

But in her heart Amanda knew it wasn't too soon. She might use her still fairly recent widowhood as an excuse, should he press her, but it was Choice himself she wasn't comfortable with, not the idea of disloyalty to Len's memory.

She stood at the kitchen screen door and watched him ride up to the hitching post near the woodshed. He saw her, she knew, but he said nothing until he had dismounted and walked to the door.

Even his walk was disturbing, the lithe movements of his long legs, the deceptively lazy grace of his stride.

"Amanda."

She cleared her throat. There was nothing in his voice to alarm her, but still the tension in her system prickled her spine. "Choice."

"Did you speak to the sheepherder?"

There were a few things to relate about the sheepherder, specifically that he wasn't alone in that wagon. And she must do so calmly, with none of the girlish giddiness that seemed to have implanted itself in her midsection. Amanda pushed the door open. "Come in, if you like."

Choice was noticing her dress. She was beautiful in a dress, although the blue garment was high-necked and without adornment. The hem of its skirt brushed Amanda's insteps, and its sleeves buttoned around her wrists, a proper garment for a proper lady. But the dress was darted to fit, and soft, curving breasts filled its bodice. Choice clenched his teeth against an overwhelming urge to touch what he dare not touch, to do what he dare not do.

Stone-faced, he walked past her, unconsciously sniffing the powdery scent that always emanated from her. She made him think of softness even when she was wearing britches, but in a dress she seemed like woman personified. The woman lonely men dreamed of during long, cold winter nights.

The kitchen was growing dim in the fading light. Amanda gestured toward a chair. "Please sit down."

He moved to the chair, but waited until she had seated herself. There was something in the air, something that made him suspect that all had not gone well at the sheepherder's encampment. "What's wrong?" he demanded.

"I didn't expect you to... return today."

"I thought about it and figured I should. What happened with the sheepherder?"

Amanda wanted to present the story without emotion, but there was a lump to swallow in her throat. Sensible or not, she was not emotionless about the family at the wagon. "The man is not alone," she said.

Choice's system tensed. Amanda seemed distraught, and if that sheepherder, no matter how many men were with him, had said one thing out of line to her, he—or they—would answer to him.

"There's a family living in that wagon," Amanda said with a catch in her voice. "A family, Choice, a woman and two small children. One of them is an infant, the other a little boy.''

''A family,'' Choice echoed, suddenly uncertain. When Amanda had said the sheepherder wasn't alone, he had pictured other men, but that really had little to do with sheep in the valley. ''It doesn't matter who brought the sheep in, Amanda. They're here, and they can't stay.''

''It doesn't matter? Of course it matters!''

''How?''

Amanda searched for the right words to express the anguish she was feeling. ''Those people have nothing!''

''They have two hundred sheep! What did you tell them?''

Just as she'd always suspected, Choice was completely without compassion. Maybe Len wouldn't have been compassionate about sheep, either.

It seemed so terribly sad to Amanda. What difference did it make whether a person raised sheep or cattle? Winter was coming on, and that family couldn't survive it in that wagon. They had to get established somewhere before the bad weather struck, erect some kind of house, a soddy if nothing else.

''Did you make it clear that sheep are not welcome in this valley?'' Choice demanded.

''Yes!'' Amanda was startled by the anger in her own voice. ''Yes, I made it clear. I told the man he couldn't stay. I told him that the cattlemen around here dislike sheep to the point of violence. I warned him to leave on his own, to think of his family.''

Choice leaned forward. ''Is he going to?''

Amanda clenched her hands in her lap. ''I don't know.''

Even while discussing what he considered to be a very serious subject, Choice absorbed the female essence of the woman across the table. She had the most glorious eyes of any woman he'd ever seen, a deep, true green fringed with thick, long lashes. Her eyebrows were two perfect arches below a short forehead and a mass of auburn hair. He wanted her. He wanted to unpin her hair and catch it in his hands. He wanted to peel away her blue dress and kiss her naked breasts. He had always wanted her, but his desire was becoming more explicit and thus more painful.

"I'll go out there in the morning. I'd go yet today, but it's nearly dark."

Amanda stared across the table, realizing that she wasn't resigned to his intrusion. If the sheepherder was still there in the morning, she would convince him to leave herself. Somehow. "No," she said flatly. "I will not stand by and see that family harmed."

"Do you think I would harm a woman? And babies?" Choice's eyes narrowed with frustration. How could she think he would hurt a woman and children? Didn't she know him at all?

But Amanda remained unmoved. "This is my land, Choice, and I will tend to it, whatever is involved."

"It's only been yours for a year," he bluntly pointed out. "And those sheep affect the entire valley."

"I don't happen to believe they're hurting anyone but me. They're eating Spencer grass, not Brenton. If they were on your land, I would not presume to suggest how you deal with them. Please give me the same courtesy." How brave she sounded, when she was really sick with worry about how she would handle the situation should the sheep still be there in the morning! Maybe she would have to appeal to Choice in the end, but not yet, not without making every attempt to maintain peace.

Choice rarely felt helpless. In fact, he couldn't remember the last time he'd felt like his hands were tied about something. But that unfamiliar, practically unknown sensation held him to his chair while he regarded Amanda with a brooding expression. "Why are you doing this?" he finally questioned.

"Insisting on fighting my own battles? Does that strike you as uncharacteristic? I had a life before I married Len, Choice. I took care of myself from the time I was sixteen. Younger than that." Since she was ten, if one wanted to get down to hard facts. Her father had bought her food and— very seldom—something to wear, but that had been the extent of his interest. More often than not, she'd worn castoffs from the other miners' ragtag children.

She leaned forward slightly. "Do you want to know something, Choice? I'd be willing to bet you've never known any kind of need. Len didn't. He grew up with a mother and father who doted on him. He worked hard, granted, just as you do, but he never knew hunger or homelessness."

"And you did?"

"Yes, I did." Amanda's chin had risen for that admittance. She couldn't help being proud of her own survival, not when she had been solely responsible for it.

But trials and tribulations had not made her hard, nor had they given her experience with kicking hapless people off a piece of land. "That family out there means something to me," she stated quietly. "They will leave, I promise, but they will leave with good feelings about this place."

"Good feelings!" That was too much for Choice to take, and he stood up. "Listen to me. No one in this valley gives a damn if a sheepherder has feelings of any kind, good *or* bad. Amanda, it's not the people, it's their animals. But even if they had brought cattle with them, would you want them squatting on Spencer land?"

Amanda got up, too. "That isn't the point, is it?"

She was making him mad. "Fine! It's your land, and you do what you want. But if that herd isn't gone by tomorrow afternoon, I *am* going to do something about it, whether you like it or not!''

He stormed out the door.

That night, Amanda lay in bed and listened to the wind that had come up. She had infuriated Choice, but she was right and he was wrong. Well, maybe not wrong. She knew the sheep had to go as well as he did. But it was a matter of methods. He would storm into that encampment, just as he'd stormed out of the house, and who knew what might happen if Jed should resist?

At least Choice hadn't attempted to hold her hand again, although he did look at her so peculiarly at times. Like he was thinking of something she was better off not knowing.

Amanda finally fell asleep thinking of Lucy and her children. She would bring some food with her in the morning, just in case the family was still there, a nice basket of vegetables, and some of those molasses cookies she had baked last week. The little boy would welcome a cookie, and Amanda strongly suspected that Lucy would welcome fresh vegetables. She would make Jed understand the danger of obstinacy... she would manage it all... without Choice's intervention ... somehow.

Chapter Four

Rather than the wicker basket she had planned to use, Amanda packed a small burlap bag with carrots, potatoes, onions and the green beans picked only yesterday, then fitted a tin of molasses cookies on top of the vegetables. The bag would be more manageable than a basket on horseback, she reasoned, tying it to the pommel of her saddle.

She halfway expected Choice to show up and tag along with her to the sheepherder's encampment, and was relieved to ride away from the ranch buildings alone. Last night's wind had gentled to a breeze again, but signs of the waning summer were evident. The air, still warm, was beginning to feel different, fresher somehow.

The long ride to the south pasture was accomplished with much soul-searching for Amanda. Try as she might, she could not rid her memory of Choice holding her hand. Such a simple gesture should not have had such a lasting effect, but that same insistent mood had shown in his eyes again last evening, even though he hadn't said or done anything untoward.

Pairing herself with Choice Brenton was the most disconcerting idea Amanda had ever had, but it was present, mingling with thoughts of the possible unpleasantness that lay ahead of her, how Buck, Woody and Jess were faring with the strays, and the knowledge that autumn was just around the corner.

She found herself thinking of Len and puzzling over why she had felt so much from the merest contact with Choice when she had loved Len and felt so little. The physical side of marriage confounded her. Len had derived such pleasure from it, while she had wondered if maybe a woman never did. Now, the sparks in her system whenever Choice was near were creating questions that wouldn't be put aside, although it seemed more sensible to bury and forget them.

When Amanda heard the sound of sheep, her shoulders slumped. Even though she had burdened herself with a bag of food for the family, she had prayed that Jed had heeded her warning and left the valley. Her mind raced in a hasty attempt to formulate some commonsense arguments to diminish the man's obstinacy. He *had* to be made to understand!

As she crested the hill, Amanda gnawed uneasily at her bottom lip. A smoky odor hung on the air, and one look at the scene by the creek made her eyes widen with horror. The sheep were scattered, grazing far afield in small groups. Amanda sought the wagon, whispering, "Oh, dear Lord," at the pile of twisted, charred wood and chunks of iron she saw. The wagon was destroyed, burned down to its metal parts. Wild-eyed, she noted the horse lying on its side and knew it was dead. She froze, fearing for the family.

When her gaze found the woman sitting beside the creek, Amanda nearly wept with relief. Nudging Ginger forward, she urged the mare into a gallop. As she got closer, Amanda could see the small boy huddled in his mother's skirt and the baby in Lucy's arms. The family was safe.

The woman looked up dispiritedly as Ginger carried her rider into the encampment. Amanda jumped to the ground, sickened by the sight of the dead horse, and hurried over to the woman. "Lucy! Are you all right? What happened?"

Lucy looked away, her eyes pale and dull.

Amanda kneeled beside her. "Where's your husband?" No response followed and a terrible premonition flashed in her mind. "Lucy, where's Jed?" she demanded sharply, giving the woman's arm a shake.

Lucy nodded to the west. "I buried him over there."

Nausea churned in Amanda's stomach. "What happened? Who burned your wagon?"

"The lantern ... toppled. Men were here," Lucy mumbled tonelessly.

"When? When were they here?"

"In the night."

A cold anger began spreading through Amanda. Her first thought was that Choice hadn't waited, that he had either told someone about the sheep or brought his own men out here last night.

But that notion was so staggering, she shied away from it. Rising, Amanda looked around. "You can't stay here," she declared, half ill from the destruction everywhere she looked. The burned wagon, the dead horse—the animal had to be buried, too.

Oh, poor Jed. Poor, stubborn man. If only he'd listened yesterday!

Heaving a sorrowful sigh, Amanda kneeled beside Lucy again. The woman was clutching her baby so tightly, Amanda worried for the infant's well-being. The little boy, although obviously scared to death, didn't appear to be physically injured. But the baby was concealed by a dirty pink blanket, and Amanda couldn't tell if the child was even alive.

"Is the baby all right?" she asked fearfully.

Without warning Lucy thrust the bundle out, and instinctively Amanda took it. Through the blanket she felt the infant's warmth, and when she peeled the top of the blan-

ket away, two blue eyes peered out at her while the baby
suckled a tiny fist.

Amanda's heart melted in her breast, and she brought the
baby closer and cuddled it. "Is it a girl?" she asked softly.

The woman nodded. "Her name's Elizabeth."

"She's beautiful, Lucy." Amanda sighed sadly and sur-
veyed the scene again. "Do you have anywhere to go?"

Lucy shook her head, and Amanda saw the first sign of
tears in her eyes. "Jed . . . he sold everything we had to get
the wagon and things we needed to come west."

"You must have family somewhere," Amanda said gently.

"I have a sister in Pennsylvania," Lucy sobbed, wiping
her eyes on the sleeve of the old jacket she was wearing over
a nightgown.

Thoughtfully Amanda looked at the saddened woman,
then at the small boy who hadn't uttered one sound, and finally at the baby in her arms. An overwhelming anger began again and quickly gained momentum, but connecting
Choice to the horrible incident made her feel ill, and she
couldn't quite allow herself to lay the blame on him. It was
a strange sensation, a deep, inner battle of recrimination and
defense. She didn't want to believe Choice was involved.

Amanda rose abruptly. "I want you to come home with
me. I live alone and you and your children can stay until we
figure something else out."

Lucy stared at her strangely.

"It's all right, you'll be safe with me."

The woman gave the sheep a fretful glance. "What about
the animals? They're all I got now."

Amanda frowned, reluctant to answer too quickly. Sheep
on her land would cause her trouble. The men who struck
this family in the night might be friends and neighbors, but
they wouldn't tolerate sheep in the valley, not even from one
of their own. Yet she couldn't turn her back on Lucy and

these children. They had nothing, not even clothing, and the sheep would give them a new start.

She made a decision that she knew was dangerous. But the whole situation was senseless, and she was being ruled by compassion. "I'll have my men drive them farther onto my land. They'll be safe, too, I promise."

With only one horse between the four of them, getting the family to the house was a problem, and Amanda decided that Lucy and the children should ride and she would walk. "Come, Lucy," she said gently, holding the infant in one arm and extending her other hand to the forlorn woman.

After food and a bath, Lucy gratefully accepted the bed Amanda offered. With her son, Tad, beside her, the woman closed her eyes and slept.

Carrying Elizabeth to the kitchen, Amanda prepared a bath for the infant. The child was beautiful, with bright blue button eyes and soft blond fuzz for hair. Amanda removed the baby's soiled clothing and carefully dipped her into a pan of warm water. While she washed Elizabeth's tiny limbs and delicate skin, Amanda crooned sweet nothings, thrilled beyond measure to have this precious life in her hands.

When the child was clean, Amanda wrapped her in soft flannel and brought her close in a loving hug. "You sweet, sweet child," she whispered, moved to tears by affection. This dear baby girl would never know her father because some people didn't like sheep!

It took monumental effort for Amanda to contain the hot tide of rising anger. She cleared her clogged throat and whispered, "Now, we must make you something to wear."

Laying the infant on the table where she could keep an eye on her while she worked, Amanda cut a soft, worn flannel blanket into squares for diapers, then took one of the squares and cut a hole in the center of it. Another slash of the scissors produced a short length of cord from the same fabric and, satisfied with her handiwork, Amanda proceeded to dress Elizabeth in her new garments. A diaper was pinned into place, and the square with the hole in it was dropped over the baby's head and tied around her little middle with the cord. Amanda held Elizabeth up for inspection. "It will do, little love," she murmured, adding, "until I can buy you some proper clothing."

Then, carrying the baby in one arm, Amanda tidied the kitchen and sat down. Her thoughts became painfully speculative. Choice was the only other person who knew about the sheep. Dear God, was he responsible for Jed's death? For that charred wagon? For that dead horse? Could he do such terrible things? Did she know him well enough to doubt it?

She was holding Elizabeth up to her shoulder and patting her diapered bottom when the door flew open and Choice burst in. He stopped dead in his tracks when he saw the baby in Amanda's arms.

"You know," he said soberly.

All sense of reason fled Amanda's system. "Yes, I know," she retorted angrily. "You didn't waste any time, did you?"

Choice recoiled, his expression icy cold. "I'll say it once, Amanda, only once! I told no one about the sheep and that family. Whatever happened out there, I had nothing to do with it."

Amanda studied him, wondering if he was lying. A man who could do murder could certainly lie about it. It was an awful few moments. Choice's lips were set in a thin line, his steely eyes daring her to accuse him again. Gradually, her anger drained away. Instinct told her that, whatever else she thought Choice Brenton might be, he wasn't a murderer and a liar. "I apologize for thinking you did. Someone else must have seen them out there."

Choice felt some of the tension that had grabbed him hard at Amanda's accusation release, but not all of it. She had a mighty strange opinion of him, and he didn't know whether he felt relieved that she had apologized or permanently injured because she had thought of him when she'd seen the destruction at the sheepherder's camp.

"Obviously," he agreed dryly. He looked at the baby. "You brought the whole family here?"

"I brought the woman and children here. The man is dead," she said with some bitterness. "They killed him, Choice."

He must have been a few hours behind Amanda, he realized. When he had decided to check on the encampment this morning, no one had been there. He'd come directly from there to Amanda. Choice's gaze narrowed. "How? Who? What happened?"

"I don't know. Lucy didn't talk about it and I didn't press her." Realizing the baby had fallen asleep, Amanda rose cautiously. "I'll only be a minute," she told Choice and left the kitchen to carry the sleeping child to the bureau drawer she had earlier emptied and padded with a blanket for the baby's bed.

When she returned, Choice was standing at the kitchen window, looking out. He turned at the sound of her approach. "I'm not sure you should keep them here," he said quietly.

"Should I have left them out there?" Amanda returned bitterly. "They have nothing, no food, not even something decent to put on their backs. They were in nightclothes, Choice. You wouldn't have left them out there, either." Her eyes narrowed. "Would you?"

His gray eyes were dark with things Amanda couldn't read. He finally admitted, "No, I wouldn't have left them. But the sheep are still a problem. They're running all over the place."

Amanda went to the table and began folding the diapers she had fashioned, uneasy over relating what she had promised Lucy. Choice had to be told. Maybe—*she hoped*—no one else needed to know, but Choice did. He was a part of this, at his own insistence, however she felt about it. "I'm going to have my men round them up and move them closer in."

"You're not planning to keep that herd here!"

His reaction was no more than she had expected, but it raised her hackles. "Yes!" she cried heatedly. "I'm going to keep the sheep for Lucy and her babies. Those animals are all they have in the world!"

Choice muttered a curse and looked away. When his gaze lit on Amanda again, it contained anger and frustration. "You're asking for trouble."

Unable to deny the charge, Amanda sighed. "There are times when a person has to do what she thinks best, even if it doesn't coincide with other people's ideas. I owe nothing to anyone in this valley, and if I'm willing to share my grass and water for a while, it's no one else's business."

"You're dead wrong. It *is* everyone else's business. It's their entire way of life, and you know as well as I do that they're not going to sit by and do nothing while you raise sheep!"

"You, too?" Amanda returned his stare without flinching, daring him to take sides. She saw a muscle in his hard jaw working and knew her challenge was causing him pain. Because of their simple contact yesterday he saw her differently, and the tension in the air became almost unbearable before he answered.

Her lips looked full and pink and ripe, and Choice found himself staring at them. He swallowed the urge to touch her again, as if it were a tangible lump in his throat. "I won't do anything to hurt you. But I think you're making a very big mistake."

Relieved despite her show of bravado, Amanda picked up another square of flannel to fold. "It's possible that no one will even notice. If I keep the herd close in...just until I can arrange to sell it . . . maybe no one else—"

Choice brusquely interrupted her extremely foolish fantasy. "Amanda, you—or someone—has to notify the sheriff about that man's death!"

Amanda stopped all movement, although her heart had started thudding fiercely. Feeling like something large and solid had just struck her right between the eyes, she realized with overwhelming shock that she should have thought of that herself. Of course the law would have to be brought into this.

But, oh, dear Lord, she didn't want the law involved! She didn't want anyone involved. There was already enough trouble to deal with without deliberately stirring up everyone in the valley.

"Choice," she said, scarcely able to speak above a whisper. "The poor man is dead, and bringing in the law won't change that cruel fact."

"He was murdered, Amanda."

She struggled to find an argument, something sensible that would still her tearing heartbeat and appease Choice's sense of law and order. "Not intentionally," she said in a near whisper. "Men came to haze the sheep, not to kill anyone."

"Are you so sure of that?"

Amanda wasn't sure of anything. She had no real facts. She stood there holding the square of flannel with a terrible sense of impending doom. The ranch had represented an almost fortresslike security to her for two years now. Events were creating a breach in that security. She could feel it slipping, and the sensation was emotionally draining.

But, as distressing as the realization was, Choice was right. Someone had to notify the sheriff of Jed's death. In the name of justice, the men who killed Jed, accidentally or not, should pay for the pain and horror they had heaped on Lucy.

"I will see the sheriff," she said unsteadily, quite shaken over the unavoidable task. Her eyes rose to Choice's. "But not until the sheep are moved."

He studied her broodingly for a very long time, until Amanda stopped staring back and tried desperately to refocus her attention on the makeshift garments on the table. Choice was perfectly capable of taking the entire matter out of her hands, she knew, and it wouldn't surprise her if he did exactly that.

Then she felt Choice's hand on her arm and she looked from it to his face. "Amanda?" He said her name questioningly and her pulse quickened. She saw turmoil in his eyes and knew she was the cause of it.

"I don't want you hurt," he said hoarsely.

What was happening to them? How could they go from mere acquaintances to this so quickly? Was it normal for a man to react so strongly to the touch of a woman's hand? Was it normal for a woman's insides to get all soft and overheated because that same man was touching her?

Amanda sighed. She had no answers to these questions, which she had never had reason to get near before. "I promised Lucy protection for her sheep. The herd has to be moved before the sheriff is notified."

His eyes assessed her face, roaming from feature to feature. "I suppose one more day won't matter," he finally conceded.

"It might be a little more than a day. My men are out rounding up strays in the hills."

"You can't put it off indefinitely."

"It won't be indefinitely."

There was a stubborn tilt to her chin, which Choice saw and interpreted as determination. His options were to let her do what she thought best or to intercede, and neither alternative felt quite right. He could make it all so easy for her, but not unless she agreed, not when dissension between them could destroy the tentative foothold he felt that he'd gained in her affections. He didn't want dissension. He wanted her warmth, her sweet and arousing femaleness, and if that meant giving her room to make mistakes in judgment, he would try to stay out of it.

For a while, anyway.

He moved his fingers on her arm. "Amanda..."

What was he doing? What did he want? Amanda tried to still the acceleration of her heart. He smelled of the outdoors, of maleness, and she was becoming dizzy.

She was still in the clothes she'd worn for the ride out to the sheepherder's camp, trousers and a rough work shirt, but her hair gleamed with gold and red highlights, and undisciplined strands had escaped their pins and floated around her face and to the back of her neck. She looked beautiful to Choice, and he lifted the hand from her arm and touched her hair.

Amanda's breath caught. Her breasts felt achy and heavy, and Choice's hand wasn't anywhere near the front of her shirt. His gaze followed his hand as his fingertips curled in her hair then drifted downward to the curve of her cheek. Amanda dampened her lips as the moment stretched.

She saw the flame smoldering in his eyes, the indisputable desire. She should back away from him this very instant! She shouldn't allow anything more between them.

But Choice was a mystery she couldn't seem to resist, and his boldness, verging on what she had always thought of as indecent, only increased the excitement developing in her own body. Amanda watched his head descending, his face and mouth coming nearer to her own, and she closed her eyes.

His mustache was silky and his mouth warm, and the kiss was a tender mating of their lips, making her feel breathless and unsettled. "Choice," she whispered, her lips forming his name within the kiss.

His arm reached out and curved around her waist, sweeping her closer to him. The kiss changed from gentle to something that caused a roar in Amanda's ears and a weakness in her knees. His size was overwhelming; Len had not been so big. Choice's tongue slid between her lips and into her mouth. Len had never kissed her so brazenly.

Nor so possessively. So demandingly. Choice's mouth molded hers until it was hot and wet and malleable. The arm around her waist pressed her forward, into his shockingly hard body. Her senses reeled. The yearning building in her own body was dumbfounding.

Choice's mind was spinning. He hadn't intended to get so carried away, not during a first kiss. But kissing Amanda was more than he had ever suspected it would be. She must know how strongly she affected him, how could she not?

But did she? He raised his head to see her face and found it flushed and glowing. She was breathless, taking air through her parted lips. His mind raced in a search for the right thing to say, but he could think of only one thing, of how much he wanted her, and instinct told him not to rush her.

His dark eyes probed hers, plumbing their depths for whatever she might be thinking. She had kissed him back, she wasn't pushing him away, but she seemed so surprised by it all.

The softness of her bosom against his chest was liquefying his bones. He took her hand and pressed it to his shirt, over the hard, excited pumping of his heart, wanting her to feel what he did. "Where do we go from here?" he asked thickly.

Amanda stared, her mind dazed from unfamiliar emotions, her palm absorbing the rhythm of his heartbeat. She was up against him, and she was overwhelmed by maleness. "Where . . . do you want us to go?"

"You were married. You know where this sort of thing leads."

Amanda recalled again the faint flutterings of something unidentifiable with Len. Was that what making love with Choice would be like, more faint flutterings?

Why did she think there should be more with a man? Why did Choice make her feel that there *would* be more? And what, pray tell, did "more" even mean?

It was all so confusing. He was thinking about making love, she was thinking about making love. Whatever was developing between them had to be slowed down.

Amanda took a backward step, eluding the hand that tried to maintain contact. She was torn up internally, but she was accustomed to inner conflict. From the time she could remember, there'd been quandaries to deal with of one kind or another.

She had found what she needed on the Spencer ranch, security, a home of her own. For a time, Len's death had seemed like a renewal of her youthful unhappiness, but she was recovering, *had* recovered.

This thing with Choice had come totally out of the blue. For her, at least, regardless of his mention of something between them all along.

"We're not alone," she reminded him in a rather prim voice, relying on Lucy and the children's being in the house without thinking of how Choice might interpret her evasion.

He looked at her queerly. "Is that our only hurdle?"

The question was rampant with innuendo, and Amanda wasn't sure how to reply. For some obscure reason she didn't want to be harsh right now. She could cut him to ribbons with lies about feeling insulted, which she didn't but knew she should be. She could tell him in no uncertain terms that she wasn't interested, but she was.

"I . . . don't know." It was, at least, an honest answer.

His eyes were dark pools, radiating desire. "We could go to the barn."

Her chest began rising and falling rapidly with harried breaths. "The barn?" she whispered, shocked again.

"The hayloft."

"Oh." Her eyes were wide while she pondered Choice's urgency. The hayloft was cool and smelled of alfalfa hay, but she had never thought of making love in such a place. With Len, everything had been conducted at night, in a dark room, beneath the covers. Her head was swimming. Was she actually having this discussion? And with a man she wasn't even sure she liked? What Choice was suggesting was... My Lord, how could he be so forward?

Amanda cleared her head with a sharp shake. "No, I'm afraid not."

He looked like a thundercloud. "How long will that woman be here?"

Amanda allowed him his little misconception. She had refused much more than a trip to the barn at this particular moment, but she saw that Choice had taken it as a temporary rejection. "I have no idea. She has a sister in Pennsylvania and I expect Lucy will write her. I must give her time."

Choice took one hasty step forward and then, as if changing his mind, turned away. The abrupt movement caused the gun on his thigh to bump against her. "You always wear that," she accused in a low voice.

"Yes," he replied tersely, offering no explanation or apology.

"You're angry with me!" She was stunned and couldn't pretend anything else. How did she think she would react to an invitation to go to her own barn with him—with open arms?

"Angry?" Choice cursed under his breath, then went to the door. He stopped and looked at her. "I've waited a long time for you."

Her mouth dropped open. "Why?"

"What kind of question is that?" he asked sharply.

"It's a perfectly logical question. Why have you waited for me?" His was the most startling confession she had ever heard. He had *waited* for her?

Choice came closer slowly, moving with that pantherlike grace she had always admired. When he stood before her, his hand rose to the back of her neck. Her system sparked from the prickles his touch evoked on her neck, and she saw the same feeling erupt in his gray eyes.

"Picking things apart makes little sense to me, Amanda. I'm not much of a talker," he muttered. "I'm more of a doer. Can you deal with a doer?" His dark gaze washed over her face. "Think about it." Abruptly, he released her and swung away. "I'll be back," he growled. "In the meantime, try to figure a way out of the mess you got yourself into today."

Amanda stared at the door he closed behind himself. He had waited for her? Dear God in heaven, what was she getting into with Choice Brenton?

She stood there until a small cry from the bedroom wafted through the house. Then she spun and hastened away to see to the baby.

Chapter Five

From the kitchen window, Amanda—with abundant relief—saw Buck, Woody and Jess ride up and dismount at the barn. It had been two anxious days since she had brought Lucy's family home with her, and the necessity of traveling to Leavitt to speak to the sheriff was a constant worry. The ongoing delay was becoming a serious concern.

Amanda had been tending Elizabeth while Lucy and Tad napped, but speaking to the men was crucial, and Amanda hurried down the hall to the bedroom she had assigned her guests. At the door she softly called for Lucy, then, when there was no response, went into the room and sat on the edge of the bed. "Lucy?"

The woman stirred drowsily for a moment, then came wide awake with a start. Lucy's panicked gaze renewed Amanda's sympathy, and she smiled reassuringly and laid the infant in her mother's arms. "My men are back. I'm going out to talk to them about moving the sheep."

Tad woke up and stared at Amanda with large, distant blue eyes. Amanda smiled at the little boy but made no other overture. So far, she hadn't heard one word from Tad, and she knew he must learn to trust her in his own time.

"I'll only be about ten minutes," she assured Lucy before leaving the family to themselves. Lucy's vulnerability touched Amanda's soul in a unique fashion. Tad's, too, for that matter. Both were heartrendingly withdrawn, with a silence that projected concealed pain.

Amanda, too, felt vulnerable. But she had taken on a massive load of responsibility with the family and vowed to see it through, however unsettling. Just talking to her men and requesting their cooperation with a list of bizarre chores was going to be difficult.

Amanda hurried from the house and across the compound to the barn. She called a greeting before reaching the trio, then, while they rubbed down the horses they'd unsaddled, she asked how they were doing with the strays.

Jess replied, "Found about sixty of 'em clear up to Quail Ridge. They wandered a long ways this summer, Amanda, a lot farther than usual."

A worried frown creased Amanda's smooth brow. Jess, Buck and Woody were lifelong cowmen and would resent a request to work with sheep. Yet she had no one else to turn to, and she paid the men well and felt they all had a reasonably good relationship.

"I need a favor," she began, at which, all three men became more alert. "There's a herd of sheep scattered in the south pasture..."

"Sheep!" Woody exclaimed.

"Sheep," Amanda repeated evenly. "They belong to a guest in my home. I'd like them moved closer in. Will you do it?" Her gaze shifted from one man to another, stopping briefly on each.

The men stirred uneasily, all the time darting questioning looks at one another. Jess cleared his throat. "Well, now, sheep ain't exactly what we're used to, Amanda."

"I know that," she retorted sharply, then heaved a remorseful sigh. "I'm sorry, Jess. Maybe if I explain..."

Quickly, Amanda poured out the story. "So, you see, Lucy and the children have nowhere else to go right now, and I'm hoping those sheep will provide them with a new start."

"You ain't aimin' to keep 'em then?" Jess spoke with a shrewd squint.

"Of course not. I don't want to raise sheep any more than you do. But someone has to help that family."

Jess's squint evolved into a deep frown. "What d'ya want us to do, Amanda?"

The stiffness in her body relented some. The men hadn't said yes, but they weren't completely negative, which was encouraging. "First, and I know it's a terrible job, that horse has to be buried. It must be attracting predators from miles around. Secondly, I would appreciate your checking on Jed's grave. Lucy buried her husband, but I don't know how well. Please make sure it's a proper grave and mark it with something so we can locate it again."

Amanda didn't add that the sheriff might want to locate the grave, too, but the thought was in the back of her mind, as it had been from the moment Choice had introduced the subject. The whole idea was extremely upsetting. Inviting the law into the situation would be like opening the door to a pack of wolves. If the association didn't stick its nose in, Wes Schuyler in particular, Amanda would be eternally surprised.

And heaven only knew what Wes Schuyler might do about Lucy's sheep. According to what Amanda had seen of the man, and from what Len had recounted of him, Schuyler was cunning, nasty and capable of almost anything.

There hadn't exactly been a feud between Len and Wes Schulyer, but there hadn't been any love lost, either. Amanda's experience with the man was limited to only a few meetings, but she had respected Len's opinion about people.

She pushed Schuyler, the association and the sheriff to the back of her mind and returned to the more urgent topic at hand. "Then, the sheep must be moved," she told her men. "Bring them close to the buildings where I can keep an eye on them."

Buck put in dourly, "They won't stay put."

Amanda hesitated. That possibility had her worried, too. "You're probably right. At this point I have no idea how long they'll be here. We might have to fence them in."

Jess looked away and muttered something Amanda couldn't make out. A tense moment passed before he turned angry eyes on her. "I ain't puttin' up no fences, Amanda. Fooling around with sheep's bad enough, but you know danged well what the association thinks of barbed wire."

"Yes, I do know. But do you have an alternative suggestion?"

"Shoot 'em," Woody said, sneering. "If someone was shootin' up the place, why din't they get rid of the danged sheep?"

Buck nodded his agreement, and Amanda's heart sank. "I know I'm asking a lot, but who else do I have to rely on?"

She never used feminine tactics on her men, but even she heard the note of helplessness in her voice. It brought a stain of color to her cheeks and she lifted her chin. "It has to be done. Please talk it over among yourselves and let me know what you decide. I'll be at the house."

Amanda strode away, forcing herself to look straight ahead. If all three men decided against her, she would be in a fine fix. Not that cowhands couldn't be replaced. But with everything else going on right now, she didn't need the additional problem of locating new men.

To Amanda's surprise, Lucy was up and dressed in the clothing Amanda had loaned her. Her hair was combed and neatly pinned into a bun at the back of her head, and she sat on a kitchen chair with the baby on her lap and Tad huddled against her legs. The little boy was wearing his nightshirt, the only garment he possessed.

Lucy looked anxious as Amanda came in. "Are they going to move the sheep?"

Apparently the return of the Spencer hands had broken through Lucy's lethargy, Amanda realized. The sheep were very important to her, which was certainly understandable when she had nothing else. Amanda's gaze lingered on the purplish bruise on Lucy's left cheek. She had also seen a startling bruise on little Tad's behind and right thigh. Amanda's heart ached for Lucy and her children and all they'd been through, and she couldn't fault the woman for worrying about her sheep when the animals were her only means to a new start. "They're deciding," she said quietly. "How are you feeling, Lucy?"

The woman sighed. "I'll get by."

"Yes," Amanda agreed softly. "You'll get by. But let me repeat that you're welcome to stay here until you have somewhere else to go." For two days Lucy had scarcely spoken and had mostly kept to her room. She seemed more alert to Amanda now, perhaps even able to discuss the situation with some degree of clarity.

Tears glistened in Lucy's pale eyes. "Thank you. I plan to write my sister in Pennsylvania."

"Is she in a position to offer financial assistance?"

Lucy shook her head plaintively. "No. But if I could raise the money to get to her place, she would take me and the babies in."

Amanda hesitated, moved by a burst of generosity and a true desire to help this woman. Clean, with her light blond hair tidy, Lucy was almost pretty. She was too thin, and the gaunt circles under her eyes and the ugly bruise on her cheek evidenced the horror she'd lived through, but with a few pounds and a little time, Amanda suspected her guest would be a striking woman.

"I could loan you the money," Amanda suggested with a warm smile, and was surprised at the vehement shake of Lucy's head.

"You've already done enough, Amanda. I couldn't take money from you on top of everything else. Couldn't I sell the sheep?"

"That's what I'm hoping for." Amanda sighed. "Around here, that might not be so easy to do." How did one sell two hundred sheep in this part of the territory where the very word *sheep* caused men to reach for their weapons?

Well, she would find a way.

Earlier, Amanda had put supper on the stove to simmer, and she went over to stir the pot of stew. One of the things Lucy and Tad needed was nourishing food, and the pot contained big chunks of beef and potatoes, carrots and onions. Amanda had pressed bountiful meals on Lucy and her son since their arrival, but for the first time, she saw a normal, healthy hunger in Lucy's expression.

"That smells wonderful," Lucy murmured.

"Yes, doesn't it?" Amanda agreed, turning to see that Tad had buried his face in his mother's lap. It happened so often, she was beginning to fear for the lad. "Is there something wrong with the boy, Lucy?"

Lucy's face lost all softness, and she caressed her small son's tousled blond hair with a protective hand. "He's seen too much," she said in a tone so bitter it startled Amanda. Holding the long-handled spoon she'd been using on the stew, she watched mother and children with heartfelt sympathy.

Lucy went on in the same bitter vein. "Anger, shouting, violence, that's all the boy's ever seen. Is it any wonder he's afraid of his own shadow? Jed . . . well, he refused to understand. He wanted his son to be strong and unfeeling, like he was. Tad's not like that. Tad is sensitive and sweet.''

As though suddenly coming awake, Lucy raised her head. ''I'm sorry. I shouldn't be talking about those things. They mean nothing to you.''

Amanda put the spoon down and, hurrying across the room, she kneeled beside Lucy's chair. ''They *do* mean something to me. I lost my husband, too. Len didn't die by someone else's hand, but his death was no less painful, Lucy. And I was alone once, too, without a home, without family. I understand what you're feeling, please believe me.''

The two women studied each other. ''You're a good person, Amanda,'' Lucy finally said. ''I'm sorry you lost your husband.''

''It's been a year and some months. I'm over the shock of it, and you'll get over losing Jed, too. I know that right now you can't imagine feeling normal again, but you will.''

A vague smile crossed Lucy's lips. ''I'm sure you're right.''

At the sound of knuckles on the back door, Amanda stood up. ''That will be my men,'' she told Lucy, and went to the door and stepped outside.

She saw the emotionless expression on the three men's faces and led them away from the house to hear their decision. Jess looked her right in the eye. ''I'll be leavin' just as soon as I get my gear together,'' he announced brusquely.

Amanda suffered an immediate, jolting anxiety. Jess was a hard man with few smiles, but there was little he didn't know about raising cattle. She would miss his expertise, but worse than that, Jess was a leader, the strongest-willed of the trio of cowhands in her employ. His decision could very well have influenced Buck's and Woody's.

Her voice wasn't very steady, although she maintained a stoic expression. "I'm very sorry to hear that, Jess." She turned to the other men. "And you two?"

"I'll be stayin'," Woody declared. "My missus ain't well and I need the job. Just so you know, I ain't happy about what yur doin', and I ain't stayin' 'cause I think it's right. I just need the job."

Relief poured through Amanda's system. "I understand. Buck?"

"I'm stayin', but at the first sign of trouble, I'll be gone."

Amanda drew a deep breath. "Thank you for being honest with me, all of you. I understand and respect your feelings." She offered her hand to Jess. "I wish you luck, Jess, and if you change your mind, I'd be pleased to have you work for me again."

Jess hesitated a bit, then shook hands with her. "Maybe it ain't my place to say, but Len wouldn't like what yur doin', Amanda."

That could be very true, Amanda admitted with a private inward wince. But Len wasn't here now, and she had to do what she thought best.

When Jess had ambled off, heading for the bunkhouse, Amanda turned to Buck and Woody. "I appreciate your both staying. I'll look for a man to replace Jess."

Buck spat into the dust. "Might be harder to do than you think. Word gets around pretty fast."

Amanda's shoulders slumped as Buck and Woody walked away. No one agreed with her, not her ranch hands, not Choice, no one. She was in this alone, wherever it might lead. It was how she had spent most of her life, alone, and for a few fearful moments, watching the men striding off, a stinging sadness enveloped her.

Neither she nor anyone else could operate a ranch of this size without adequate help. She'd expected resistance from the men, but losing Jess was a blow she really hadn't seen coming.

That night, after blowing out the lamp, Amanda settled down in bed with a weary sigh. The day had been long and tiring. In the dark it was even easier to doubt the wisdom of her actions. She would never be sorry for helping Lucy and the children, but she could have taken them in without harboring their sheep. Would she live to regret it?

It wasn't too late. In the morning she could explain a change of heart to Lucy and insist the family accept the money for the trip to Pennyslvania. Buck and Woody would be more comfortable with such a decision, and maybe Jess would come back.

And Choice? He would be greatly relieved, wouldn't he?

Of course he would. Everyone concerned—other than Lucy—would be relieved.

Why, then, did some obstinate part of Amanda recoil from the idea of taking the easy way out?

The answer was really very simple. Lucy had nothing except those sheep, and even if she only got five dollars a head for the herd she would have a thousand dollars. That amount of money would go a long way toward giving her and her two sweet children a fresh start in Pennsylvania. While Amanda could certainly come up with enough cash to pay for train tickets for the family, she couldn't afford to hand over a thousand dollars.

Ignoring that scattered herd of sheep was like throwing money down a well, which was utterly ridiculous. She would have Buck and Woody round them up and drive them closer in, just as she'd been planning. And Lucy would have her money, just as soon as Amanda figured out how to go about selling the animals.

There was another reason behind her stubbornness, too, Amanda admitted, thinking about her own unstable past. She knew so well what Lucy was feeling now, that wrung-out sensation of rootlessness, of having nowhere to turn. Only a person who had experienced the torment of being completely alone, without any security whatsoever, could possibly comprehend its terrifying reality.

No, she would not turn her back on Lucy. She would never turn her back on anyone in Lucy's predicament, but especially not a widow with two babies to care for. Somehow she would deal with the law and with Wes Schuyler, too, should he intrude.

With that final and irrevocable decision, Amanda let her thoughts wander to Choice Brenton. What exactly was going on with her and Choice? He was such a strange man, with his dark, unfathomable gray eyes and unsmiling mouth. There was a dark side to Choice, and while it attracted her, it also troubled her.

Did she want Choice as he seemed to want her? A sensation of warm liquidity rippled through Amanda. It was so strange to think of Choice in that way, and yet there had been something indistinct in the back of her mind from their first meeting.

Surely she hadn't thought—even subconsciously—about making love with Choice while Len had been alive!

No, she could not believe such a thing about herself. She may have noticed Choice's good looks. She might even have appreciated his unquestionable streak of animal magnetism, but she had not placed him in her bed, not ever!

The distinct degrees of morality she had encountered throughout her life flicked through Amanda's mind. As a young single woman, she had remained chaste for her future husband. Until Len and their marriage she had lived virtuously, without any sense that she might be missing something important. Certainly without any of the unusual yearning she was feeling around Choice now.

In pondering the matter, Amanda realized that she felt very little similarity between Len's and Choice's courtships, if one could label Choice's earthy pursuit so romantically. During one long-ago month with Len, she had been starry-eyed and bedazzled, startled by every familiarity from her handsome young suitor.

She wasn't starry-eyed this time, but some part of her was definitely becoming bedazzled. Keeping Choice at bay while she made up her very confused mind about him would be an extremely dangerous game.

He hadn't returned to the ranch since he had kissed her, but he would, and just how was she going to react the next time he attempted familiarity?

Chapter Six

At dawn the next morning Buck and Woody rode south to tend to the horse's body and move the sheep. Amanda again requested that they check and mark Jed's grave, certain in her heart that once Lucy regained normal feelings she would want to visit it. Amanda could only hope that no one else would want to, but doubts that the sheriff would listen to the story and remain detached kept her deeply unsettled.

Most of Amanda's concern had to do with Lucy, although a disruption of her own privacy was a gnawingly discomfiting prospect. But Lucy was so defenseless right now. She was dealing with grief in a strange way—without tears or references to that night—but her heart had to be full and heavy and aching.

Amanda hadn't mentioned contacting the law to Lucy, deep down harboring a hope that Lucy would not have to be involved in whatever action or investigation the sheriff might institute. What a miracle it would be if the sheriff accepted the story from her and then dropped it. She did see a certain amount of logic in that wishful speculation. Accidents happened with disturbing frequency, and how would anyone ever ferret out which wild, possibly even drunk cowboy was responsible for the bullet that had found Jed that night? Perhaps Sheriff Lawrence would see the regrettable incident from that judicious point of view.

When Amanda went to the house after seeing the men off, Lucy was in the kitchen with the children. Elizabeth was having breakfast at her mother's breast and Tad, as usual, was clutching Lucy's skirt. Putting her worries aside, Amanda smiled affectionately at the family and busied herself preparing some oatmeal and bacon.

She was wearing a dress, as she planned to stick close to the house to await her men's return. It was pleasant having guests, even under these trying circumstances, and while they enjoyed the morning meal Amanda noticed that Lucy seemed quite calm. The woman saw to her son's food and talked to him soothingly, bringing an unfamiliar sparkle to the boy's eyes.

When they were through eating, Lucy got up and immediately began clearing away the dishes. "I will clean up," she said firmly. "I'm sure you have other chores to tend to."

Lucy's offer pleased Amanda, heartwarming proof, she felt, that her guest's emotional state was strengthening. "Let's both clean up, then take a walk," she suggested, turning and smiling at little Tad. "Would you like that, Tad? Would you like to have a nice long walk and see the horses? There are three cats living in the barn and one of them is quite friendly. Would you like to play with a kitty?"

Tad sank deeper into his chair and stared at Amanda with big eyes. His mother smiled softly. "He would like it, Amanda. Thank you."

The day moved on agreeably, and Amanda found herself genuinely liking Lucy McMillan. Lucy talked about her past, relaying her beginnings on a small farm in Pennsylvania. She spoke of her sister, of the Pennsylvania countryside, of friends she had left behind.

She never directly mentioned her husband, and Amanda bypassed Jed, too, giving her new friend all the leeway she apparently needed to handle grief in her own way. One day Lucy would want to talk about Jed, and when the time came, Amanda would listen and sympathize. For today, Amanda was only grateful that Lucy seemed to be accepting the sad situation so well.

The women exchanged stories while they strolled. Amanda spoke of the mining camps of her youth and of her awful train trip from Nevada to Wyoming. "I was nearly paralyzed with fear," she confessed with a small laugh. "I had never traveled alone before."

"And then you met your husband?" Lucy inquired.

"Not for nearly five years. I worked as a cook's helper in a restaurant for a while, then I answered an advertisement in the newspaper placed by a small farming community some distance away that needed a teacher for its youngsters."

Amanda smiled at the memory. "I'm sure that if anyone with any real training had applied for the position, I would never have been considered. But the community welcomed me and I taught very young children how to read and write and do sums in the four years I lived there."

"And *then* you met your husband?"

Amanda sighed wistfully. She related the story from her and Len's introduction to their wedding and finally their journey to the Spencer ranch. "Len had talked about the ranch, of course, but its beauty amazed me."

"You liked it immediately."

"How could I not?" They were walking along slowly, with Amanda contentedly carrying Elizabeth so Lucy could hang onto Tad's hand. "Anyone would, don't you think?"

"I'm not sure I—" Lucy stopped abruptly. "I'm sorry. I don't mean to sound ungrateful. It's just that your ranch is so far from other people."

Amanda looked at her friend. "Didn't you realize what the territories would be like before you came west, Lucy? How immense and vacant this land is?"

Lucy sighed. "No, I don't think I did. Jed was all fired up about going west. My sister hated my leaving, and I...well, I really didn't have much to say about it."

That was Lucy's only mention of Jed all day, but Amanda saw it as a small step on the path to healing for her new friend. Buck and Woody rode in around six, and while Lucy and Tad finished up their dinner, Amanda left hers and went down to the barn to speak to the men. "Did everything go all right?" she questioned.

The two men looked at each other with frowning, uneasy expressions. "Amanda, did ya notify the sheriff about that fella gettin' killed?" Woody asked.

"I plan to." Something was wrong, Amanda sensed. The men were unnerved, and their talking about the sheriff, when she hadn't thought about involving the law until Choice had brought it up, signified something amiss.

"Well, there's somethin' funny about it, Amanda. We checked the grave like you said and it was pretty poorly done, so we thought we should do a better job. The man was killed with a knife."

"A knife!" Amanda's entire system recoiled.

"Yeah, a knife. Buck and me expected a bullet wound."

"So did I," Amanda admitted thoughtfully. A knife. Lord above, what had gone on out there? What kind of animals could brutally knife a man in front of his wife and children? Not that a bullet wasn't brutal. The scene Amanda had been carrying in her mind had been one of confusion, the noise and dust of riders shouting and scattering the sheep with guns pointed to the sky, a stray bullet hitting the horse, Jed running out of the wagon with his rifle...

There was nothing accidental about a fatal knife wound.

"Did you bury the horse?"

"All done. We started gatherin' the sheep and got them moved as far as Wolf Draw. Hope they stay put for the night."

Disappointment that the sheep were still too far away from the buildings for any real protection tautened Amanda's nerves. But the men had done the best they could in one day, and she kept her misgivings to herself. "Thanks for everything you did today. I have a nice pot of stew ready for you. I'll bring it down right away."

Deep in thought, Amanda started back for the house. It seemed utterly impossible that Jed McMillan had been killed with a knife. Notifying the sheriff was crucial now that she had such horrifying information. Lucy must be suffering the tortures of hell. Had she seen it all? Had little Tad? Was that why the boy shrank from everything but the touch of his mother?

Tad had barely noticed the cats, the horses or anything else Amanda had pointed out to him that afternoon with the hope of seeing some boyish enthusiasm instead of that blank, withdrawn expression on his handsome little face.

She would have to see the sheriff with all possible haste, but how could she keep her intention from Lucy now?

Amanda's stomach churned. The thought of even mentioning a knife to Lucy was abhorrent. Sheriff Lawrence was not going to listen to the story, label Jed's death an accident and forget it, not when the cause of death had been a knife wound.

Everything seemed to be falling apart. Quickly, Amanda went into the house for the men's dinner. Lucy was clearing the table. "I left your plate, Amanda."

"Thanks, Lucy, but I'm through eating." There was a loaf of freshly baked bread to go with the pot of stew, and she wrapped it in a clean cloth.

"Can I help you carry supper to the men?" Lucy inquired.

"You stay with the children, Lucy. I'm used to the chore."

When the food had been delivered to the bunkhouse, Amanda avoided returning to the house and went to her garden instead. The sun was waning, dropping in the western sky, casting longer shadows. A wooden bench was situated near the denuded and drying corn stalks, and admitting weak knees over this new development in the McMillans' plight, Amanda gratefully sank down upon its smooth, weathered surface.

This had always been a favorite thinking spot and felt doubly so with guests in the house. What wouldn't she give right now to have someone to really open up to, Amanda thought rather frantically. She had enjoyed talking to Lucy today, but she could only guess at what lay behind Lucy's impassive blue eyes. One would think a woman with such a horrifying memory would be forced from within to pour out the dreadful story.

Instead, Lucy didn't even hint at it. Amanda wondered how she could make the aftermath of revealing the story to the sheriff easier for Lucy, or if there was any possible way of keeping Lucy completely out of it.

And there were the sheep to consider. She should see the sheriff first thing tomorrow, but one more day would alleviate the tension that herd of sheep was bound to cause. By tomorrow night, Buck and Woody would have the herd moved closer in. Its proximity to her buildings would be a declaration of her decision to shelter the animals for Lucy and her children. The sheriff might notice and even disapprove, if he came to the place, but surely he wouldn't lodge a complaint with the association.

The situation was worsening by leaps and bounds, Amanda realized, stifling an urge to just let go and bawl. What Sheriff Lawrence might do about anything was only a nebulous conjecture in her mind. Like so many of the valley's other inhabitants, John Lawrence was barely an acquaintance. Distance between ranches and the nearest town, Leavitt, made making new friends difficult. In some ways she was still a newcomer to the valley.

There was something else. In the past year she had spurned the attentions of the several men who had called with amorous intentions. Not that any woman should accept suitors when she wasn't interested, but perhaps she should have promoted better relations with her neighbors since Len's death. An appeal in Lucy's behalf now would carry a lot more weight if Amanda were on a sounder footing with the other members of the Stock Growers Association and with the citizens of Leavitt.

A tear formed and dropped from the corner of Amanda's eye. Jed's dying from a knife wound made matters worse, and they had already been bad enough. What on earth was she going to do about it all?

A horse and buggy approached in the distance. Amanda squinted at the rig in the silvering evening light, then recognized the person driving the buggy. Choice. She dried her eyes while her system reacted in a completely female fashion. Choice was a man who went after something he wanted with persistence, and he apparently wanted her.

This evening, however, she had much too much on her mind to worry about where she and Choice Brenton might be heading. She had to talk to someone about Jed McMillan's death, and it was becoming more evident every day that whatever she did about the sheep, Choice was likely to intrude. She may as well talk to him.

What she needed right now was some support, Amanda admitted during the walk around the house to the front porch, where she sat down to wait for the buggy to arrive. If only one person would tell her she wasn't being a complete fool about Lucy and her sheep, just one, she would feel much better.

That was an improbable hope, though. Choice wasn't apt to suddenly reverse his opinion and compliment her generosity.

The buggy finally arrived, and Amanda walked out to meet it. Choice jumped down. "Evenin', Amanda."

As though seeing him for the first time, she was stunned by how handsome he was, how tall and lean, how strikingly masculine. His clothing was clean, his boots polished. He was wearing a good hat, a dark gray felt with a silver band and a wide brim. He was freshly shaven and smelled of soap.

He had come calling, obviously, and Amanda couldn't help smiling, in spite of her voluminous worries. "Good evening, Choice. Out buggy riding?"

His dark eyes washed over her dress, which was plum colored and pretty, with white lace on the sleeves and collar. "I came to see you." He glanced to the house. "Still got company?"

"Of course."

"Then come for a ride with me. I need to talk to you."

Buck and Woody's revelation nagged at Amanda's mind again, sobering her expression. "I need to talk to you, too."

Choice helped Amanda up to the buggy seat, then sat beside her. He flicked the reins and turned the horse in a wide circle, and they were soon trotting down the trail. Neither spoke, and silently Amanda studied the man beside her. In profile, Choice appeared as ruggedly handsome as he did full face.

She was enjoying Choice's company more and more. Denying it to him was probably only sensible, but denying it to herself seemed utterly childish. Amanda reminded herself, however, that enjoying a man's company did not necessarily have to go beyond friendship.

The Leavitt River wound through the valley, slow and sluggish at summer's end. During spring runoff it became a raging torrent, and many years flooded its banks and caused ranchers all sorts of hardships. The river was beguiling and serene now, with cottonwoods fringing its banks, and Choice directed horse and buggy to a secluded spot within a group of the tall gnarled trees and called a soft whoa.

Amanda watched the river for a few moments, absorbing its calming, gentle burble, then murmured, "It will be dark soon."

"The horse knows the way home in the dark."

"Did you bring the buggy to take me out here?"

"We can't be alone at your place."

Her eyes flashed to his. "No," she agreed, then deliberately reminded him, "you needed to talk to me?"

"Yes. I was in town today and stopped by the association's meeting hall."

Amanda's heart leaped into her throat. "Was anyone there? You didn't . . . ?"

"I told them nothing. But they already knew. Seems that Leon McElroy and Clint Edmunds are braggin' all over town about how they rousted the herd of sheep that snuck into the valley."

Amanda's eyes sparked. "Bragging! About killing a man?"

"I heard nothing about any killing, but people are talking about the sheep."

"Well, Jed McMillan's dead all the same. And—" Amanda's voice broke "—they used a knife on him, Choice."

"Sweet Jesus," Choice muttered. "Are you sure?"

"I sent Woody and Buck out there to bury the horse and check on Jed's grave." Tears were coursing down Amanda's cheeks, and she could barely speak. The situation was becoming more appalling by the minute. Poor Lucy. And those babies. Not to mention Jed, who was lying in a makeshift grave. "I was worried. I couldn't see how Lucy could have managed a proper grave, and I wanted the men to mark it."

Gritting his teeth, Choice lifted an arm around Amanda's shoulders and pulled her close. "This is a damned mess, Amanda," he said huskily.

She wept on his chest for a few minutes, admitting to herself that it felt good to be held and comforted. Maybe Choice did have some sensitivity, some compassion. She accepted the handkerchief he offered, sat up straighter and wiped her eyes. "Lucy still hasn't talked about it. It must have been terrible for her. I hope whoever went out there that night didn't harm her—she has a bad bruise on her face."

Frowning, Choice lifted a boot to the rail at the front of the buggy. "It doesn't add up. Leon and Clint are notorious big mouths, but even those two half-wits wouldn't knife a man and then brag about doing something that could lead the law directly to their door."

Amanda released a sad sigh. "One wouldn't think so. Anyway, I . . . I plan to see the sheriff."

Choice nodded. "Let me handle it for you, Amanda."

It was a generous offer, but Choice would probably take off for town at first light tomorrow morning, and she had to put the disturbing chore off until the sheep were moved.

"Thank you, but I have to go to Leavitt anyway. Lucy and the children don't have a stitch of clothing, and I'm going to buy a few things for them to wear. Besides, it's not fair to involve you in this."

Choice's arm was still resting on the top of the buggy seat, and he lifted his hand to her hair. His gaze, dark and somber, traveled her face. "There isn't much I wouldn't get involved with for you," he said softly.

His tone and words mesmerized her. Her thought of maintaining nothing but friendship with Choice returned but with little impact. "I'm beginning to believe that," she whispered, finding herself lost in the mysteries of his eyes.

"Believe it," Choice murmured, drawing her closer.

His mouth brushed hers once, then again. A shivering thrill spiraled through Amanda, but when he attempted a more uniting kiss, she ducked her head and eluded his lips.

Choice raised his head. "Don't push me away. We're alone tonight," he whispered urgently.

Her eyes darted around. Shadows were creeping in, and the sun was only a partial ball of fiery orange on the western horizon. They were truly alone. Had he brought her out here for kisses? For more?

The sum total of Amanda's sexual experience had occurred in one place, the bed she and Len had shared as husband and wife. Such modesty had narrowed her imagination, and she had never envisioned making love anywhere else. *Choice's* imagination stunned her.

"Let me kiss you." Choice caught the back of her head and looked into her eyes. There was so much heat and desire in his gaze, Amanda's skin turned warm and rosy.

Her tongue flicked, dampening her suddenly dry lips. She said the first thing that popped into her mind. "Choice, I need some more time."

"To do what?"

"To understand what's happening."

"What's there to understand?"

"For heaven's sake, we scarcely spoke for two years, and now you're all over me!" The hot flush on the heels of her heedless words scorched Amanda's face. "Oh, blast," she groaned, wishing she could disappear. She could have said no without embarrassing both of them. "I'm sorry. It's just that..."

"You don't feel the same way about me as I do about you."

"I don't *know* what I feel." Choice had sat up and away from her and she braved a glance at him. "If you could go a little slower..."

"Slower," he repeated sourly, as though the word tasted bad. "We're not kids, Amanda."

"I don't think age has a great deal to do with improper behavior."

"Oh, you see kissing me as improper."

Amanda dropped her eyes. "You don't only want kisses."

"What do *you* want?"

"Choice, you're so... forward. Must you put everything into words?"

"Ah, I see the problem. I offend your sense of propriety. You would rather I came around and hid what I'm really feeling. Amanda, I'm no good with flowery words and beating around the bush."

How true. Amanda saw him reach for her hand. She studied the length of the fingers grasping hers, and the large, masculine thumb shaping almost dainty circles on her skin. Something vital and alive was traveling from Choice to her through their hands, and the vitality continued up her arm and spread through her chest and internal organs. It was a rich feeling, one she found herself savoring.

She lifted her eyes to his and the feeling expanded again. There were flecks of black and gold within his gray pupils. He had unusually thick eyelashes. The hard lines of his face had softened, although the intensity remained in his eyes.

"Don't be afraid," he whispered. "Do you think I would hurt you?"

She swallowed. "Not intentionally."

"How, then?"

Heaving a sigh, she closed her eyes. "I don't know."

Was she deliberately blocking him out? Choice impulsively leaned forward and pressed his lips to hers. She started, then sat very still, with her eyes squeezed tightly shut, and let him kiss her.

His mouth was firm and soft and very warm. She noticed scents, soap, leather, wool, tobacco, and something spicy. She liked Choice's smell, although it was different than what she remembered from Len.

Choice was nothing like Len, and she had to stop making comparisons. Guilt awaited those who dwelled too much on the past, and she had nothing to feel guilty about. No one expected her to live without male companionship for the rest of her life.

Her lips began to yield beneath Choice's. He felt the shiver that passed through her body and knew she wasn't unaffected, even though she seemed to be trying very hard to appear so. He held his explosive feelings in check and played Amanda's game, kissing her as though she was something fragile and breakable instead of the warm, flesh-and-blood woman he believed she was.

She had demanded a slower pace? He would give her slow and easy if it killed him, which it might. Her lips were sweeter than any he had ever kissed. His body pulsed and ached and wasn't the least bit cooperative. He was not a man who lived with restraints or wasted time on reluctant women.

But Amanda was not just any reluctant woman. She was the woman he thought of during long, solitary horseback rides or while hauling hay to hungry cattle in the dead of winter, with a freezing wind numbing any exposed skin and making the simple routine of breathing a powerful exertion.

He raised his head and watched her eyelashes sweep upward. Her green eyes had a silvery cast in the dusky light, and he wished he had the gift of eloquence so he could tell her how special she was to him.

The kiss had been gentle, without demands, and Amanda felt a great tenderness for the man who had administered it. She lifted a hand to his arm, and when he moved to take another kiss, she willingly closed her eyes again.

Only this kiss deepened quickly. Choice's arms dropped around her and she was brought to his chest with a rustle of clothing and a squeaking of buggy springs. Amanda's hands rose to push him away, but at best, the effort was weak. His lips were leading hers in a very artful way, teasing hers into parting, persuading hers to return the pressure of his.

She felt the tip of his tongue and the possessive way his big hand was clasping the back of her head. She could hear his breath and her own crazy heartbeat. The evening air seemed suddenly too warm, but she still didn't push against him.

Choice's pulse went wild. He took Amanda's sigh into his own mouth with another kiss and brought his hand down to caress the curves of her hip and thigh.

She melted into him and the kiss grew hungrier. Choice stopped thinking altogether and began working her skirt up. Beneath it he encountered all the female garments he'd expected. She allowed exploration until he pressed into the valley between her thighs. "Stop!" she cried then, grabbing his hand.

"Let me," he urged hoarsely. "I can give you pleasure."

"You want too much," she gasped.

"Not too much." Her undergarment was between his hand and her body, a dry barrier to the heat and moisture he ached for. "Don't hold back. Let yourself go," he pleaded, beginning to understand that her own desire was unfamiliar and frightening to her.

This was her own fault, Amanda knew. Kissing led to other things, and she already knew what Choice wanted from her. Thinking she could maintain a friendly relationship with him had been a preposterous idea.

He looked at her long and hard, then shook his head. "You really have no idea what's going on with us, do you? Or you won't admit it."

"Is that a crime?"

His eyes smoldered while he studied her. "No, but it's damned confusing."

It was confusing for her, too. She liked—more than liked—his kisses, but he went too fast.

Amanda said it again, this time meaning it. "I need more time." Choice was who he was, a take-him-as-he-was-or-leave-him-alone type of man. The question was, what sort of woman was she? It wasn't something she'd thought about in years, not since she'd been fourteen years old and wise enough to decide that prostitution was not the easy way out for a woman of little means.

She wasn't fourteen now and she wasn't a virgin, either. If she decided in Choice's favor, it would be her decision, not his.

In either case, nothing further was going to happen between them tonight. For one thing, she still needed to pick Choice's brain. Never had it been necessary for her to deal directly with the law. Choice had to know all about it, having been a lawman in the past.

Amanda clutched his hand and forced her gaze to hold steady while she looked into his eyes and inquired, "What do you think the sheriff will do when he learns about Jed McMillan's death?"

Choice frowned at the abrupt change of subject. His blood was running hot and heavy, and he wasn't in any mood for conversation about the McMillan family or their damned sheep.

He answered slowly. "He'll ask questions, but a few questions never harmed an innocent person."

"Of course not," Amanda quickly agreed. "And I fully intend on talking to him myself, but... Well, I guess what I'm wondering is, will Lucy have to talk to him, too?"

Apparently this was important to Amanda, sensible or not. Choice aligned his thoughts, forcing them from her to what she was saying. "That will be up to John, but I don't see how Lucy could be kept out of it."

"She's been through so much. How much more can she take? Choice, if I tell John exactly what happened, couldn't—"

"Do you *know* exactly what happened?" He saw on her face that she knew nothing more than she'd already told him. "Lucy hasn't explained that night, has she?"

"Well, no, but..."

"Don't you find that a little odd?"

"No, I don't find it odd. The woman's in shock."

Choice felt impatience in his gut. Amanda shouldn't be involved with murder and a herd of sheep, and she wouldn't be if she wasn't so damned stubborn. "I'll talk to John. I'll do it first thing tomorrow."

"No!"

"Why not?"

The sudden suspicion in his voice put Amanda on the defensive. "Would you please let me handle this?" she said with some exasperation.

"What are you up to?" he questioned with very little warmth, much like she supposed John Lawrence might do. "You've put it off too long already, Amanda. When are you planning to go to Leavitt?"

How perceptive he was! Amanda swung her eyes to the right, preferring the darkening vista to Choice's darkening face.

"Amanda?"

"Stop judging me!"

"Then stop hedging, dammit!"

Her eyes jerked to his. "All right! I'm not going to Leavitt until day after tomorrow. Buck and Woody got the sheep moved only to Wolf Draw today, and I want the herd closer in before the sheriff interferes."

"Interferes! What are you afraid of?" Choice's eyes narrowed. "Oh, I get it. You want the sheriff to know where you stand on the McMillans' sheep."

"I know you don't approve, so please stop glaring at me."

Choice took her chin and held it. "Let me say something. No, I don't approve, but maybe worse than stupidity or stubbornness, I hate lies."

Amanda gasped. She'd had just about all she could stomach for one day. "So I'm stupid, stubborn and a liar? Take me home, Choice. And from now on, stay *out* of my business!"

"No!" he exploded. "I'm not staying out of it!"

Furious, she wrenched free of his grasp. "You *will* stay out of it if you ever want to see me again! This is my land, and anything that happens on it is my affair, not yours!"

A muscle jerked in Choice's jaw. Her ultimatum stabbed him to the quick. She had kissed him, and would again if he remained neutral about the sheep and that sheepherder's death. If he didn't, he could forget about anything further between the two of them.

It was an almost unendurable test of his willpower to sit there and do or say nothing in reaction to her overbearing attitude. He had never come close to violence with a woman before, but he had to forcibly stop himself from reaching for her and shaking her until her teeth rattled.

"Let's get a few things straight," he said in a lethally soft tone that brought Amanda's head around in surprise. "First, either you or I will see the sheriff tomorrow. I'll let you decide which, but one of us is going to Leavitt in the morning. Second, I don't give one damn about those sheep, nor whether Lucy McMillan has the money to make a new start. If she was in my house, I'd put her and her babies on the first train east, so don't think you can play on my sympathy because that woman has nothing.

"But most important of all, Amanda, don't ever make the mistake of thinking that I'm at your beck and call. I've got some real deep feelings for you, but they're not going to turn me into a man who jumps just because you suggest it. You want from me exactly what I want from you. A man can tell with a woman, in the way she warms to him, in the way she kisses him. You need a man. You need me, and when the time's right, it's gonna be the greatest thing that ever happened to either one of us. I'll give you some time, like you asked, but I won't wait forever."

He picked up the reins and gave them a flick. The horse started walking. Amanda could scarcely breathe. She had never heard anyone convey so much tension in such a soft tone of voice. She knew he was angry even if he hadn't sounded angry. He'd stated his case as though there was no possible argument against it, and she couldn't think of one, no matter how hard she tried.

Besides, his reference to sex between them—that's exactly what he had meant—had started her blood thrumming. And that part about his having "some real deep feelings" for her seemed lodged in her brain.

After a few minutes of riding in silence, Choice asked, "Are you going to Leavitt in the morning, or am I?"

Amanda turned her head to look at him. "I'll go, but I don't like being told what to do any more than you do."

"You're a woman."

"Which doesn't automatically make me stupid or in need of a keeper."

"No, but you're in over your head with the McMillan family." Choice sent her a glance. "You aren't denying what's between us, at least."

She hesitated, reluctant to admit something she didn't fully understand.

"Be truthful, Amanda," Choice said quietly.

"All right," she finally conceded. "I never expected what's happening with us, but yes, there's something quite . . . powerful."

The corners of Choice's mouth curled up in a satisfied smile. "It's going to get a lot more powerful."

Amanda turned her face away, shaken by the impact of his opinion. She wished she felt nothing at all for Choice. No good would come out of the sort of relationship he had in mind. What about romance? What about hints of love and a future together, the kind of lovely intimations that Len had made almost from the first? It wasn't romance that was in Choice's mind, it was sex, and Lord help her, that's what he made her think of, too, which was almost unbelievable when she had never enjoyed the physical side of marriage!

Choice stopped the buggy near Amanda's house. "I'll see you tomorrow," he said.

It was getting very dark, and she could barely make out his face. "I'll be busy tomorrow. Good night."

Choice shook his head as she jumped down from the buggy before he could offer assistance. "I'll see you tomorrow," he called, letting her know that, busy or not, he wasn't going to let her ignore him.

There was more than Amanda's reluctance to face the reality of their relationship bothering Choice, however. *He* should be the one going to the sheriff in the morning, not her. Why in hell was she so determined to prove herself equal to any situation? Was there anything wrong in a woman's accepting help from a man?

Maybe he'd ride to Leavitt in the morning, too, just in case Amanda ran into trouble. One thing was certain: if there was any trouble to run into, Amanda would find it.

Chapter Seven

Amanda made the trip to Leavitt as seldom as possible, only enduring the long, solitary miles when she needed supplies. Today she rode the wagon and clutched the reins with a feeling of dread.

Events of the past few days made today's trip mandatory, but Amanda also carried a list of items needed at the ranch, thus making the most of a journey that, other than the welcome duty of purchasing baby and toddler garments, didn't promise much pleasure. Especially when she was going a day sooner than she thought best.

The prospect of seeing Sheriff Lawrence had Amanda sitting on the edge of the wagon's padded seat. The man was too hard and opinionated, to her way of thinking. Like too many of the Stock Growers Association members, John Lawrence felt a woman's place was in the home—a home that was under the strong, protective hand of a husband. Widows and maiden ladies were exceptions, of course, but only because so many of the women in those situations earned their living in feminine enterprises, such as sewing, hand laundry or selling home-baked pies and cakes.

Those who didn't—women who ranched on their own, or operated a regular business—displayed a strength that made some men uncomfortable. Amanda knew she was a topic of gossip because of her preference for masculine clothing, and her firmly denying the several men who had ventured out to the ranch with courtship on their minds hadn't garnered her any favors, either.

Wyoming Territory was a strange mixture of contradictions. Created in 1868 by Congressional passage, the brand-new and tiny territorial legislature gave its female citizens the right to vote the very next year. Less than nineteen hundred of the territory's population had been female at the time, and nowhere else in the entire country were women allowed to vote or hold public office. Even their right to own property was heavily restricted elsewhere in the United States.

But Wyoming was isolated, and men depended on their female partners for countless responsibilities. The right to vote, to hold office and to own property for the ladies seemed only fair to the majority of the male population.

Still, there were pockets of extreme prejudice. Around the Leavitt area, Amanda knew, the consensus of opinion was that women should behave with female decorum. It seemed so awkward to her. Legally she was equal to any man in the territory; socially, she had to affect a certain amount of pretense.

To appease the gossips Amanda usually wore feminine apparel to Leavitt, a major concession, she felt, when trousers would be so much more manageable than yards of skirts and petticoats on the tiresome trip. Nevertheless, she had trussed herself into a corset and long stockings that morning, dug out her best hat and boots, and donned a long-sleeved, high-necked dress, choosing the severe garment because of the relentless sun she would be exposed to for most of the day.

At dawn, she had bade Lucy and the children a good day and had driven away, turning to wave at the family on her front porch with a feeling of guilt. She still hadn't told Lucy she would be visiting the sheriff, although several times it had been on the tip of her tongue to do so. But hope that

Lucy would not be drawn into any investigation John Lawrence might make into her husband's murder was still at the front of Amanda's thoughts.

And while she held the reins and directed the horse, Amanda felt that hope rising again. Poor Lucy had enough problems to overcome. She was a sweet woman, loving and tender with her children, thankful for Amanda's smallest kindness. The thought of John Lawrence forcing Lucy to relive that terrible night in an insensitive inquisition broke Amanda's heart, and hers was a heart that was already very vulnerable today.

Amanda sighed, recognizing the turn of her thoughts. Choice was always there, present behind everything else that happened. He was a purely physical being, and she had been making a big mistake in comparing his attentions with the considerate, gentlemanly courtship Len had honored her with.

There was very little about Choice that could be labeled gentle. He was a rough man, hard as nails in everything he did. There wasn't a man in the valley who would stand up to Choice in a fight, not even John Lawrence.

Maybe she should have let Choice speak to John about the whole horrid situation. But it had happened on Spencer land and it was her problem, not Choice's.

When she finally drove the wagon into Leavitt, Amanda was as hot and uncomfortable as she'd known she would be. She stopped the horse in the shade of a building, and with the clean handkerchief she'd placed in her reticule, dabbed at the perspiration and dust on her face.

Leavitt looked as it always did, two rows of various businesses paralleling a dusty street, fronting, Amanda knew, several more streets containing the residences of the townspeople. When rain fell the dust turned to clay, making passage from one side of the street to the other a perilous undertaking. The mercantile, where she would buy her supplies and the clothing for the McMillans, and also post the letter Lucy had written to her sister in Pennsylvania, was directly across the street from where Amanda sat. Then there was a dentist's office, a bank, the Stock Growers Association meeting hall and a café. A hotel, the Wyoming Inn, easily the nicest building in town, was at one end of the street, and at the opposite end was a saloon, a rowdy place that Amanda had never given much thought to, let alone visited.

Today her gaze rose to the saloon's second story, and she wondered, for the first time, if Choice ever climbed those stairs to call on the women who lived there. There was a seedy side to life that good women rarely got near, but growing up in mining camps, Amanda had been aware of brothels and their inhabitants since childhood.

Placing Choice in that picture was extremely discomfiting, however, and Amanda thrust the image away and climbed down from the wagon.

The sheriff's office was two doors down from the building she'd parked the wagon in front of, and determined to get the worst chore of the day over with, Amanda marched down the wooden walkway.

A few people were out and about, Choice saw from the window, but Leavitt was quiet most mornings, and it was still fairly early. He watched Amanda get down from the wagon and head for the sheriff's office, her chin high, her back straight. He didn't know what to expect from her mission and had decided to keep an eye on her. Althea's room on the second floor of Foxy's Saloon offered a clean, unbroken view of the entire street.

"Whatcha lookin' at?"

Choice shot a quick glance to the woman behind him and immediately returned his attention to the street. "Nothing important."

He heard Althea plop into a chair. "Gonna be hot today," she said, sighing.

"You shouldn't be too uncomfortable dressed like that," he returned absently, noting Amanda entering the sheriff's office. Frowning reflectively, he drew away from the window. Althea's carrot-red hair was pinned here and there, only enough to evidence a desultory attempt at control. The thin wrapper she was wearing left little to the imagination, and Choice took a long look.

Oddly, Althea's blowsy beauty and hopeful expression left him cold today. Amanda was embedded so deeply into his brain, other women could parade naked in front of him with little or no effect.

With a strangely forlorn sigh, Choice went back to the window.

"There's gotta be somethin' interesting goin' on out there," Althea remarked with a laugh, and got up and peeked around his shoulder. She shook her head. "I don't see nothin'."

"I've got a friend who might be in trouble," Choice said quietly.

"Oh?"

"A good friend."

"A woman?"

He turned surprised eyes on her. "How'd you know?"

Althea shrugged. "Just a hunch. You never looked and turned away before, Choice."

He grinned. "I guess not."

"So, what'd you do, fall in love?"

Startled, Choice stared at her. "Why would you think something like that?"

Shaking her head again, Althea walked away. "If you don't know, how could I explain it? You're just different, Choice. That's all I can tell you."

"Different how? What do you see that I don't?"

Althea rolled her eyes. "Men! You're all alike, aren't you? Don't you know when you're in love?"

Choice looked at the street again. "Maybe not," he said softly, very much to himself. "Maybe we don't."

Sheriff John Lawrence got up from his desk when Amanda walked in. "Mornin', Amanda."

"Good morning, John. Do you have a few minutes?"

"Of course. Would you like to sit down?"

"Thank you." Primly Amanda perched on the edge of a chair, feeling John Lawrence's curiosity as he settled himself behind the desk. He was a big beefy man with enormous shoulders and a thick neck, intimidating in size and demeanor.

"Now," he said. "What can I do for you?"

Amanda cleared her throat. "I'm here to report..." She paused, shaken by the enormity of what she had to tell this man. With a few words Lucy's life could take a drastic turn, but she had no choice. Learning that Jed had died from a knife wound had made the decision for her.

"I must report the death of a man on my land, John."

Not so much as an eyelash flickered in the rigid features of the sheriff's face, yet Amanda sensed his immediate alertness. "What man?" he asked. "Who died on your land, Amanda?"

She took a quick breath. "A sheepherder. Jed McMillan. I have his wife and children staying at my house for the present."

John Lawrence leaned back in his chair. "I've heard a few rumors about those sheep. Where is Jed McMillan now? His body, I mean."

"Buried. I can show you where."

"Good. Do you know what happened? Did he die from natural causes?"

Amanda's stomach turned over. "No. That's why I'm here. He was killed with . . . a knife."

"A knife. I see." The sheriff stared across the desk with a penetrating look that gave Amanda a shiver of apprehension. "Tell me what you know, Amanda."

"Yes, of course. Last Sunday I became aware of a herd of sheep in my south pasture, approximately two hundred animals. At first I hoped the wagon and the sheep were just passing through and did nothing about them. The next day I entered the encampment and spoke to the herder."

"Go on."

Amanda had to force herself to do just that. She hated what she was having to do, not because she was against law and order in the territory, but because she was so concerned about Lucy and her children.

"I learned the man's name was Jed and that there was also a woman—his wife, Lucy—and two children in the wagon. I told Jed he was trespassing and asked him to move on. I also told him the cattlemen in the area would not permit sheep in the valley. He . . . he was rather belligerent and said he was going to stay.

"The next morning I rode out again to see if they had gone. The sheep were scattered and the wagon was burned. The family had a horse and the animal was dead, shot. The woman and children weren't seriously injured, but I didn't see Jed. Lucy told me he was dead and that she had buried him herself. I asked her what happened and she said that men had come in the night."

Amanda blinked back some threatening tears and met the sheriff's unwavering gaze. "I took Lucy and the children home with me and had my men, Buck Connors and Woody Samuels, go out to the site and bury the horse. I also had them check Jed's grave to make sure it was secure, and they told me it had been poorly done, so they . . ."

She stopped, unable to go on. She pulled the handkerchief from her reticule and blew her nose. "I'm sorry," she murmured. "Anyway when they returned they told me Jed had died from a knife wound."

"That's everything you know?"

Amanda nodded. "Yes."

"You saw nothing of the men who supposedly intruded on that family?"

"No, it happened at night. I was home."

The sheriff got to his feet. "Well, it looks like I better take Doc Lowden out there and look around. Will you be at the ranch?"

Amanda rose unsteadily. Her worse fears were unfolding right before her eyes. "I have some purchases to make, then I'll be heading back."

"Good. I'll see you out there some time this afternoon."

Very anxiously Amanda asked, "Will you have to question Lucy?"

"She's the only witness, Amanda, unless... How old are the children?"

"The oldest is only three."

"Then I have to talk to her."

The finality of John Lawrence's proclamation created an immense, cold void in Amanda. Barely managing to utter a simple good day, she hurried out to the sunshine, glad for the warmth.

She would finish up in Leavitt without delay and get back to the ranch and talk to Lucy before the sheriff did. Perhaps she could buffer the shock of having to relive every horrible moment of that night for her friend.

Even the enjoyment she had thought she might derive from choosing tiny garments for Elizabeth had failed her, Amanda realized as she paid for the merchandise she'd purchased. A cloud of despair seemed to have settled upon her, and now she only felt haste to get home.

Carrying the first bundle of several out of the store, Amanda was startled to see Choice standing near her wagon. "I didn't expect to see you in town," she exclaimed.

Choice took the package from her and placed it in the wagon. "I wasn't sure what you'd run into with John. Are there more parcels?"

"Yes."

"I'll get them."

Perplexed, Amanda watched his long-legged stride carry him into the mercantile. They hadn't parted on the best of terms last night. Why was he here today? What did he mean about not knowing what she would run into with John? The meeting hadn't been pleasant, but she had handled it well enough.

Choice came out of the mercantile with an armload of packages, deposited them beside the first parcel in the wagon and went in for the final load. "Looks like you bought out the store," he remarked dryly.

"I stocked up on staples as long as I had to come to town," Amanda explained. "Were you worried about me?"

Choice regarded her for a long moment. "Is that what you want from me, worry?"

Flushing, Amanda looked down the street. "Of course not."

"What did John say?"

He *was* worried. Something fluttered in her breast. "He was nice enough," she responded. "Curious, of course. He said that he would be out to the ranch this afternoon. What were you worried about?"

Choice hesitated. He didn't want to alarm her, and maybe he was a tad too jumpy. But she seemed to think that she could float through a crisis, and that *did* worry him. "I just wanted to make sure you got home all right."

Her breath caught. "Who would... I don't understand."

"I know you don't. That's the problem. Are you ready to leave now?"

Amanda nodded blankly.

"Then let's get going." Taking her arm, Choice helped her onto the wagon. Then he loosened the reins he'd looped over a nearby hitching post and swung into the saddle on his horse's back.

Summers in Wyoming were usually only pleasantly warm, but as August progressed this year, each day had seemed hotter than the previous one. Today was a scorcher, another factor to make Amanda ponder her bad luck. The sun was merciless, and after an hour she felt wrung out. Her clothing was drenched through with perspiration, and she cursed the corset around her waist and the long stockings on her legs.

If Choice hadn't been riding beside the wagon, she would stop and get rid of some of the feminine nonsense she'd trapped herself into that morning.

Heat waves played tricks with her vision, and Amanda drank often from the canteen of water she'd brought along, noticing Choice repeatedly tipping his own canteen. He made her tell him exactly what John Lawrence had said and how he'd said it, but when that narration was completed, they plodded along side by side without speaking.

"The horses need water," Choice announced as they approached Red Rock Canyon. "Turn in and drive to the spring."

Wholeheartedly agreeing, Amanda directed her animal onto the bumpy trail leading to a scenic spot that she'd always enjoyed stopping at. Today it was doubly pleasing, for the massive red boulders of the canyon provided some much appreciated shade. She drove the horse right up to the spring, and the animal dipped its muzzle into the water and began drinking immediately.

Amanda got down, pulled off her hat and fanned her overheated face with it. Choice dismounted and led his horse to the spring. Removing his hat, he tossed it to the ground and followed it down to stretch out in the shade.

"I can't linger long," Amanda warned, but she couldn't resist cooling off a little, and sat on a sizable rock next to the pond. The water was crystal clear and inviting, and she bent over to trail a hand in the cool liquid.

"If you were alone, would you take a dip?" she heard.

Turning her head, she looked at Choice. "I've done so before." She watched a rare smile form beneath his mustache.

"Probably everyone in the valley has at one time or another," he remarked.

She stared with unconcealed admiration. "You should smile more often. It makes you very handsome."

The smile vanished. "Don't tease, Amanda."

Her green eyes widened. "I was serious. You don't smile often enough."

"Is that what you want from me, smiles?"

"You amaze me with your questions, Choice. Perhaps I should ask what you want from me."

He sat up, and his eyes were dark and stormy again. "You know what I want."

"Yes, I guess I do." She sighed, looking back to the spring.

"Not just once," she heard, spoken softly. She dropped her hand to the water again, hoping to quieten her suddenly erratic heartbeat with the pool's radiating coolness.

"Maybe you're worried about that," Choice went on. And after a pause, "Are you?"

She couldn't find an answer, nor could she look at him.

"Do I strike you as a man who wants a woman only once?"

He was the only man she'd been attracted to since Len, and she felt his pull very strongly in this quiet canyon. Understanding his ways a little better now, Amanda knew that if she gave the slightest sign, he would come to her.

Sighing, Amanda raised a perplexed gaze to the red boulders forming the canyon. Behind her, Choice was waiting for a reply, and she finally conceded, "No, you don't strike me as a man who wants a woman only once."

"At least you know that."

As he had stated, Choice would never delude a woman with flattering phrases, Amanda thought with some cynicism. Sitting here, with him speaking so candidly, it was entirely possible to envision telling him what a woman really hoped for from a man. *"It doesn't make you less masculine to speak of tender feelings."* But then, maybe he didn't have any tender feelings, or wouldn't recognize them if he did. For that matter, were her feelings for him tender?

The cuff of her long sleeve was getting wet, and Amanda unbuttoned it and rolled it back from her wrist. Quite naturally, she repeated the process with her left cuff, then unbuttoned the collar of her dress to get some air on her throat.

Choice laid back again, propping himself up on an elbow to watch Amanda. Her breasts moved with her arms, lifting with each new position, and the memory of how that softness felt against his chest seared his senses. He wondered if Althea was right, if a man really didn't know when he was in love. Could he be in love with Amanda? Was that why he wanted to coax her to the ground and peel away that gray dress? How did a man know if he was in love with a woman? If a desire to possess was any measure, he was insanely in love.

Amanda was quietly driving him crazy. For years he'd stayed away from her, purposely stayed away from her, and now he couldn't be with her enough. All because she'd breached the invisible barrier between them by laying her hand on his. In a flash he'd realized that she wouldn't live the rest of her life without a man. He wanted to be that man. He was *going* to be that man. And if it took a little grin-and-bear-it type of suffering for a while, he'd live through it.

But he'd make damned sure Amanda knew he was around.

Besides, as strong and independent as she was, she was making some bad mistakes in judgment. Maybe taking in that woman and her children was to be expected, even admired, but protecting Lucy McMillan's sheep was just begging for trouble.

Trouble was brewing, all right. Choice could feel it in his bones. And Amanda was smack-dab in the middle of it. She was a hardheaded woman, a lot more determined than he would have guessed while Len was alive. Amanda wasn't above getting her hands dirty, often working right along with her men, and it was plain to Choice that she was accustomed to doing as she damn well pleased.

But this time she was getting in too deep. Courage was one thing, foolhardiness another. Riling the cattlemen in the valley over a herd of sheep she didn't even own was pure idiocy, and Choice was uneasy over what some hothead might take a notion to do to a person daring to break the rules.

Oddly, Choice knew that if he ever decided to raise sheep, which he wanted no part of, he'd do it and face anyone who tried to interfere. But Amanda doing it was a whole different story. Despite courage and determination and maybe even being right, she was still a woman, and she would stand little chance of coming out on top should a real battle erupt over her actions.

Watching Amanda in the cool silence of the canyon gave Choice a soothingly peaceful sensation, even with unrest about those stinking sheep eating at him. He'd known pretty women in the past, although none of them had been the lady of quality that Amanda was. She had depth, intelligence, a logical mind—normally—and a wonderful smile. Yes, she was headstrong, and a man would have a hell of a time taming her natural instincts toward determination and independence. But taming Amanda just might be the most satisfying event of his life.

Choice didn't question wanting her. He'd always wanted her, even when she'd been the blushing bride of his best friend.

He frowned with the discomfort that thought always gave him. Amanda noticed his creased brow and became very still. "What are you thinking?" she asked, positive it touched on the two of them.

"I was thinking about how the sun dances in your hair," he finally replied, which certainly wasn't a complete lie. "Even here in the shade."

His comment took her by surprise. She was positive his mind had been on something else and that he was eluding whatever it was with an uncharacteristic compliment. Why was he being so evasive?

Any worries Choice might have right now were because of her, Amanda realized abruptly and with no small alarm. Lord above, she didn't want to be the cause of him having problems with the association!

"I don't need protection, Choice," she said, low and emotionally.

He bolted up to a sitting position. "What makes you so sure of that?"

"That's what you were thinking about, isn't it?"

Choice got to his feet. "No. But as long as you brought it up, I think you just might have bitten off a little more than a woman alone can chew." His feet were spread in an authoritative stance, and his right hand went to the butt of his pistol, resting there with what looked like deceptive casualness to Amanda.

She stared. In the wink of an eye, he could draw that gun and fire it with deadly precision. He was afraid of nothing, and he would fight for her if it became necessary. Amanda's stomach roiled at such a ghastly possibility. Gunfights, bloodshed, violence of any kind, had always sickened her. Jed McMillan's murder on Spencer land was horrifying, an abomination. She had feared trouble the moment she'd seen those sheep, but the whole thing was getting out of hand. Choice was threatening anything that threatened her, and she didn't want him involved. If he got hurt—or hurt someone else—because of her, she would never forgive herself.

"Let me spell it out," Choice said flatly, shaping the words distinctly, as though explaining something to a child. "I know you see what you're doing as charitable. To a point, I agree with you. But that point stops at those sheep."

"What would you have me do, run them off? Scatter them in the hills?" Amanda struggled to her feet, defensive anger making her almost awkward. How quickly their attitudes had changed! It seemed that there were lines neither of them dared cross with the other. "Didn't I ask you last night to stay out of it? I don't need your help, Choice."

He was tight-lipped, as angry as she had ever seen him. "A man looks after the woman he... The woman in his life."

Her senses went flying. Had he been on the verge of saying "A man looks after the woman he *loves?*" She wanted to question him, to hear what he really felt for her. The urge was so strong, Amanda couldn't combat it. "Am I the woman in your life?"

"I think you know the answer to that."

Amanda's hackles rose at his continued evasion. "And just how would I have that answer?" she inquired with acerbity.

Choice came back with a slowly drawled, "Are you deliberately trying to pick a fight?"

Was she? It was all beginning to get to her, the heat, Jed McMillan's murder, Choice's unexpected change of heart, Lucy's predicament, her own mixed-up feelings.

She turned wearily. "I have to get home. The sheriff will be along, and I want to warn Lucy."

Choice followed her to the wagon. "I don't want bad feelings between us," he said quietly.

"Neither do I." Nevertheless, Amanda climbed up to the seat without taking Choice's proffered hand. Holding the reins, she looked at him. If nothing else ever occurred between the two of them, she had to get across to him that she didn't want him and his gun involved in her problems. "I ask no one to fight my battles, Choice. Please stay out of it."

His eyes darkened. "I've admired your spunk, Amanda—living alone, running the ranch, keeping everything going. But you don't know what you're dealing with now. I attend most of the association meetings, and no one in this valley is going to accept sheep on your place. Not even temporarily."

"That's ridiculous!"

Choice looked away, frustrated at her stubbornness. "I thought you were smarter than that."

He was an infuriating man, protective in spite of her objections. Nothing she could say would keep him out of it. "We've been acquaintances for years and yet I don't know you," she said with some bitterness.

"What do you want to know?"

"Does anyone know you? Have you ever let anyone really know you?"

He scoffed. "You're talking nonsense!"

"I'm not!"

"Maybe I don't know you, either, but how are we ever going to get to know each other if you keep backing away from me?"

The frustrating exchange was going nowhere. Flicking the reins, Amanda urged the horse backward a few steps so she could turn the wagon. She saw Choice give her a perplexed look, then climb onto his horse.

When they resumed the journey, Choice kept his horse just behind Amanda's line of vision. She avoided looking back at him but couldn't ignore his brooding presence. They rode in heavy silence, Amanda gnawing her bottom lip and worrying, Choice scowling.

Behind his dour expression, Choice was remembering. He'd received news of his father's illness right after a long hard trip into Texas. He'd been following the trail of a murdering polecat by the name of Tom Juarango, whom he'd nailed just north of San Antonio. Slapping the man in a Texas jail, he'd immediately headed for Wyoming and home.

His father had survived for another six months but was never able to run the ranch again. Shortly after Choice's return, Len married Amanda and brought her to Wyoming. In all the women Choice had met during his travels, he'd never been as impressed by one as he was by his best friend's bride.

He'd tried to ignore the attraction. He and Len had grown up as friends, and he was determined that a woman wasn't going to destroy their relationship. But he'd always felt something from Amanda herself, something in her shy smiles and in the few words they exchanged.

He stayed away from the Spencer place as much as possible, laying his noticeable absence on his father's illness and the demands of the Brenton ranch. And then, less than a year after his wedding day, Len was killed. It had been nothing but a freaky damned accident that shouldn't have given Len so much as a scratch. Everyone in the territory had lost a buggy wheel at one time or another, and Len dying from something so common had been tough to accept.

The tragedy had deeply affected Choice. Already guilty over his furtive feelings for Amanda, he vowed to honor Len's memory by staying away from his widow. Neighborly calls had been infrequent and brief.

And then . . . Amanda had touched his hand.

Choice cursed under his breath, forcing himself to face the truth. He couldn't stay away from her anymore, guilt or no guilt. And now, even though she hated admitting it, she was heading for a passel of trouble. She was a stubborn, strong-willed woman, and he wished he were able to express himself better, to make her see the danger.

Underlying it all—the questions, the uncertainty, the problems, the quarrels—Choice believed that Amanda was as drawn to him as he was to her. He knew now that he would take her any way he could get her, do anything in the world for her. There was really only one thing he wouldn't do for Amanda Spencer, which he'd more or less spelled out to her last night—play an indefinite waiting game.

When they at long last reached the turn to the Spencer ranch, Choice stopped for a final word, which wasn't about the sheep or the association.

"I'm sorry we argued last night. I'm sorry we argued again today. It's not arguments I want from you, Amanda, and it's not arguments you want from me." He tipped his hat. "I'll see you soon."

Amanda sat on the wagon under the broiling sun with the reins in her hands and watched him ride off.

Sighing, she continued to the house. In all honesty, she didn't know why they argued so much. But now she had another worry, Choice's determination to defend her stand, even though he was dead set against it.

Chapter Eight

Approaching the heart of her ranch, Amanda could hear the distant bleating of sheep. Although Woody and Buck had brought them close in, as she'd asked, she now wished she had sequestered the herd a little farther from the buildings. She had foreseen the possibility of John Lawrence coming to the ranch, but not Doc Lowden. Flaunting her good intentions to the sheriff *and* the crusty old doctor wasn't very wise, she worried. It would have made better sense to move the sheep farther out, perhaps near the foothills.

News spread quickly in the valley, and after today everyone would know that there were sheep on the Spencer ranch, with Amanda's blessing. What if the association members became incensed? Would John Lawrence go from the Spencer ranch to the association? Would Doc Lowden take it upon himself to interfere?

Amanda questioned whether she was doing anything right these days. One charitable act should not cause so many problems. While the horse and wagon kicked up a fine dust that filled Amanda's nose and throat and clung to the perspiration on her face, she pondered the changes in her life that one short week had wreaked. More than a year had passed more or less uneventfully since Len's death, and now, all within a few days, she was involved with murder, a homeless family, defiance of the Stock Growers Association's strict policy against sheep in the valley and, maybe the most provoking for her, Choice Brenton.

All things passed with time, even troublesome issues. She would somehow deal with the murder investigation, and caring for Lucy and the children was more a pleasure than a problem. The sheep would eventually be sold and gone—she would find a way—which would eradicate any dissension with the association, but where Choice was concerned she had no answers. He had been a peripheral influence since their first meeting, a distant but noticeable drumbeat in the rhythm of her life, and it wasn't sensible to assume that awareness of his drawing power would abate.

Whether their newly gained personal relationship floundered or flamed was up to her. Though the thought of Choice reverting to the seldom seen neighbor he'd been for so long was astonishingly discomfiting, it was highly unlikely he would ever channel what he was feeling into the type of emotion a large part of her deemed acceptable. If she wanted Choice Brenton, she would have to take him as he was, incommunicative, somber, guarded. *And* with that enormous pistol on his hip.

The thought of Choice's ever ready weapon presented Amanda's most current misgiving again. Somehow she had to get this matter resolved before any more violence erupted. She knew now that Choice would retaliate for any threat to her, and the very thought created fingers of ice on her spine, never mind the stifling heat of the day.

Squinting against the sun, Amanda saw Lucy come out of the house and wave eagerly, and the weight of what she had to tell the woman reappeared.

She delayed the unhappy task until the parcels had been opened and their contents inspected to the accompaniment of Lucy's tears, effusive thanks and promises to repay Amanda when the sheep were sold.

Then, with a cup of tea and a bowl of warmed-up soup before her, Amanda knew the moment could not be put off any longer. John Lawrence would arrive any minute, and Lucy should be prepared.

Baby Elizabeth was napping and Tad was playing on the floor with the set of wooden building blocks Amanda hadn't been able to resist as a special gift for the little boy. Lucy was having a cup of tea, too, sitting across the table from Amanda while she ate the late lunch.

It was difficult to begin, but finally Amanda said, "There's something I must tell you, Lucy."

Lucy's unsuspecting expression created an ache in Amanda's heart. Lucy had made very few references to her deceased husband, which Amanda interpreted as self-protection. Grief was devastating, and the shock of remembering, of being forced to remember, might very likely shatter the veneer of normalcy Lucy was managing.

Still, after relating the day's events, Amanda wasn't completely prepared for the frozen expression on Lucy's face, nor the fearfully cried, "No! You shouldn't have! Why? Why did you go to the sheriff?"

Sick at heart, Amanda sadly defended herself. "I had to, Lucy. Please try to understand. Jed was killed on my land. I really should have reported it the morning I discovered it." She watched Lucy get up and pace the kitchen, wringing her hands as she moved around.

"Please don't be upset," Amanda pleaded. "Sheriff Lawrence will talk to you about it, that's all. I know it will be hard for you, but you're the only one who can tell him what happened that night."

Lucy stopped, a look of relief washing over her. "Why, yes, you're right. I am the only one, aren't I?" She returned to her chair and sat down again. "Oh, Amanda, it was so dreadful," she moaned.

Amanda expected the young woman to finally open up about that night, but she remained silent. Surprised that Lucy wasn't going to begin reciting details, Amanda resigned herself to remaining uninformed. Reaching across the table, she patted the woman's arm. "Just remember that I'm with you in this, Lucy. John Lawrence doesn't take his responsibility to the community lightly. He'll do his best to ferret out the heartless men who left your babies fatherless."

Lucy listened to every word and nodded stoically. "I'll tell him . . . everything, Amanda."

"That's all he or anyone else can ask," Amanda concluded with a comforting smile. Lucy's reticence was understandable, she told herself. Having to speak of the nightmarish episode to the sheriff was bad enough; Lucy probably couldn't force herself to spill the appalling tale to anyone else.

At any rate, Amanda was tremendously relieved that this portion of the day was behind her. She only wished she could rid herself of her own worries as smoothly as she had eased Lucy's.

Russell Lowden, Leavitt's only doctor, acted as coroner in instances of violent death. Doc, as everyone called Russell, arrived with John Lawrence and, to Amanda's dismay, two other men, one of whom she knew to be a deputy by the name of Runnell Petersen.

The second man was Wes Schuyler, to whom Amanda said an extremely stunned hello. If anyone scared her, it was Wes Schuyler. Everything Len had told her about the influential rancher swarmed in her brain like a hive of buzzing bees. Len had said that the man was shrewd, cold, callous and best given a wide berth. John Lawrence must have gone to Wes with Amanda's story, involving him even before coming to the ranch. It was a blow she hadn't anticipated.

The four men looked formidable in her parlor. Striving for composure, Amanda invited them to sit down, then went to the guest room where Lucy had secreted herself at the first sign of the approaching caravan. "They're waiting for you, Lucy."

Lucy's hands fluttered over the baby. "I must see to Elizabeth first," she demurred huskily.

"All right. But please come to the parlor as soon as you can."

Leaving Lucy's room, Amanda paused in the hall to collect herself. Her heart was pounding. She took several deep breaths, forcing her shocked system to calm down. What could Schuyler do? she asked herself in a rush of courage. Lucy's sheep were on Spencer ground, not harming one blade of anyone else's grass. Schuyler had no business coming here on this unnerving occasion. John Lawrence had no business inviting him to come. This was her place, and the sheep on it were no one else's affair.

With studied determination, Amanda returned to the parlor and told the men, "Mrs. McMillan will be here shortly. She's tending her baby."

Wes Schuyler hadn't sat down. He was standing near the piano, directing a hard-eyed gaze at Amanda. Around fifty years of age, Schuyler had a broad, flat face with swarthy, coarse skin and a thin, disdainful mouth. His shoulders and chest were immense, but no part of him was as intimidating as the cold expression in his dark eyes. "We took note of the sheep, Amanda. They're the cause of this whole bloody mess, you know."

And so it begins, she thought with a sinking sensation. She opened her mouth, prepared to relate her plans to sell the animals with all possible haste. But she didn't get the chance.

"You can't keep them," Wes declared in a tone that carried anger and disgust.

Amanda's spirit ignited. She had no intention of keeping the sheep, but to be spoken to as though she was incapable of making a sensible decision on the matter was galling. "They're on Spencer land, Wes," she bluntly pointed out.

"I don't give a tinker's damn where they are! As long as they're in this valley, me and every other cattleman in the valley are telling you, you can't keep 'em!"

Amanda drew herself up in a chilly response. "Is that why you came along, to give me an ultimatum?"

Wes didn't back down an iota. "Call it what you like. We've fought squatters and sheep for years, and we're not going to jeopardize a hard-won way of life for you or anyone else who thinks he can bring sheep into this valley. You know what those stinking animals do to grass. They don't just bite it off, they rip it up by the roots!"

The other men had remained silent throughout Wes's tirade, but a glance at their faces showed Amanda that all three were in complete accord with the rancher. John Lawrence had brought Wes Schuyler along purposely to give Amanda Spencer a lecture, which the man had done in no uncertain terms.

Amanda had to consciously stop herself from showing Wes the door. How dare he speak to her in that manner in her own home? She understood the policies of the association as well as he did. What's more, she was no fonder of sheep than any man in the room.

But she couldn't antagonize Schuyler or anyone else, not with Choice so steadfastly involved. Dear Lord, what had she gotten herself—and Choice—into? All she'd intended was to help Lucy and her children.

Amanda didn't lack courage, and she felt very little friendliness toward this group. Deviating from her own beliefs about sheep to assist a homeless family was perhaps foolhardy, but she was stuck in the middle of it now, too deeply enmeshed to back away. Even concern about

Choice's involvement couldn't make her buckle under. She stood as tall as possible, presenting a resolute countenance.

"The sheep are going to be sold," she stated coolly.

"When?" Wes asked, barking out the word.

"When?" repeated Amanda, putting a question of her own into her voice. "I think everyone here understands the nature of the problem. Sheep buyers aren't hanging from the rafters in these parts. Obviously I'm going to have to go to Cheyenne to contact them."

Wes and John Lawrence exchanged glances. "The animals are only here temporarily," Amanda continued in the same cool tone. "I understand Leon McElroy and Clint Edmunds have been boasting about hazing the sheep the night Jed was killed. I suspect they know something about Jed McMillan's death, but be that as it may, it might be a good idea for one of you to pass a message on to them. If they try the same thing on Spencer land again, they'll end up with a lot more trouble than their good time is worth."

"Brave words, Amanda," John Lawrence observed softly. "Let's just say that it would be best if you got rid of those sheep very quickly."

Four sets of hard eyes regarded her, presenting a united front. "Temporarily" was only a word to these men, just as Choice had predicted. Sheep were in the valley, and the cattle people's biggest fear was that if they relented on one herd, more would follow.

"I'm doing it for Lucy McMillan and her children," Amanda said, resorting to a plea in spite of her wish to remain strong.

"If Len were alive . . ." Wes muttered.

The implication was insulting, especially coming from a man who hadn't liked Len. Amanda felt that she had proven her ranching abilities since her husband's death, but to Schuyler, she was only a woman making decisions based on female whims. Success in any venture was not accidental, but that was even truer in ranching. Amanda faced harsh weather, animal diseases, feeding problems and fluctuating prices, the same as any male rancher. But any mistake she might make was laid on her sex.

Well, Len might not have taken in Lucy's sheep, but he would not have left that family out there without food, clothing and a roof over their heads.

Amanda's lips parted to say so, and to tell Wes Schuyler a few other facts of civilized behavior, too. But then she spotted Lucy peering around the door. "Come in, Lucy," she said, glad that Lucy had arrived. Releasing her frustration and outright fury about Schuyler's prejudiced attitude wouldn't even make a dent in the man's overbearing armor, and the situation was bad enough already. Wes Schuyler was easily as angry as she was, but he wasn't trying as hard to conceal it. The man's black eyes nearly burned. He saw her as dead wrong and too stupidly female to realize the trouble she was causing.

Feeling a little sick to her stomach, Amanda made introductions. John, Doc and the deputy got to their feet and said hello, then the sheriff turned to Amanda. "Would you prefer we speak to Mrs. McMillan outside?"

It was a bald-faced hint for Amanda to make an exit, but she wasn't comfortable leaving Lucy at the mercy of these four harsh men. "Lucy?" she inquired.

"It's all right, Amanda. You go on. I'll be fine. I'm not scared anymore."

Nodding, Amanda spoke to the group. "I'll be in my room. You may close the parlor door if you wish." Her gaze returned to Lucy. "I'll listen for the children."

"Thank you. I left Tad watching the baby."

It was a major advance in Tad's introverted behavior to have let go of his mother's skirt, but Amanda felt that watching the baby was a bit much to expect from the frightened little boy, and instead of going to her room, she went to Lucy's.

She opened the door cautiously and peeked in. Tad was sitting on the bed beside Elizabeth, who was wide awake and waving her little arms and kicking her feet. "Hello, Tad," Amanda said softly.

He only stared.

"May I come in and sit with you and Elizabeth?"

Several seconds passed, but Tad finally nodded his head. Amanda walked to the bed. Lucy's children were adorable, beautifully innocent, handsomely featured. Like their mother, they had blond hair and blue eyes, and Amanda's heart warmed while she perched on the edge of the bed and fondly regarded the youngsters.

Whatever else Lucy McMillan had or didn't have, she had these two precious children, and in maternal instincts alone Amanda felt a rare bond with the woman. Someday she was going to have children, too, she ardently vowed, sweet babies like Elizabeth and Tad. She had so much love to give a child, so much untapped tenderness and affection.

It was quiet in the room, so quiet Amanda became aware of the drone of voices from the parlor. She wondered how Lucy was faring. Wes Schuyler's presence was a staggering shock. Choice wouldn't like the rancher laying down ultimatums, even ones he agreed with in concept, but then, she didn't like it, either. The difference was, there was little she could do about it, and Choice might not feel that way.

Amanda shivered. She did not want Choice challenging Wes because of her. Her insides were in a tumult, part of her ruing her generous impulses with the McMillans, another part knowing she could have done nothing else. She had done what any compassionate person would do.

Shaping a smile and putting the awful mess out of her mind, Amanda began talking to the two children. She spoke soothingly and in soft tones, and after a while, she was pleased to hear a few words from Tad. There was nothing physically wrong with the little boy, which she had feared despite Lucy's assurances to the contrary. Tad's timidity was emotionally related, apparently, and Amanda wondered again just what the small child had witnessed in his short lifetime to affect him so adversely.

Then, quite suddenly, Lucy was in the doorway. Her face was streaked with tears, but she offered Amanda a weak smile. "It's over. I told them everything," she stated wearily.

"Thank goodness." Amanda got to her feet. "I'll go back to the parlor now," she said before hurrying away.

The four men were standing, talking quietly, but when Amanda appeared, they fell silent. John Lawrence stated, "It's getting late. Are you free to show us the site now?"

"Yes. I'll saddle my horse and be ready in a few minutes."

Amanda had washed up and changed to a clean skirt and blouse before the men arrived. She hastily exchanged her skirt and house shoes for trousers and riding boots before going to the barn.

With all of them mounted and heading away from the buildings, she couldn't resist asking John, "Did Lucy clarify what happened that night?"

"She gave me her story," the sheriff replied noncommittally, leaving Amanda still in the dark.

"What about Leon McElroy and Clint Edmunds?" she asked, implying that the two men knew something about Jed McMillan's death.

The sheriff never even blinked. "I plan to talk to them when I get back to town."

As they topped the hill from which Amanda had originally viewed the McMillan encampment, Amanda pulled Ginger up. "You don't need me any longer, do you?" she asked John.

"Doc?" John questioned.

Russell stirred. "Is the grave marked?"

"I haven't seen it," Amanda admitted. "But my men told me they marked it with three large rocks."

"In that case I don't see any reason for Amanda to linger," the doctor told John.

As Ginger trotted away, Amanda glanced back to see the four horsemen heading down the hill. She didn't envy them their grisly task. Law and order sometimes demanded a high price from its participants and yet she'd detected only calm acceptance from John Lawrence, Runnell Petersen and Doc Lowden in their roles.

Wes Schuyler was another matter. He'd come to speak his piece, and he'd done so without a drop of tact. Her being a woman seemed to infuriate him in a strange way, to make him take a harder stand than he might have with another man.

Amanda thought about it while she rode. Schuyler had taken a hard stand, all right, but wasn't that exactly what she was doing, too?

Sighing, Amanda lifted her hat to wipe away the perspiration that had gathered on her forehead. There was only one person in the valley who was the least bit sympathetic, but Choice's sympathies were not because he agreed with her, but because he wanted to make love to her.

That fact was becoming less shocking, Amanda realized, somewhat startled by the knowledge. She was getting used to the idea.

If he wore down her resistance and she let him make love to her, what would come after? For that matter, what would come during? Would the feverish feelings he aroused in her system mature? His touches and kisses promised something, and she couldn't help being curious about what that something was.

But how foolish dare she be with a man who only wanted pleasure from her? Crossing that line with a man, any man, would forever alter who she was. If only she didn't feel so giddy with Choice, so flushed and damp and overheated. How could her body react so opposingly to her own sense of right and wrong? She had admitted to something powerful between them, and he had said it was going to get more powerful.

Amanda shivered, although there was little coolness in the late afternoon air. Maybe she had no choice in the matter. Maybe whatever was gripping her was stronger than common sense.

She was glad the long, exhausting day was nearly over. She unsaddled Ginger quickly, intending to linger no longer at the barn than was necessary. Coming out of the tack room, where she had put away the saddle, she spotted Buck and Woody riding in.

They hailed her from horseback, and she stood by while they approached and finally dismounted. Both men seemed stiff, grim. "Saw the sheriff from a distance," Woody announced.

"And Wes Schuyler," Buck added dourly. "What'd he want, Amanda?"

Something sad and unsure sighed in Amanda. She hadn't expected that her own men would see Schuyler and question the man's presence, but she realized now that Buck and Woody were uneasy because they had helped with the sheep.

A great weariness drained what felt like the very last of Amanda's strength. In the face of more pressing concerns, she hadn't yet attempted to locate a man to replace Jess. She was neglecting the ranch to help the McMillans, and with roundup just around the corner, she would not only need a third full-time man, she should hire on extras.

Her tired gaze went between the two stone-faced men. They didn't like Wes Schuyler on the place, knowing that the man could think they were condoning sheep in the valley. But it was all so ludicrous, and Amanda was becoming impatient with men and their misplaced ethics.

"Schuyler wanted to give me a lecture," she finally said flatly. "Which he did. His disapproval of me has nothing to do with the two of you."

Buck and Woody exchanged meaningful glances, which set Amanda's heart to racing. "It doesn't," she insisted rather frantically.

Woody spat in the dust. "I ain't gittin' anywhere near those sheep again, Amanda."

"I ain't either," Buck agreed.

"Fine," she said quickly. "I won't ask you to. I'll take care of them myself."

Woody squinted at her. "How're ya gonna keep 'em from wandering off Spencer land?"

How, indeed. For a moment Amanda stood there feeling helpless. But then, from somewhere deep inside herself, she felt a burgeoning fury. She had struggled too hard with life's cruelties to admit defeat over this. The security she had found here was being threatened by small-minded men, and damned if she was going to give it up without a fight!

Where had her backbone been hiding these past few days? She'd been mealymouthed with Choice, concealed her indignation with John Lawrence and Wes Schuyler, picked her words carefully with her own men. Enough was enough.

Her eyes glazed over with anger. "Neither one of you need to worry about how I deal with those sheep, all right? Take care of your regular chores and forget that herd is even on the ranch!"

She had never spoken so harshly to the men before, but even their surprised expressions couldn't daunt her fighting spirit. No one was going to intimidate her again, not even Wes Schuyler. This was her land, and by damn, everyone was going to know it.

Amanda drew a deep breath. "I'm going to the house now. Your supper will be ready in about an hour." Turning, she walked away, leaving her two hired hands to stare after her. At the moment, she didn't give a damn if they both rode off for good. Roundup or no roundup, she'd had just about all she could take of masculine stupidity!

And one thing more, she thought defiantly as she marched to the house, the next time Choice tried something, he just might get a surprise, too. She was not going to be pushed into anything with him, either, damn his overbearing hide. She was all through being pushed by anyone.

Chapter Nine

Amanda's courage held, although she felt abnormally on edge. Lucy and the children were tucked in and probably already sleeping when Amanda took a basin of warm water to her bedroom for a sponge bath before retiring. Despite a dozen sound reasons for exhaustion, she suspected that she would put in a restless night.

Her mind seemed to be on fire with provoking thoughts and worries. A warm bath would help to relax her, she hoped as she soothed her taut skin with a wet cloth and scented soap. Deep down she knew she shouldn't have talked so heedlessly to Buck and Woody. She hadn't been wrong in letting them know who was boss on the Spencer ranch, but she could have picked a better time to assert herself, and done so without anger.

It was a warm night, unusually muggy. A storm was brewing, still some hours away but weighting the atmosphere. Amanda bathed her feet and legs, her arms and body, then dropped a clean nightgown over her head. Removing the pins from her hair, she gave it a vigorous brushing. It all helped relieve some of her tension. Donning a long robe and slippers, she carried the basin of water through the silent house to empty it. Kitchen debris and wash water were discarded in one particular area beyond the woodshed, and Amanda stepped into the dark night without a qualm.

An owl hooted, and Amanda stopped near the shed to glance at the sky. Stringy, thin clouds scudded from a high wind, but the quarter moon was relatively clear, as were some stars. It probably wouldn't rain tonight, but rain was in the air. Strange that it was so warm at this hour, she thought, proceeding to the compost pile to empty the basin.

Retracing her steps, she hesitated at the back door of the house. She had too much on her mind to fall asleep quickly, and she hated rolling and tossing. Setting the basin down beside the back stoop, she started toward the barn.

The bunkhouse was dark. Buck and Woody were probably long asleep. A single lamp burned in the house, illuminating one small window. Animal noises seemed muffled and far off. Amanda occasionally walked around at night and had no fear of the dark. Besides, the moon was giving off quite a lot of light and she had no trouble finding her way. She stopped at the corral and, sighing, leaned her back against the pole fencing. Her nerves were stretched a little too thin, and the night quiet was soothing.

It was a few minutes before she felt uneasy, as though she wasn't alone, although she heard nothing to alarm her. She looked around and saw the glow of a cigarette in the shadow of the barn. Her heart leaped into her throat. Buck and Woody didn't smoke!

The small glowing light arced and fell to the ground. "Amanda?"

Choice stepped out of the shadows. "My God, you scared me half to death!" Amanda exclaimed. "What on earth are you doing here at this time of night?"

He walked toward her. "Couldn't sleep, so I took a ride. I saw your light."

"Why didn't you come to the door?"

"I was going to, but you came out instead. You having trouble sleeping, too?"

She rubbed her arms, although the night air wasn't the least bit chilly. "It was a long day."

"Made you restless?"

Something had made her restless. Maybe it was finding some genuine courage after behaving like a jellyfish for too long. Maybe it was the raw emotions that seemed to be eating her up inside. Or because she was still uncertain even with courage. But right now it was because she was remembering that the Brenton place was too far away for a casual ride over just because Choice couldn't sleep.

She was in nightclothes. And while Choice might not suspect her state of undress, she was incredibly aware of her nakedness.

"Have you done this before?" she questioned uneasily.

"Rode over here after dark, you mean?"

"That's what I mean, yes."

"Once or twice."

"And never knocked on the door?"

"Would you have welcomed me?"

Amanda swallowed and looked away from his dark visage. His hat was low on his forehead, its brim hiding his eyes. His voice, all soft and silky, bothered her. A thrill rippled her skin, raising gooseflesh.

"I don't think you would have," he said, answering his own question. "You weren't ready."

Her eyes jerked to his face. "And I'm ready now?"

"Aren't you?"

Her voice contained a challenge. "Ready for what, Choice?"

He took a step closer. "For me, Amanda."

Her breath caught. "You're crude."

"Honest," he rebutted. "Why is it that an honest woman doesn't like honesty in a man?" He peered at her. "You are an honest woman, aren't you?"

"Don't make fun of me. I'm in no mood for it."

"No?" He inched a little closer. "What kind of mood are you in, then? Reckless, maybe? Lonely?" He raised a hand to her hair. "God, it's beautiful down like this."

Amanda ducked her head and backed up a step. "Don't!"

"I make you nervous."

"Making a woman nervous is hardly something to boast about."

"Who's boasting? I feel a hell of a lot more like crying than boasting." She was backed up to the corral fence again, and Choice swung around and put his back against the pole rails. "Do you have any idea what you do to me?"

Amanda felt as if she was about to choke on her own wild heartbeat. They were standing side by side, neither looking at the other. "Maybe I don't want to know."

"You're a baffling woman."

"You're a baffling man."

"Dammit, Amanda!" Choice spun to face her, moving so quickly she had no chance to get out of his way. He curled his hands around the top pole of the corral, one on either side of her.

"Don't you dare think you can hold me here," she said furiously, doing her best to avoid contact. His body was crowding hers without quite touching it. His size and scent were smothering her, making breathing a chore. "I won't be treated this way. And just why are you sneaking around here at night? Do Buck and Woody know you do that? What would people say if they knew you—"

"Cut it out, Amanda. In the first place, I don't give a damn what people might say about anything. In the second, I wasn't sneaking. But since you're so worried, no one knows I've ever been here without your permission." He finally registered her long robe, figuring out what it was. "You were getting ready for bed."

"Uh..."

"That's a robe you're wearing." He tried to see better in the dark, narrowing his eyes on the garment. What was under it? His pulse was suddenly loud enough to hear. "Honey...Amanda..." He dipped his head, seeking her lips.

Amanda turned her face away, and his mouth landed in her hair. He left it there, and his hot breath heating her scalp was almost as arousing as a kiss on the mouth would have been. "Please don't," she whispered huskily.

"Don't ask me to not want you. It wouldn't do any good anyway." He moved closer until his body pressed into hers. "Kiss me the way I want you to," he whispered.

Amanda squeezed her eyes tightly shut, knowing she was on the verge of doing something very foolish. The pressures of the past week had put her in a strange mood, those of today in particular. Her newly galvanized courage was satisfyingly real, but it was still mingled with loneliness and sorrow that she should be so singularly different from her neighbors when she had almost desperately wanted to fit in.

Maybe she hadn't tried hard enough. Maybe she shouldn't have worn men's clothing and gotten all silly and sentimental over a homeless family. Maybe she should have let the sheep run wild and put Lucy and her babies on the first train to Pennsylvania.

And maybe she shouldn't crave and ache and respond when Choice Brenton leaned into her. When he rubbed against her. When he breathed into her hair and asked her to kiss him the way he wanted her to.

But she had reacted to Lucy's plight with uncontrollable compassion, and her reactions to Choice were even more unmanageable. How did he have the power to create so much need in her? So much unrest?

Amanda's head came around slowly until her lips were only a breath away from Choice's. "You're very... persistent," she whispered.

"Don't say I wore you down, Amanda. Tell me, instead, that you want what I do."

"It's so simple for men, isn't it? You function so..." Amanda stopped, stunned that she would speak so plainly.

Choice pushed his hat back on his head and tried to see into her eyes. "That remark raises some real interesting questions," he said quietly.

"Please forget it." Embarrassment scorched her face. "I better go in."

"Not yet." Choice dropped his arms around her and urged her forward. "You're tight as a drum. Relax." He held her to himself, soft female flesh against sinewy maleness, and gradually felt some yielding in her.

She did feel reckless, just as Choice had suggested. But being held by strong, certain arms was even more influencing than her own unusual mood. She wasn't lonely in Choice's arms, she realized. She felt drawn to that security, and she wondered again about his power.

His hands moved on her back. Her cheek was on his chest, and she could hear his strong heartbeat. If it were only possible to maintain this closeness without advancing to his true goal with her.

But the ripples of awareness in her mocked such a foolish hope. If even she couldn't share this sort of embrace and feel nothing but friendship, how could he?

"You smell like roses," he whispered, his lips in her hair again.

"Scented soap." She knew she should stop this from going any further, but that didn't give her the strength to push him away. He felt like nothing she had ever experienced, like safety and seduction all mixed up into one tempting package.

Her legs were trembling. Her hands rose to his shirt, her fingers curling into the fabric for support. She felt his hands leave her back and slide around her, rising to cup her face and lift it to his. Even in the pale moonlight she could see the desire in his eyes.

"Amanda..."

It was a low, hoarse call, different than anything she had ever heard. She dampened her lips. His head came down, and then his mouth was on hers, moving, taking, possessing. A long breath shuddered out of her as a flame darted through her body. His big hands caressed her face while he kissed her lips. She wilted into him and began kissing him back.

His tongue slipped into her mouth, and the flame within her blazed higher. Emotion filled her, taunted her, dared her. The pleasure of the kiss was flawed only by a need for more. She strained to him as objections to this sort of intimacy faded into obscurity.

There was such potent strength in his kiss, his hands, his body. His mouth was like heated satin on hers, shaping, leading. His breathing was no longer smooth and even, nor was her own, and the sounds of arousal were almost as seductive as Choice's powerful embrace.

Amanda felt his hands leave her face and go behind her, tracing her shoulders, her back. They splayed on her hips and drew her even closer to him, and he moaned deep in his throat, a growling, purely masculine sound that prickled Amanda's spine.

She let his tongue play with hers, tease hers, and the resulting sensations made her dizzy. Her arms went around Choice's neck, her hands exploring the dense, springy hair at the back of his head. She flicked his hat away, baring his head, and explored further.

Choice could feel the layers of her garments, the robe and a gown. But there was nothing else beneath his fingers, and his mind exploded when he realized she was naked under the nightwear. Desperately needing to touch her bare skin, he began working up the skirts of her clothing.

Kisses were melting into kisses with barely a breath in between. Amanda vaguely wondered about her own wild response, but something she couldn't name controlled her senses. Something too intense and demanding to combat. Heat...so much heat...so much wanting. She leaned her weak and trembling body into his, silently agreeing to everything that was happening.

But then, shocked even through the overwhelming passion fogging her brain, she felt his hot, searching hands beneath her clothing, moving on her hips, cupping the curves of her bottom. She tore her mouth from his, breathing hard, gasping for air and for reason. "Choice...no..."

He held her fast. "Don't stop me," he whispered raggedly.

"This is...crazy." She could scarcely speak, and her voice sounded hoarse and scratchy. His right hand slid around her, squeezing between them. It move up to a breast and closed around it, and another onslaught of flames licked at Amanda's insides. Her eyes closed at the intense pleasure. "You...have to stop," she whispered. "We can't do this."

Choice hesitated, surprising himself. He knew now that he could lead her into making love, and it was a heady sensation. He'd always suspected she had a weakness for him, and he sure as hell had one for her. But he wanted her without protests, without her conscience or inhibitions or whatever the hell was bothering her getting in the way, and he hadn't known that before. It wouldn't be long. Every meeting, every touch, every familiarity brought Amanda closer to admitting her own desire.

He could wait. He wasn't a patient man, but he would try to be for Amanda. He'd already been more patient about those damned sheep than he'd ever been about anything, and that sure wasn't for any other reason than because she kept asking him to stay out of it.

She probably didn't realize just how much he *had* been staying out of it. It wasn't like him to lurk on the fringes of a problem, but that's exactly what he'd been doing.

That generosity could only go so far, however, and the reason he'd come over here tonight was to find out from Amanda what had happened with the sheriff this afternoon. The kisses hadn't been planned, and it was satisfying that she had responded with so much abandon, but... He'd be patient.

Slowly and deliberately, he removed his hands from under her clothing and let her skirts drop. His heart was pounding, and he was achingly, painfully hard.

Amanda stood there in the circle of his arms, amazed that he had respected her wishes. Oddly, she felt a sense of loss and no small amount of disappointment.

He pressed a long kiss to her forehead, holding her while he attempted to calm his system. But he wasn't going to calm down as long as he touched her, so he dropped his arms and backed off.

Amanda reeled and reached for a corral pole to steady herself, grasping for something to say. "Uh...where's your horse?"

"Right over there."

She glanced to where he indicated and saw the black bulk of Bolo. "I didn't see him."

"You seemed fixed on something."

"On something...yes." She didn't want to tell him about Wes Schuyler coming with the sheriff, but now she realized that curiosity about the afternoon was what had prompted Choice's visit. "I best go in," she murmured.

"In a minute. What happened with John Lawrence? Did Doc Lowden come with him?"

"Yes, Doc and Runnell Petersen."

"Runnell, too?" Something in Amanda's voice made him ask, "Anyone else?"

Amanda hugged her robe around her, remembering much too vividly how Choice's hands had felt beneath it.

"There was one other person," she admitted reluctantly.

"Who?" The word was snapped out.

Amanda hesitated, but there was no evading an honest answer. "Wes Schuyler."

"Wes!" Choice looked away and cursed under his breath. That was exactly what he had thought might happen and what he'd tried to warn Amanda about. If the association, Schuyler especially, decided to do something about those sheep, anyone who got in their way was liable to get hurt.

For that matter, someone already had been hurt, Jed McMillan, and Choice couldn't ignore the possibility of the association being involved. Maybe Schuyler had sent Clint and Leon out to roust the sheepherder, although it did seem that a bullet was more Wes's style than a knife.

"What did Schuyler have to say?"

Choice spoke in that lethally quiet voice that alarmed Amanda whenever she heard it. She kept her torn-up emotions out of her voice, hoping to relay the conversation with Schuyler in an unthreatening way. "He merely said I couldn't keep the sheep, which I had no intention of doing anyway. He didn't scare me, Choice, so please..."

"Did he threaten you?"

"Of course he didn't threaten me. John Lawrence was standing right there, Doc and Runnell, too. Schuyler was no more upset about the sheep than you are, for your information."

"But I'm not going to do anything about them and he might. Amanda, don't confuse me with the other ranchers. If it was anyone other than you protecting that herd, I'd be lined up with the association."

She drew a long breath. "I guess that's clear enough."

"I hope so."

Something drove her to accuse, "You're denying your own beliefs because you want to... to... take me to bed." She stumbled over the words because she had never said anything so bold to a man before.

"That's it in a nutshell," he replied grimly.

"I hate that."

"Well, don't think I'm wild about it," he drawled sarcastically. "The whole situation rubs me the wrong way. If I'd gone into that camp the first day I saw those sheep, that herder might still be alive, and he and his family and his stinking sheep would be a long way away from here by now."

They both froze. Choice hadn't meant to accuse, but what he'd said sounded exactly like an accusation. Amanda was nearly struck dumb from the reproach. If she hadn't insisted on handling the situation by herself, Choice might have made Jed see the wisdom of leaving the valley.

The idea kept sinking deeper into her soul, and she moaned suddenly and turned to the corral. "My Lord," she whispered, horribly shaken.

Choice stood there, wishing to God he'd watched his tongue. He moved closer and put his hand on her shoulder, which she promptly shook off. She didn't want to be touched. She was miserably unhappy, worried that her own selfish desire to operate the ranch without anyone else's help or interference, especially Choice's, had resulted in Jed's death.

"Amanda, I shouldn't have said that. I didn't mean it the way it sounded."

"How could I have been so blind?"

"It wasn't your fault."

"I have to make it up to Lucy. I *have* to protect her sheep. I owe it to her."

"You don't owe anybody anything. Will you listen to reason?"

Amanda felt sick to her stomach. She hadn't thought of Jed's death in that way before, and all she could think of now was helping Lucy. She was the only one who would do it. Certainly Choice wouldn't bend enough to care for the sheep until the herd could be sold, nor would anyone else in the valley. Even her own men had made their distaste abundantly clear.

The only assistance Choice might give her now would be to stand up to Wes Schuyler, should Schuyler become a problem, and that was the one area in which Amanda didn't want his help. She still had to keep Choice out of it, although her reasons had nothing to do with independence. The thought of any more bloodshed because of her was repugnant.

She turned to face Choice. "I don't want you confronting Wes because he came here with John today."

Choice struggled with a sudden burst of impatience. "You're still insisting I stay out of it."

"More than ever."

"Why? Dammit, Amanda, don't you see that you just keep digging a deeper hole? Look, I could have my men drive those sheep out of the valley in the morning and everyone would forget 'em in a few days. That makes real good sense."

"Drive them out? To do what, die in the cold and snow this winter?"

"Do you really care?"

"Choice, that herd is worth at least a thousand dollars. Do you have so much cash lying around that a thousand dollars means nothing? I don't mind admitting that I do not. I'll tell you something, Choice. It's possible that every rancher in this valley bears some responsibility for Jed's death. I have half a notion to go to the next meeting of the association and appeal to the members."

"Amanda," he said softly. "They would laugh you out of the hall, unless they got mad. They are not going to relent on a herd of sheep."

"If I explained how temporary..."

"Did you explain that to Schuyler? You did, didn't you? And did he tell you that a temporary herd was all right?"

"You know he didn't," Amanda said in a low voice.

"Yes, I do know. Even without being there, I know what Schuyler's response was. There's no gray area on this issue, Amanda, that's what you have got to understand. It's black or white, and temporary doesn't mean diddly to anyone but you."

Maybe for the first time, Amanda comprehended how adamantly against sheep the cattlemen really were. She'd assumed that she understood, but she hadn't, not really. It still made little sense to her, but the cattle people didn't care if their attitude made sense to anyone but themselves. There were not going to be sheep in this valley and that was the final word on the matter.

She heaved a discouraged sigh, facing the urgency of that trip to Cheyenne to locate a buyer for the sheep. She almost mentioned it, but didn't want an argument from Choice on that, too. They had argued enough. They had kissed enough, as well. She didn't know what she felt for Choice. No one she had ever known could turn her upside down and inside out the way he could.

"It's getting late," she said. "And I'm tired. I'm going in now." Instantly she sensed his reluctance to say good night. He would stand around out here and talk—or argue—indefinitely, probably hoping in the back of his mind for further intimacy. "Good night," she said firmly and started for the house.

Choice snagged his hat from the ground and walked along with her. "If you didn't have company, I'd go in with you," he said at her door.

She turned. "No, you wouldn't. Not tonight, at any rate."

He touched the collar of her robe. "Soon," he said softly.

"I...don't know." She couldn't make promises, not when she had so little understanding of their almost explosive relationship. They were either arguing or kissing, and while he might believe she was "ready" for him, she felt no such clarity on the matter. "Good night."

"Just a minute. Did you hear what Lucy told the sheriff?"

"No. John made it very clear that he wanted me to leave the room."

"But she did tell you what happened that night."

Amanda hated admitting this, too. "She hasn't talked about it."

"And you still don't find that strange?"

"What are you getting at?"

Choice looked off. "I don't know. Something about it doesn't feel right. Seems to me that's just about all a woman would talk about, if she went through it."

Amanda defended her friend. "She's in shock, and everyone handles grief differently."

"I guess so."

"Good night."

"Good night, Amanda."

Choice waited until she was inside and the door was closed, then, forgetting Lucy McMillan, he strode to the barn and Bolo, whistling softly between his teeth. Maybe he shouldn't feel so silly, not when there were a dozen hurdles still to get past with Amanda.

But she had melted into him and kissed him with all the honeyed heat a man could hope for in a woman. She was getting used to the idea of having him in her life. He was a lucky man.

Mounted on Bolo, Choice set off in the dark. He was nearly home when he started thinking of marriage. The thought made his blood run faster. Amanda was the marrying kind of woman, but was he the marrying kind of man? He wasn't dissatisfied with his life. Routines were set and comfortable. His hired men slept in the bunkhouse, but wandered in and out of the main house at will. A wife would change everything.

But a wife would be in his bed every night, warm and soft and rose-scented. And if he didn't marry Amanda, other men would try. There were a lot of lonely men in Wyoming. Even plain women didn't have to remain unmarried, and Amanda was not only beautiful, she owned a ranch that would whet any man's appetite.

It was a subject that should be given consideration, Choice decided. Some very serious consideration.

Chapter Ten

Amanda was keeping a close eye on the weather. The humidity was unusually high, although the threatening rain never quite matured. The temperature was dropping daily, and Amanda wore a jacket when she rode out to bunch up the sheep each morning. Buck and Woody rode right past the animals as if they weren't there, annoying Amanda to exasperation, but she said nothing to either man about it.

She made plans for the trip to Cheyenne, talking it over with Lucy. "It shouldn't take more than three days, two for travel there and back and one to locate a buyer."

"No, I suppose not," Lucy sighed.

The journey would consist of catching the stage that passed through Leavitt to the railroad, then the long train ride to Cheyenne. Amanda wasn't looking forward to the trip, but it had to be done.

She directed Buck and Woody to begin roundup, although it was still a little early to move the main herd back to lower ground. But she was worried about having only two men when she needed at least three and should really have a couple of extras.

No transient cowhands asking for work through roundup had come along, though she remembered very well that last fall and the one before, which had been her first on the ranch, quite a few men had stopped in asking for work.

That struck Amanda as odd, but something else struck her as even odder. Twice when she was out riding, she saw distant, unrecognizable men on horseback who appeared to be doing nothing more than taking a look at what was happening on the Spencer ranch. The second time she spotted them, a chill went up her spine. She was being watched. More precisely, the sheep were being watched, and she knew again that she had to get the herd sold and out of the valley with all possible haste.

Something else was bothering Amanda, probably caused by Choice's questions the other night. Lucy still hadn't talked about the night Jed was killed, and while Amanda truly liked Lucy, the woman's reticence was beginning to feel like secrecy. At mealtimes, they talked about any number of things, cooking, the children, the ranch, Lucy's past, Amanda's past, but never anything about Jed, never anything about the man or men who had killed him and if Lucy had seen it happen.

Other than that, Amanda found Lucy to be a pleasant companion. She cared for her children, keeping them fed and clean, and took over the housekeeping, the laundry and most of the cooking, leaving Amanda with a lot more free time than she usually had.

It occurred to Amanda after seeing the distant riders for the second time that it might not be safe to leave Lucy and the children alone while she went to Cheyenne. She could ask Woody and Buck to stay alert, of course, something they obviously didn't do since Choice could ride right up to the barn after dark and neither man heard him.

But Amanda didn't completely trust Buck and Woody anymore. There was rebellion in their eyes these days. They hated the sheep on the ranch and couldn't pretend otherwise. Maybe they would turn their backs if a group of cattlemen rode up and started shooting up the place.

Since Choice's disturbing remark about Jed's still being alive if he had gone into the sheep camp the first time he'd spotted it, Amanda was more determined than ever to give Lucy a new start. Rationally she knew she wasn't directly responsible for Jed's death. But she'd been a part of it, just as Choice and every other cattleman in the area had been, and the image of her standing in the association's meeting hall and saying so was tempting, despite Choice's warning that it would do no good.

Riding on Ginger, Amanda muttered, "What a pickle," meaning every single development over the week and more that had passed since she had first seen Jed McMillan's sheep. Warily she glanced at the sky. Oppressive gray clouds seemed close enough to touch, and the air felt like the storm was holding its breath. It could break any minute or hold off for an indefinite period. Amanda had no instinct about the strange weather, and it made her uneasy. The animals, too, felt it, she saw from the milling, unsettled movements of the sheep.

Turning Ginger's head, Amanda rode away from the herd. The weather had been unstable for two days, since the evening Choice hadn't been able to sleep and dropped in after dark.

Amanda sighed. Why couldn't she put Choice out of her mind? Why was his absence bothering her so much? She should be relieved that he was leaving her be.

But she wasn't relieved. She didn't want to leave for Cheyenne in the morning without talking to Choice. He might agree to keep an eye on the Spencer place while she was gone, and . . .

Admit it, she told herself grimly. Admit that you *want* to see him. You can't forget how his hands felt under your gown, and you won't ever forget it, even if your present worries multiply a hundred times.

It was true. Disconcerting, troubling, but true. Choice had wormed his way into her private self, and she couldn't shake him no matter how hard she tried.

Actually, she wasn't trying very hard. There was something painfully pleasurable about reliving the other night, a sweet torment that she kept going back to. Her body was behaving strangely, trembling at odd moments, aching at others.

She wondered if she was falling in love but discarded the notion. She felt none of the desire to share laughter and affection with Choice that she had with Len. Her desire with Choice was for him, for his kisses, for his dark and magnetic aura. She had never before experienced the primal urges she felt with Choice.

Amanda pulled on the reins when she realized where she was heading—Brenton land. She sat atop Ginger, frowning and chewing her bottom lip. Had she become so bold that she would seek out Choice? The next time he kissed and held her, as he'd done the other night, she might not stop him.

She looked around, as if hoping someone would be there to tell her to stay on her own land. There was no one, of course, nothing but miles of summer-dried grass, miles of leaden sky, miles of emptiness and the miniature forms of the distant sheep. Whatever decision she made about Choice, she must bear the consequences by herself. There would be no one to blame should she end up miserably unhappy.

But that's how it had been her whole life. Every decision she had made had been without reassurance from anyone. She had grown up very young, Amanda thought, recalling that her first major decision had been not to sell herself for a few dollars at fourteen years of age.

She nudged Ginger into a walk and proceeded onto Brenton land. She was an adult now. She had been married and was widowed. She'd known true happiness and the deepest sorrow. She made her own decisions and lived with their aftermath. The sheep on her land were proof of that.

But she hadn't known passion, and that's what Choice promised.

Amanda had been to the Brenton homestead only twice, once to meet Choice's father, Riker, and the second time for the old man's burial. After that, the few times Len had announced a ride over to see Choice about one thing or another, Amanda had looked for excuses to stay at home.

Her former reluctance to see Choice was making some sense now. She *had* felt something for him then, an uncomfortable hint of what she was feeling for him now, and she hadn't been able to face it, let alone label it.

She still couldn't label it, but she was driven to explore it. She kept on going, riding deeper into the Brenton ranch.

Approaching the heart of Choice's home ground, the buildings, Amanda searched the area for activity. No one seemed to be around, but horses stood in the corral, and Amanda spotted Bolo.

Amanda's heart skipped a beat. She wanted to see Choice, but denying that he still made her jittery would be a lie. What she'd told him, about not knowing him, was the God's truth. He didn't know her, either, not really, and yet they were rapidly advancing to intimacy.

She would never admit this to his face. Today they would probably only talk. She would tell him about her trip to Cheyenne and ask him to keep an eye on things while she was gone. It was a logical reason for coming here, and he might never catch on that there was more in her thoughts.

Ginger's hooves thudded on the hard-packed earth. Nearing the barn, Amanda heard another sound, the ring of steel on steel. Someone was working at the forge.

She slid off Ginger's back and looped the reins around a post, then walked around the barn. The hammering stopped abruptly, and Amanda stopped, too. "Choice?"

He appeared in the wide doorway of the forge, his gun in his hand. "You shouldn't sneak up on a man, Amanda."

He was naked to the waist, perspiring from the heat of the forge, his dark skin glistening over rippling muscles.

"I didn't mean to... sneak." Her gaze went to the black hair on his chest, then to his flat belly. She swallowed.

Choice never could have imagined her coming to his place, not for a while yet, anyway, and the fact that she was here was satisfying.

Amanda couldn't seem to stop staring. Without a hat, a shirt and that constant gun belt, Choice was almost too beautiful to be believed. His thick, heavy hair, damp with perspiration, curled slightly at his temples and on the back of his neck. His pants had slipped down his slender hips lower than usual, and a narrow strip of black hair trailed from his navel to the drooping waistband.

He held the gun, pointing it upward, and stood there without moving, until finally she forced her gaze away from him.

A faint smile tugged at his lips. "Let me turn the forge down. Wait here."

She could see him through the large doorway. His gun belt was hanging on a wall hook, and he holstered the gun. Then he closed the draft to the forge to kill the flames.

He picked up his shirt and gun belt and stepped outside. "I'm gonna wash up. I'll only be a minute."

Amanda cleared her throat. "I didn't mean to interrupt your work."

"Don't worry about it." He walked off, still nude to the waist, and Amanda shivered in her jacket.

She followed along. "Aren't you cold?"

He glanced at her. "Got plenty heated up in the forge." He was plenty heated up from her, too, but that wasn't something that needed to be said. He stopped at a pump and trough.

"I'll hold your things," she offered.

"Thanks." He handed her the shirt and gun belt, smiled mysteriously and turned to the pump. Working its handle, he soon had a nice stream of water flowing, and he bent over and splashed it over his upper body.

Amanda took it all in. She could smell his scent on his shirt, and she furtively lifted it closer to her face. He was throwing water around, and she smiled pensively as she realized that she had never seen Choice do something so ordinary before.

Water dripped from his hair and skin as he straightened and reached for his shirt. As she handed it to him their eyes met for a long moment.

Choice finally took the shirt and slipped it on, positive that he could see the fluttering of the pulse at her temples. Excitement wracked his body, but he did his best to ignore it. "Nice of you to ride over."

She was still holding the gun belt and watched while he buttoned his shirt. "Surprised you, though."

"Yeah, you surprised me." He pushed the tails of his shirt into his pants, a process that Amanda deliberately looked away from. "Let's go up to the house."

"Fine . . . thanks."

Choice took his gun belt from her but didn't put it on. They walked together. "Storm's coming," he commented.

"Summer's over."

"Afraid so."

"I've started Buck and Woody on roundup."

"I'll be starting soon, too. My men are still working on strays. Lots of them this year."

"Yes."

"Buck and Woody? What about Jess?" They had reached the house, and Choice pushed open the back door and waited for her to precede him in.

"Jess quit. Didn't I mention that?"

They were in the kitchen. "No, I didn't know Jess quit. Take your jacket off and sit down. I'll stoke up the fire and make a pot of coffee. Why did Jess quit?"

Amanda slowly buttoned her jacket. There was little point to beating around the bush.

He sent her a glance. "Because of the sheep?"

She sighed. "Yes. If you hear of anyone needing a job..."

"I'll send 'em over. In the meantime, you're short-handed."

Pulling a chair away from the table, Amanda sat down. "That's why I started Buck and Woody on roundup already. It's funny there haven't been any men stopping by and looking for work for roundup this year."

Choice turned slowly. "No one's been by your place?"

"No. Have they been by here?"

"A few, yes. If I'd known you were shorthanded... Amanda, you realize what's happening, don't you?"

"I'm beginning to," she said grimly. "Would they really spread the word that the Spencer place has sheep on it and to stay away?"

"In a heartbeat." Disgustedly, Choice slammed the metal coffeepot onto the stove. "You can't handle roundup with only two men."

"It's all right," Amanda said quickly. "That's why I started roundup early."

"It's *not* all right."

"I'll find another full-time man, Choice. When I get back from Cheyenne..."

"You're still planning to go to Cheyenne?"

"I don't see any other way to sell the sheep, do you?"

Choice moved across the room and stood near the table. "When are you going?"

"In the morning."

"*Tomorrow* morning?"

The reproach and disapprobation in his voice were so distinct, Amanda felt every spark of affection for him die a sudden death. She drew a long, slow breath. Since those sheep turned up Choice had done little more than judge and find her lacking. He heartily disapproved of what she was doing and couldn't be generous enough to support her in spite of it.

She would not become involved with a man who couldn't bend enough to see more than one side of an issue.

And she couldn't ask Choice to watch out for Lucy and the children while she was gone, either. He was all set to do battle because she was shorthanded. What he might do if someone actually threatened the peace on the Spencer ranch was anybody's guess.

"I really can't stay," she said, getting to her feet.

Choice's eyes narrowed. "You didn't make that long ride over here just to stay five minutes, Amanda. What's wrong?"

She almost said that nothing was wrong, but the lie caught in her throat. "Can you take the truth?" she asked instead, bluntly.

He liked having her in his house, but he wasn't pleased by the hard glint in her green eyes. Her mood had changed drastically from the one he'd sensed when she arrived.

"Yeah, I think I can take the truth," he said with some caution, not certain where this was going.

"Good. I know you don't like what I'm doing, but I do not need nor appreciate repeated reminders of your negative opinion. I'm not a child, and I'll live with my own mistakes."

He stared at her. "Are you through?"

Amanda's chin came up. "Not quite. I don't want you coming around the way you did a few nights ago. I'd just as soon keep our relationship purely platonic."

"Purely what?"

"Neighborly," she responded, ignoring the literal meaning of the word.

Choice's face took on some color as he grasped the gist of what she was saying. "Is that why you couldn't look hard enough when I was only half-dressed?"

"I don't appreciate crudeness, which I've told you before." Amanda turned toward the door.

Choice moved fast, and before Amanda could open the door, he had her turned around. "Don't you dare!" she yelled.

But he did dare. Her back was to the door and he was against her front, his hands holding hers over her head, his body pressed to hers. "What's going on with you?" he said quietly, his eyes glittering dangerously. "A few minutes ago you were eating me up with your eyes, and now you're telling me that I'm a neighbor, nothing more."

"It's your own doing. Don't you think I'm tired of being judged?" She was trying very hard to ignore the pressure of his body, but her breasts were reacting, and so was another very personal portion of her anatomy. "Get away from me."

He glared at her. "Tell me you didn't like seeing me half dressed. Say it. Lie through your pretty teeth."

"Don't be absurd!"

"Do you want me to force you into something, Amanda? That would make it real easy for you, wouldn't it? No decisions to make. You know something? I think you *did* make a decision about us. That's what brought you over here today, but after you got here you lost your nerve."

"You *are* absurd," she scoffed.

"Oh, yeah? Suppose we find out." He lowered his head, aiming for her lips, but she turned her face and eluded the kiss. Her hat toppled off her head, bouncing to the floor. "Don't do that, Amanda," Choice said very softly. "You're so determined to keep us in the neighbor category, a few kisses shouldn't do one damned thing to you. Stand here right now and prove I'm wrong about us. If you can do that, I'll never bother you again."

"No," she whispered, knowing very well she couldn't meet that kind of challenge from him, not when her heart was already pounding like a wild thing. She closed her eyes to shut him out. "I'll never forgive you for this."

But with her eyes closed, she didn't see his kiss coming, and when she felt his mouth on hers it was too late.

The kiss started out rough, but quickly gentled. Choice's mouth moved on hers, working her lips apart, asking for yielding, for softness.

With a low moan, she gave what he asked for. The kiss stole her breath and her strength. She teetered on weak knees while he released her hands and peeled down her jacket, letting it fall to the floor. Then, without breaking the kiss, he began unbuttoning her shirt.

His tongue slowly moved into her mouth. He seemed in no hurry, which had a hypnotic effect on Amanda. Beneath her shirt she wore a white cotton chemise, a plain, everyday garment without frills or ribbons. It had tiny, colorless buttons from top to bottom, and she knew when he began working them open.

Dazed and yearning, she let him go on kissing her and unbuttoning her clothing. The shirt stayed on her shoulders and arms, and the chemise stayed on, too. But the garments were opened, and he raised his head to see what he had uncovered.

Amanda was breathing in short bursts, looking at his face as he stared at her bared breasts. A muscle moved in his jaw. His eyes grew darker, smokier.

"You're beautiful," he whispered raggedly, and lifted a hand to touch her. She gasped as his fingers teased a nipple. His eyes flashed to hers, and his urgency stalled at the defenselessness he saw. "You're so very innocent," Choice whispered. "I didn't expect that." His eyes closed for a moment, then opened again. "Don't look so scared." He began closing the buttons on her chemise.

Amanda felt tears in her eyes and batted her eyelashes to keep them from spilling. Choice didn't notice. His eyes were cast downward, watching his fingers working the tiny buttons through the tiny openings. Her breathing calmed some as he finished with the chemise and went on to her shirt buttons. He had gone only so far and then stopped because... Why? Because he'd seen her fright?

Her teeth clenched. He'd proclaimed her innocent, and maybe innocence wasn't what he wanted. But she wasn't innocent. How could a woman married a year be labeled innocent?

She was hanging on the edge of an emotional cliff, regretting whatever it was that she had done to stop him. She wanted him to continue, and an immense void in her mingled with yearning and unfulfilled longing.

But his expression was closed and guarded again. He bent over and picked up her hat and jacket off the floor, straightened and held them out to her. "I'll ride home with you."

She was very close to uncontrollable tears. "No. I'd like to be alone."

He studied her, and the idea of marriage flashed through his mind again. Maybe she was holding out for marriage, but he didn't really think so. She was genuinely confused about the rich, wild feelings between them. Len had loved her, he had no doubt, but Len had neglected her in an unforgivable way.

He hated her going off to Cheyenne by herself. He hated everything she was doing. But he said no more about it.

"We can't be only neighbors," he said instead. "Don't expect it."

Amanda didn't know what to expect. He could have taken her, and he hadn't. But if she had displeased him, why was he talking about more than friendship again?

She felt behind her for the doorknob. "I'll be going."

"Are you sure you don't want me to ride back with you?"

"Yes, I'm sure." She desperately needed to be alone, to think this through.

Choice followed her outside. "The storm could break at any time."

The storm had already broken for Amanda. Her insides felt as if a tornado were ripping a destructive path within her.

They walked to where Amanda had left Ginger. She took the reins and swung quickly into the saddle before Choice could offer assistance. "Goodbye," she mumbled, not looking directly at him.

Choice watched her ride away, a lone figure beneath the gloomy, leaden sky.

He could not imagine his hard, taciturn father ever saying "I love you" to a woman. To anyone. He didn't remember his mother, and had never heard the words "I love you" from anyone's lips. He had never said those words to anyone.

But what else besides love would make a man want a woman to the point of obsession then deny himself because he'd discovered that she possessed an impossible innocence?

Chapter Eleven

It was starting to rain. Dully, Amanda looked at the heavy, dark sky. She felt the way it looked, dreary, overloaded, sorrowful. Why couldn't she let her feelings be known when she was with Choice? They wouldn't be easily explained, but an attempt would be better than the constant tumult beneath them. The confusion. They had no understanding of one another.

She was nearly home. In the distance the buildings seemed to be huddling in the rain, their wood siding growing dark and blotchy from the absorbed moisture. Everything looked bleak, even the ranch she loved so much.

Darkness was falling early because of the breaking storm. Ginger's pace picked up and Amanda let the mare have her head. Ginger, too, was anxious to be home and out of the rain.

At the corral, Amanda dismounted and led Ginger to the barn. Buck's and Woody's horses were not among those in the corral, and she hoped the two men came in before the storm got too bad.

Inside the barn, Amanda lit a lantern and hung it on a hook. The atmosphere was murky and damp. She unsaddled Ginger and forked some hay into a feed trough for the mare.

"Amanda?" Lucy darted into the barn, a jacket tented over her head. She lowered the makeshift umbrella. "I've something to tell you."

Was Lucy's face wet from tears or rain? Amanda's spirit sank even lower. "What is it?"

"Your men . . . they left."

Amanda stared blankly. "Left?"

"They're gone. They came to the house looking for you."

Icy fingers began to squeeze Amanda's heart and soul. "You mean they quit their jobs?"

"I saw some other men before that. They were down here, by the barn, talking to your hands. A little later, Buck and Woody came to the house and asked for you. Amanda, what does this mean?"

Amanda was more than stunned, she was numb. "It means," she said with strangely little emotion, "that I have no help for roundup. It means that my herd is in the foothills, the weather has broken, and I . . . have no help." *Dear God!* This wasn't possible. Maybe Lucy had misunderstood. "Buck and Woody have wages coming. What did they say, exactly?"

Lucy hugged the jacket around her. "I left the children alone. May we speak in the house?"

Amanda drew a long, shaky breath. "Yes, of course. You go back. I'll be along in a few minutes." When Lucy had scurried off, Amanda headed for the bunkhouse.

She opened the door, but the light was so poor she could see little. Hastily, awkwardly, she located and lit a lantern. There was no clothing hanging on the wall hooks, no personal belongings evident, nothing at all of Buck and Woody.

She slumped against a wall, too shaken for tears. Damn prejudice! Damn narrow-minded men who forced their own bias on others! Lucy's sheep were harming no one, certainly not Wes Schuyler, whose ranch was clear at the other end of the valley. But Schuyler was the man behind this, she felt. She hadn't gotten rid of the sheep soon enough to please him, and he had sent men to talk Buck and Woody into leaving her high and dry at the most crucial time of year.

It was a master stroke of manipulation, evil in its brilliance. Without threats or open hostility, Schuyler had shown her how powerful the association was, how powerful *he* was. He would never try something like this with Choice. She should ride right back to the Brenton ranch and—

Dear God, no! What was she thinking of? The thought of Choice and Wes Schuyler squaring off was horrifying.

Amanda pushed herself away from the wall and extinguished the lantern. She would see Wes Schuyler herself. She would leave first thing in the morning and ride to his place.

She was almost to the house when she remembered that she had been planning to go to Cheyenne in the morning, and she wavered for a moment, bogged down by the enormity of her situation. If she didn't catch tomorrow's stage, the trip would have to be delayed for another week, until the stage came through again.

But this was too crucial to put off. The weather had turned. Roundup must get underway without delay. She had to see Schuyler and convince him that what he was doing was only making matters worse.

The thought of pleading with that arrogant, hateful man made her sick to her stomach. And there were no guarantees that Schuyler would even discuss the matter with her, certainly none that he would admit culpability.

Her only course was to speak to her neighbors, perhaps every single one of them. But it made sense to begin with Wes Schuyler, and that's what she would do.

The Schuyler ranch was probably the largest in the valley, Amanda figured. She had visited there only one time, when the Spencers had attended a summer barbecue along with a horde of other guests.

It wasn't raining today, although the sky remained dark and overcast. After four grueling hours on horseback, Amanda approached the core of the Schuyler ranch with stiff joints and an ache between her shoulder blades. She reined in Ginger some distance away from the buildings and absorbed the scene with an admittedly nervous quiver in her stomach.

Schuyler's large, sprawling house was constructed of native rock and massive, unpeeled timbers. The logs forming the walls of the house had to have been hauled to the valley from the mountains, where tall, straight pines and firs abounded, a journey of many miles. The house had a hand-split cedar shake roof, small windows, large, heavy doors and a wide front porch. While the Spencer place ran around a thousand head, the Schuyler spread could support four times that number. Schuyler employed a dozen men year round, and probably twice as many during fall roundup and spring branding.

Amanda could pick out the barns, the toolsheds, the bunkhouse and several other buildings of unknown usage. Men moved around, some near the corrals and pens, some working around the barns. A group of riders were way off, heading away from Amanda. Cattle were scattered everywhere, but sparsely. Schuyler's main herd was yet to be brought down from higher country, as was hers.

Moving with deliberation, Amanda removed the gun belt from her waist, wrapped it around itself and tucked it into the leather bag behind her saddle, which also contained the food she had brought with her. She would not speak to Wes Schuyler wearing a weapon, although she had felt it necessary for such a long ride. Not every stranger who rode through the valley was to be trusted, and Amanda felt particularly wary today.

Settling her hat a little more squarely on her head, Amanda clicked her tongue and nudged Ginger forward with her knees. During the long ride she had gone over in her mind what she would say to Wes Schuyler. She would speak firmly, with confidence, and try not to let him know how furious she was with the situation. Anger would get her nowhere.

Not that she was physically afraid. Surely no one meant her any bodily harm. Schuyler and the other cattlemen merely wanted to bend her will to theirs. Any challenge of the association's policies wasn't going to be ignored, obviously, but a challenge from a woman probably made it doubly unpalatable.

She had avoided thinking about Choice during the tiring ride. She knew he would be furious that she hadn't come to him first. But her way of life and the Spencer ranch were in jeopardy, and it was up to her to stop this ridiculous clash.

Her approach had drawn attention, Amanda realized when she spotted two men on horseback coming her way. As they got closer, she saw that one of the riders was Schuyler.

His mount was an elegant animal, one with some Arabian blood, Amanda determined with an admiring assessment of the horse's lustrous hide and splendid lines. Schuyler's companion was armed with two revolvers in crossed holsters and a rifle in a saddle scabbard.

Schuyler's expression revealed no emotion as the three horses came abreast. "Amanda," he said in a toneless greeting. "You're a long ways from home."

"As you were the day you came to my place. I'm here to speak to you, Wes."

"What about?"

Amanda threw the other man a glance. "In private?"

Wes pondered the request, then nodded. "All right. We'll talk at the house." A cool twitching of his lips passed for a smile. "You could probably stand to stretch your legs about now, anyhow."

Indeed she could, Amanda thought. But she kept her back straight and her head high during the ride to Schuyler's house. She sensed nothing beyond a trace of curiosity from Wes, which made her wonder if she was wrong about him being the instigator behind Buck and Woody quitting their jobs.

No, she was not wrong, she adamantly told herself. The man was just very clever. This rugged country produced men of monumental strength, but that strength sometimes resulted in stringent, unyielding attitudes. Choice was like that. Maybe he wasn't quite as unbending as Wes Schuyler, but then her opinion of Choice was biased in his favor. She had no such feelings for Schuyler.

In fact, it was impossible to like the man. Not that he had ever attempted anything beyond the most casual of friendships. His wife was dead, Amanda knew. He had three daughters and two sons, all of them grown and married. To the best of her recollection, she had met only one of his offspring, a son, a burly ape of a man with an enormous red beard. She couldn't even remember his given name, only that awful beard.

Amanda sent a sidelong look to Schuyler's companion and wondered if he was the rancher's second son. There really was no family resemblance, but then Red Beard didn't look like his father, either.

"You take the horses, Rocky," Schuyler said to the man upon reaching the house.

"Right."

"I'll hitch mine here," Amanda said calmly.

Schuyler dismounted and shrugged. "Suit yourself."

Amanda's legs felt rubbery, but she managed to follow the rancher into the house with a semblance of dignity.

"Maude?" Wes bellowed just beyond the front door.

A middle-aged woman with a severe hairstyle and ballooning skirts appeared. "What is it?"

"Bring some coffee to the study."

Maude gave Amanda—particularly her britches—a thorough appraisal. "Cream and sugar?"

"Yes, please," Amanda replied evenly, refusing to be cowed.

"Bring some cookies, too," Wes shouted after the woman. "We'll talk in there," he said to Amanda, indicating an open doorway.

The room, a parlor, was large and comfortably furnished. "Have a seat," Schuyler said while he went to a table, set his hat on it and opened an intricately carved wooden box.

Amanda saw the cigar he extracted from the box and chose a chair near a partially opened window.

To her surprise, Wes Schuyler's cigar had a most pleasant aroma. He held a match and puffed on the cigar to get it lit, then took a chair near hers. "Now, tell me what brought you clear across the valley."

She drew in a deep breath. "I'm being harassed."

The man's eyes narrowed. "Is that so?" He puffed on the cigar.

She wanted to accuse him right out, but he wore a bland expression, as though he had no idea what she was referring to. She wasn't being treated discourteously on the Schuyler ranch, but, from the lack of introductions, either to the man with Wes or to Maude, it was quite obvious that she wasn't a valued guest. And Schuyler's expression was maybe a shade too bland to be genuine.

Oddly enough, now that she was here and facing the man, she felt less angry than she had last night or during the ride over. Or rather, more controlled. Neither Wes Schuyler nor the association was going to beat her into the ground, and she just might make that point very clear to Mr. Schuyler before she left his house.

In the meantime, she would pick her way through with caution. "A group of men came to my place yesterday afternoon. My two hired hands quit their jobs immediately afterward."

"Ah, I see." Wes sighed. "And you believe the men who visited your place were sent by...who, Amanda? The association?" The cigar rolled back and forth between his fingertips. "That's a very strong accusation."

"It's a difficult situation."

"Yes, it is. Are those sheep still on your land?"

"Temporarily."

"So you said the last time we talked."

"I understand the association's policies. I even agree with them, but—"

"But there is still a herd of sheep in this valley," Wes interjected softly. "How long have you lived here? One year? Two?"

"Two, but I love—"

"I've lived here for fifty-three years. My father homesteaded the very land this house is sitting on. There wasn't a neighbor within fifty miles back then. I grew up here and raised my own family here. *That's* roots, Amanda, very deep and very abiding roots."

"The Spencers—"

"Were great people. I had only the highest respect for Bud and Mary. You didn't know Len's parents, did you? Len was all right, too."

Amanda didn't know how to respond to that obviously glib lie. If she believed what Len had told her about Wes Schuyler, it was a lie. She suddenly felt like an onlooker rather than a participant. If she had grown up in these parts, like Wes had, like Len and Choice had, she would have firsthand information to rely on.

Maude came in carrying a tray, which she deposited on a table. Silently, with her dark and somber eyes on Amanda, she poured coffee into two large cups and brought one to Wes. To Amanda she said, "Tell me how much cream and sugar you want."

"A splash of cream and one spoon of sugar," Amanda replied quietly, deeply troubled by the way the conversation with Schuyler was going. In a moment, a cup was delivered to her hand. "Thank you."

Maude passed a plate of cookies and Wes took a handful. Amanda refused with thanks, and finally the woman left.

"Maude is my sister," Wes volunteered.

Amanda made no comment.

"She's a widow. Life is hard for widows."

Amanda took a sip of the strong, rich coffee. Wes was referring to her, of course, pointing out that a widow should turn to a man for protection. She thought of mentioning Choice. She did have a man to turn to, should she choose. A very strong man, one who would make even Wes Schuyler sit up and take notice.

She said nothing of her thoughts, but merely thinking of Choice at this moment was surprisingly comforting. "Life is hard for most people. Why should a widow be an exception?"

"Do I detect a note of bitterness?"

"I prefer to call it reality."

"Then you consider yourself a realist? I would have thought differently."

"I've been a realist all my life. Helping a homeless family doesn't make me a dreamer."

He regarded her through hooded eyes, maybe because of the cloud of smoke around his head, Amanda mused. "All women are dreamers to a point, Amanda. They offset the reality men must live with. One balances the other."

Wes Schuyler's philosophizing startled Amanda. Her formal education had been extremely limited, but she had passed many a lonely night with books and recognized a thinking person when she saw one, even if he was almost laughably inaccurate.

The pale blue eyes resting on her so studiously aroused some unease in Amanda. She was roughly clad. Her hair was hidden beneath her favorite old hat. Her jacket had been chosen for warmth, not attractiveness. But Wes Schuyler's expression was speculative, and an unexpected flush heated her skin.

She took another swallow of coffee and nearly choked on it when Wes said, "You should remarry, Amanda. It's not healthy for a young woman to live alone. A woman is ... fragile."

The man amazed her. She hadn't thought he would have the gall to give her personal advice. "I'm not the least bit fragile, Wes."

He puffed on the cigar, then examined it with great care. "Perhaps not, but you are vulnerable."

"Who isn't?"

He smiled slowly. "Come now. Do you actually believe you're as capable of doing a man's job as I am? I'd say the division of labor is fair to the weaker sex. In your case, and a few others in the territory, however, the weaker sex is rather headstrong."

The conversation was wandering, and arguing with Wes Schuyler would resolve nothing. Amanda got up and set her cup on the tray. She turned to face the man. "I'd like to explain my plans for the sheep."

"Didn't you do that the day John Lawrence and I came to your house?"

"Yes, but I wasn't sure you understood how temporary—"

"And the next herd might be only temporary, also, but it would be here. News travels on the wind, Amanda. It's probably all over the territory and beyond that sheep are already in our valley." Wes sucked on the cigar, creating a fresh burst of smoke.

How smug he looked, sitting there with his fat cigar, so positive he was on the side of right. Further explanations would be for naught, Amanda realized uneasily. He was right and she was wrong. Exactly as Choice had told her, Schuyler saw black and white and nothing in between.

His gaze was fixed on her. "So... why did you come to me? Why not another member of the association?"

The questions dared her to be so bold as to issue an indictment. A quick and certain reply was in her mind. *Because you're the person who sent the men to my place, Schuyler. You're the one who decided to bring me into line by leaving me without help during roundup.*

The hair on the back of Amanda's neck prickled as a renewed frisson of hot anger traveled her system.

Yet she spoke slowly and without dramatics. "You're a power in the valley, Wes. I thought you might speak to the association on my behalf."

"A power in the valley," Schuyler repeated in a musing, rather pleased tone, as though the idea had never occurred to him before. Amanda saw it as an act. The man knew exactly how much power he wielded. He was the cornerstone of the association, the fire and zeal that devised then inflicted unwritten laws upon the valley's inhabitants.

"But," Wes said in that same musing tone, "if I speak in your behalf, Amanda, wouldn't I be condoning sheep in the valley?"

He allowed no respect for her intelligence, Amanda realized. He would never use that condescending, almost amused tone with another man. Schuyler was not ever going to forget her sex, not even if she built the Spencer ranch to one ten times the size of his.

Her voice became colder. "What would you have me do, kill the sheep?"

His expression became colder. "What you do with those sheep is your problem. You made it your problem."

"I helped a destitute family."

"Which any person in the valley would have done. *But,* Amanda, they would have done so without protecting their sheep."

As infuriating as Schuyler was, he'd spoken the truth. Not even Choice would have herded the sheep onto his own land.

"I have no men for roundup," she said flatly.

"If I had any extra hands, I would loan them out to you. Neighbors always help neighbors in these parts, but during roundup experienced men are at a premium."

She was not going to get an ounce of sympathy from Wes Schuyler. Not only that, he had admitted nothing. But standing in Schuyler's house, Amanda knew with every certainty that he had sent those men to talk Woody and Buck into deserting her. Frustration created a knot in her stomach.

But more than frustration was roaming her feverish soul. Fury was making calmness nearly impossible. She wanted to lash out at this man, to somehow wipe that smug, superior expression off his face.

Words of rage and outrage had to be forcibly beaten back. "You won't help me."

Wes got to his feet. "I would if I could. Tell you what I can and will do. If anyone comes along needing work, I'll send them directly to your place."

"And after the sheep are gone?"

A smooth smile curved Schuyler's lips. "We'll all have reason to celebrate, won't we?" His eyes dared her to speak more boldly and warned her against doing it.

Every line of Amanda's body was clenched with rigid accusation. "I wonder if the other ranchers feel the way you do," she said softly, unconsciously using the same tone that Choice did when feeling threatened.

"I cannot speak for them. Maybe you should call on them and find out for yourself."

"Maybe I should." It was an empty threat. Schuyler had everyone in the valley—other than Choice and her—under his thumb, and they both knew it.

She thought again of mentioning Choice, but she could not bring Choice into it, not even now. Schuyler was beating her, and even while despising her own weakness she could not force Choice's name out of her mouth.

"I'll be going. Thanks for your time."

Wes led her to the front door and held it open. "Drop in again sometime, Amanda. My door is always open to my neighbors."

Nearly choking on a cutting reply, Amanda crossed the porch, skipped down the stairs and hurried to Ginger.

Wes stood on the porch and watched her ride away. Rocky came around the house. "She's real good-looking, boss. Surprised the hell out of me."

"Got a pretty face, all right," Wes agreed.

"Who's courtin' her?"

"Don't know."

"I'd like to court 'er. Give 'er a taste of a real man."

"She's too damned headstrong, Rocky. Her kind of woman makes a man miserable." Wes rubbed his jaw. "Tell you what. I don't want her hurt, but let's give her a little scare. Take a ride and..."

Chapter Twelve

That same morning Choice rode to Leavitt. He knew how dead set Amanda was against him barging into what she considered her business, but he had a few questions of his own that needed answers.

He ambled into the sheriff's office around ten and saw Deputy Runnell Petersen sitting in John Lawrence's chair. Runnell got to his feet. "Howdy, Choice."

Runnell was a tall, stringy-looking man, with bony, angular shoulders and a skinny body and legs. He wore a gun belt low on his hips, but Choice had wondered in the past if Runnell had much experience with the weapon.

"Have a seat," Runnell invited cheerfully. "Take the load off."

"Thanks." Choice sat down and Runnell settled back into John Lawrence's chair. "John around?"

"Nope. Went down around Looper yesterday. Should be back sometime today."

"Trouble at Looper?" John Lawrence's legal authority encompassed a wide area, including the small settlement another half a day's ride south.

"Nothing big, just a drunk shootin' holes through people's windows. I volunteered to take care of it, but John's got a daughter down there. He wanted to stop by and tell her hello. I guess. How you been? Ain't seen much of you lately."

"Been busy, like everyone else at this time of year."

"Startin' roundup, huh?"

"Workin' up to it. Runnell, you went out to the Spencer place with John the other day."

"Sure did."

"What'd you think?"

Runnell leaned forward and spoke low and conspiratorially. "That sheepherder was killed with a knife, Choice. It was murder, plain and simple." He sat back again. "I ain't sure I should be talkin' about it, though."

Choice almost smiled. Runnell took his duties seriously and enjoyed his increased authority when John Lawrence was elsewhere. But Choice knew that he was apt to get a lot more out of Runnell than he ever would out of John. "Leon McElroy and Clint Edmunds probably know something about it. I heard they were boasting about being out there that night."

"Yeah, but John talked to them real hard, right to the point, if you get my drift, and they swore up and down that they never even seen the man."

"And John believes them?"

Runnell scratched the back of his neck. "Well, that's hard to say."

Choice moved his chair a little closer to the desk. "What's going on, Runnell? You can talk to me. It won't go any farther, you know that."

"Yeah, but..." Runnell frowned for a few moments, then sighed. "What the hell? You were a lawman." He leaned forward again. "Listen, Choice, there's something real odd about that killin'. Leon and Clint weren't out there alone that night. There were three other guys, and all five them swear that no one even got near the wagon. One of them is Rudy Cole, and Choice, Rudy ain't a man to hurt no one or to stand by no one who does. Rudy says they went out there to ride down the sheep and scatter them to hell and back, that's all. When they caught on that one of them had accidentally shot a horse, they got a little nervous and hightailed it back to town.''

"Then who killed Jed McMillan?''

"That's the big question, all right.''

"Okay, so that's Rudy's story. What did Lucy McMillan have to say about it?''

"She claims some men came into the wagon. One of them hit her and knocked her colder'n a cucumber. When she came to, her husband was dead and the wagon was on fire. She got the kids out, then dragged out Jed's body. She don't remember what the men looked like.''

"What does John think of her story?''

Runnell hesitated for a long stretch. Finally he admitted, "Well, John don't tell me what he thinks about much of anything, and he don't ask for my opinion too often, either.''

That was easy enough for Choice to believe. John Lawrence wasn't the sort of man to ask for anyone's opinion about anything.

Except maybe for Wes Schuyler's. Bringing Wes along to the Spencer ranch that day seemed to Choice like John and Wes might be a little closer than he'd known.

He got up. "Well, guess I'll be headin' back.''

Runnell grinned. "Gonna stop at Foxy's first? Althea was askin' about you the other day.''

"No, I don't think so. See you around, Runnell.'' On the street, Choice's expression lost all signs of friendliness. He stopped to roll a cigarette, thinking about what Runnell had said. The two stories, Lucy's and the five men's, were too far apart. Someone was lying.

His eyes narrowed to a reflective squint. One would think that a woman who'd been knocked unconscious and awakened to a burning wagon and a murdered husband wouldn't be able to shut up about it. Grief-stricken or not, she should have confided in Amanda.

He shouldn't have deliberately avoided meeting Lucy McMillan the way he'd been doing. It was time to rectify that mistake, to look the woman in the eye, to see for himself what she was or was not capable of doing. He didn't like to think that maybe she was the one doing the lying, but all along he'd felt that something was just a little out of kilter with Lucy McMillan.

Choice stuck the rolled cigarette between his lips and lit it. Then he stalked off to where he'd left Bolo tied, mounted and headed out of town.

"I'm sorry, Amanda's not here. If you give me your name, I'll tell her you called when she returns this afternoon." A small boy peeked around Lucy McMillan's skirt, and she placed her hand on the child's head. The gesture was markedly protective.

Choice turned his attention from the handsome lad to Lucy's face. Amanda had mentioned the bruise, and he could see its yellowish remnants for himself. Someone had given this woman a hell of a clout for it to still be visible after so long.

But Amanda had told him she was leaving for Cheyenne this morning. She couldn't possibly be returning this afternoon. He'd come here to talk to Lucy McMillan, but Amanda's abrupt change of plans felt oddly suspect. "Where'd she go?"

Lucy's reluctance to tell him anything was written all over her face. "I'm a neighbor, a good friend. Name's Choice Brenton. Amanda must have mentioned my name."

Lucy's hand fluttered to her throat. "No, she hasn't."

"Look, I'm only trying to help. Is she working with Buck and Woody today?"

Lucy cleared her throat. "They don't work here any-more."

The comment took a second to register. "What happened?"

"They... quit. Yesterday. While Amanda was gone somewhere."

"Is that why she didn't go to Cheyenne?"

"I think so." Lucy looked helpless for a moment, then sighed. It was obvious Mr. Brenton wasn't going to tolerate evasion. "She went to call on Wes Schuyler."

"She *what?*" Turning his back on Lucy McMillan, Choice muttered some very angry curses under his breath. He spun around. "What time did she leave?"

Lucy cleared her throat. "Very early. She said it was a long ride."

"It is." He walked off, feeling Lucy's questioning eyes on his back, and swung onto Bolo. "I'm going out to meet her. If she gets back without seeing me, tell her I'll be by."

"Yes, of course," Lucy murmured.

A chilly wind had come up. Amanda buttoned her jacket, raised her collar and pulled her hat a little lower on her forehead. The conversation with Wes Schuyler required little thought; she fully understood its implications. The man had neatly boxed her in. She had nobody to turn to except for one person.

But Choice wouldn't accept these latest developments without anger. She didn't want to see that dark and forbidding expression come alive in his eyes, that dangerous glint. She and Choice did not communicate well. She certainly didn't convey her true feelings and thoughts to him, and she couldn't believe that he didn't omit a lot of what he was thinking with her, too.

A disconsolate sigh escaped Amanda. Ginger was moving at a walk. On a long ride, Amanda alternated easy gallops with periods of walking to preserve Ginger's endurance. The mare was a strong animal, but an all-day trek was tiring for even the hardiest of horses.

A few drops of rain fell now and again, brief and scarcely noticeable showers. Amanda had taken the most direct route to Schuyler's place and was returning by the same course, which skirted the foothills. To her right lay miles of softly rolling grassland, which was devoid of animals except for small groups of wandering beef cattle. To Amanda's left, the ground began a bumpy ascension. Rocks and boulders protruded from the earth. Clumps of brush and an occasional scrubby pine dotted the landscape. Higher, the pines thickened.

Amanda shivered. Her clothing was warm enough, and the temperature was chilly but far from intolerable. But she felt trapped, and she had not felt so helpless in a long time. Wyoming Territory had been good to her. In Wyoming she had found herself.

Amanda drew a deep breath. What next? Where did she go from here? Bending to Schuyler's will would destroy her. For the rest of her life she would remember that she had been forced to do another's bidding. Forced into acceptance of bias and bigotry.

Idealistic thoughts left Amanda feeling empty. Her reality demanded pragmatism, some sensible, constructive planning.

Facts lined up in her mind. The sheep in her pasture. The Spencer herd in the foothills. The cattle sale coming up, without which she would have a difficult winter. The herd had to be decreased for winter feeding, and she needed the cash the sale would produce.

There was no one to turn to except Choice. He would help her with roundup and the cattle drive to the railhead. She had no other option, and if he became furious enough to confront Wes...

A *zinngg* whistled past her face, followed instantly by the report of a distant rifle. Ginger reared, whinnying in a high-pitched scream of terror. Amanda felt herself falling.

She hit the ground hard. Nearly blacking out, she only vaguely registered the sound of running hooves, getting fainter. And fainter.

Amanda shook her head, trying to clear it. Awareness returned slowly. It took several seconds of dizzily watching the ground waver before it became steady again. The silence felt deadly. Ginger was only a speck on the grassland and still running.

Dear God! Panic struck, and Amanda gazed around. Someone had shot at her! Or at Ginger. Had the mare been hit?

Spotting a large rock ahead, Amanda crawled to it, seeking cover. She peered around it, searching the hills, the small pines, the boulders. Nothing moved. Whoever had pulled the trigger was well concealed or too far away to see.

She didn't even have a weapon. Everything had gone with Ginger.

Her body hurt. She had not been prepared for a sudden fall, and she had landed awkwardly.

She lay there for a long time, until her heart calmed down and rational thought returned. It could have been an accident, a hunter's stray shot. If someone had wanted to harm her, he would probably have shot more than once.

Unless it had been a warning shot, designed only to scare her.

Scare her? The idea made Amanda's blood pump faster, this time with a slow-burning fury.

She struggled to her feet, wincing at the pain in her hips and lower back. She would feel this fall for days to come, but it was miles yet to the ranch and there was no way to get there but under her own power.

She stood beside the rock, glaring up at the hill. If someone was up there and waiting for a clear target, he had it now. Defiantly she turned her back and started walking. Her first steps were a torment, and tears of frustration seeped from her eyes. She would not get home before dark.

Choice had worked Bolo into a pounding gallop. His face was set into lines of purposeful determination. He would find Amanda if he had to ride all the way to Schuyler's ranch. And she had better be all right. Fool woman, thinking she could buck a man like Schuyler.

Or maybe she thought she could reason with him. That idea was just as preposterous. Schuyler thought only one way, his way. Choice had never cared much for Wes Schuyler, but no one could doubt the man's power in the territory. Schuyler didn't confine his interests to his ranch and the valley; the man's long arm of influence reached clear to Cheyenne and the territorial government.

Obviously Amanda believed he was behind Buck and Woody defecting. It was possible. *More* than possible. But only a woman with Amanda's naïveté would think a personal appeal to the man would deter his goal to get those sheep out of the valley and send a message to anyone who thought they could bring more in.

That's what Schuyler and the other members of the association feared, that leniency on one herd would invite others. One irony had always struck Choice about the association's unyielding attitude. If the damn fools would relent on their stand against barbed wire, there wouldn't be near the problem with squatters and unwanted animals wandering onto deeded land. Fences meant something to a lot of people: keep out.

He'd brought up that point at a meeting one time, but had dropped it when it received only stony, cold silence. His fellow cattlemen, he'd realized then, were not going to change their way of life, not even when it made better sense to do so.

Choice was about two miles from Amanda's house when he spotted a horse running like a bat out of hell way off to his right. A riderless horse. Ginger.

He pulled Bolo up short, his heart in his throat. A muscle jumped in his jaw. He spurred Bolo into a run again, directing the stallion closer to the foothills, full of dread but relieved that he had a better idea of where to look for Amanda.

His thoughts raced. Ginger wasn't riderless for some trivial reason. Amanda was a good horsewoman, but even the best of riders could run into trouble. If Schuyler had anything to do with Amanda's trouble, he'd destroy the man, influential or not.

Amanda was limping, making slow headway. Her riding boots had not been designed for walking, but the pain in her back and hips was her biggest handicap. She'd broken no bones, she felt sure, or she wouldn't be upright at all. But she had to be badly bruised.

Never had she taken such a fall before. She'd seen men spill from the saddle of a bucking horse and get up immediately as though nothing had happened. Then, too, she'd seen one collision of cowboy and earth that had resulted in several broken bones, so she could be a lot worse off.

Amanda grimaced at the ludicrously optimistic thought. She could not be much worse off if she had purposely set out to destroy her own peace. She had Lucy and the babies to care for, a herd of sheep to dispose of, a wandering herd of cattle to round up, the wrath of Wes Schuyler and the Stock Growers Association to deal with and quite a lot more when she added it all up. Murder on her land, the sheriff doing God knew what about it, no hired hands and winter coming on.

And she dare not forget Choice Brenton. Although, right at the moment, her personal dilemma over Choice seemed much less daunting than everything else.

Picking her way cautiously, Amanda felt weighted down, as if burdened by a hundred extra pounds. Maybe she would attempt roundup alone, she pondered dully. Going to Choice after fervently insisting he stay out of her business seemed like the final straw. Her last vestige of pride would be completely destroyed. She would have nothing left of the independence she had been so proud of.

Her disheartened gaze swept the horizon. She had miles to go yet . . . miles.

Her eyes narrowed. Someone was out there. Moving fast. A horse and rider.

She looked around for cover and saw none. If the rider was a foe, she was at his mercy.

Her shoulders slumped. She didn't care, she realized despondently. She simply did not care anymore.

She trudged on, watching the distant silhouette becoming larger, more defined.

Then she felt recognition. "Choice," she whispered, suffering an enormous surge of self-pity. Suddenly, she was completely without dignity, a forlorn, limping woman, a victim of her own rashness. Perhaps of her own stupidity.

She lifted her chin, trying desperately to appear uncowed. With Choice she must maintain some pride, whatever the cost.

The driving beat of Bolo's hooves reached her ears, a welcome sound. The sight of the big black stallion and its masterful rider bearing down on her brought tears to her eyes.

Bolo came to an abrupt stop, blowing and heaving from his long run. Choice jumped out of the saddle. "Amanda." He ran to her and scooped her into his arms, so relieved to see her in one piece and on her feet that his legs felt weak.

She winced at the pain caused by his rough embrace, but he felt so good, so solid and real. Her head lay on his chest, her arms wound around his waist. She could hear his strong, fast heartbeat and felt his concern, with gratitude. The moment was beautiful for Amanda, a communion of spirit she had never felt with Choice before.

He took her shoulders and moved her away enough to see her face. "What happened? I saw Ginger. Were you thrown?"

She knew at once that she couldn't tell him the truth, not about the gunshot. "Yes . . . thrown," she whispered, taken aback by the lack of strength in her attempt to speak. Tears were suddenly too overwhelming to repulse, and they came spilling out like a damn giving way.

She clutched at the woolen vest he wore over a heavy shirt, and buried her face in his chest. Sobs shook her shoulders.

Choice stroked her back and mumbled, "There, there," which, to his dismay, seemed to make her cry harder. He stood there, emotionally lost. A woman's tears were foreign to his experience. He would do anything to stop them, but had no idea what that anything might be.

Just let her cry, he told his confused self. Let her get it out of her system. She'd taken some hard jolts lately, brought on by her own foolhardiness or not, and maybe a good cry would make her feel better.

But while he stood there and held her and listened to her, his thoughts began to focus on the day's events. Finally her sobs diminished to hiccups, and he let her go to dig out his handkerchief. She took it without meeting his eyes, turned her back and blew her nose.

He was uneasy with this Amanda, uncertain in the face of so much vulnerability. He wanted to comfort her but wasn't sure how. He cleared his throat. "How'd you get thrown?"

She was calmer, terribly embarrassed to have broken down so completely, but calmer. "Ginger reared. I was... daydreaming. You saw Ginger? Then she's all right?"

"From a distance." He didn't question her inquiry. A horse could get spooked from a snake, or from an unexpected chuck hole, and sustain an injury. It was natural for Amanda to be worried that Ginger might have been hurt.

But behind concern and understanding, Choice was thinking about why Amanda was out here. "Did you see Schuyler?"

Her gaze jumped to his face. "How... how did you know?"

"I talked to Lucy."

She hadn't asked Lucy for silence concerning her destination. Or on anything else, for that matter, and she could see in Choice's eyes that he knew about Buck and Woody. "I thought Wes might—" she began weakly, only to be interrupted.

"You thought wrong."

Amanda physically recoiled from the harshness she heard in Choice's voice. Two seconds ago he had been commiserating and kind. There was no trace of kindness on his face now.

"Apparently," she retorted, suddenly defensive. "You do enjoy pointing out my errors, don't you?"

"I enjoy none of this. Why didn't you come to me? Is it never going to sink in that you're fighting a battle you aren't equipped to win?" Choice's eyes were dark with frustration. "This is the end of it, Amanda."

Choice's change of heart was both discouraging and infuriating. She had thought he would be primed to protect her, and he had been for a moment, but now he was turning on her, issuing orders.

Ask him to help with roundup? Never. She would ask *no one* for anything. She would survive on her own or not at all.

The look she sent him was withering, and Choice blinked and frowned when he saw it. "Where're you going?" he demanded when she turned and started walking. Then he understood. She was walking home.

"Wait a minute!" He rushed forward and took her by the arm. "I didn't come looking for you so you could walk home."

She spun and nearly passed out from the spasm of pain in her hips. Choice grabbed hold of her to keep her from falling. "Are you hurt?"

"Take your hands off me."

"I will not, dammit! What's wrong?"

Her eyes were blazing. "I despise you."

"Because I have the nerve to disagree with you? Why in hell did you go to Schuyler? Why didn't you come to me?"

"For this very reason! You're an opinionated know-it-all. I hate Wes Schuyler. I hate *you*. I hate . . ." Amanda's voice cracked. She slumped as her fury lost impetus. Nothing she could say would make any difference.

But then, maybe she hadn't been saying it to the right people. "I'm going to the next association meeting," she announced curtly. "Which, if I remember correctly, is to-morrow evening."

"To do what?"

"Tell them everything, that's what."

"Don't you think they know what's been going on? Amanda, you can't buck the whole damned system."

"Like hell I can't. I'm not standing still for this, Choice. Schuyler talked my men into deserting me at the worst possible time of year. I doubt very much if that was an association decision. My neighbors . . ."

"Are *cattle* people. You can't do a man's job. You're a woman, and why in hell won't you accept facts?"

How dare he attack her sex? "I'm as capable as—"

"You're *not*. Dressing like a man doesn't *make* you a man."

Stung to the quick, Amanda attempted a fierce glare, only to feel herself internally wilting. He'd hit her smack in her vanity, and it was a stunning blow because she had never considered herself vain.

"Come on, let's get you home," Choice muttered, and swept her off her feet so quickly, Amanda had no recourse but to hang on. Automatically her arms went around his neck.

Choice looked at her with a worried look. "What am I gonna do with you? You keep coming up with these crazy ideas, and one of them is going to get you hurt."

She swallowed. He was holding her as though she weighed nothing. His face was no more than a breath away. Emotion filled her, the kind he always caused, awareness of his maleness, admission of his strength, a curling weakness in her belly.

"You do not have to take care of me," she said, then wished she could have spoken with more authority, told him that as if she really meant it. She did mean it, but it had come out sounding more like a plea.

"Ah, Amanda." For the first time ever, Amanda saw something akin to helplessness on Choice Brenton's face. "You weren't so stubborn before."

"You didn't know me before."

He stared, then shook his head. "So I didn't." Moving to where Bolo stood, Choice lifted Amanda to the saddle. She swung her leg over Bolo and clenched her teeth to keep from crying out. Her behind felt like her bruises had bruises. She would be black-and-blue, at the very least.

"Sit forward," Choice instructed with his foot in the stirrup. He squeezed into the saddle behind her, causing an unexpected jolt to Amanda's nervous system. His arms came around her to clasp the reins. Bolo began walking.

There was no way that Amanda could ignore the man wrapped around her, even if she had a dozen sound reasons to despise and resent him. Her sore and aching behind rested against his lap. Her back was pressed to his chest. His thighs curved with hers. His hands held the reins at the front of her waist. He was warm and he warmed her.

"Relax," he growled.

She didn't want to relax. He'd yelled at her at a particularly low point of her life. When she desperately needed kindness, he had told her again, by tone of voice if nothing else, that he thought her a fool.

Self-pity returned, striking Amanda in a massive, soul-squeezing wave. She wanted no more to do with weeping and weakness. Bawling on Choice's chest once was embarrassing enough.

But the tears would not be held back, and they seeped through her lashes and down her cheeks.

Choice sensed her misery. "You're crying again."

"Not because I want to."

"Things could be worse."

"How?"

"If I wasn't here, if I didn't give a damn about you, things would be worse."

"I don't want you giving a damn about me. I've done everything I could to keep you out of it."

"I know you have."

She was so shook up the truth came spilling out. "I don't want you getting hurt because of me."

"Is that what you're afraid of? Don't worry about me. I can look after myself just fine. I can also look after you, and I intend to."

They rode in silence for a stretch, involved in their own thoughts. Choice's would have stunned Amanda, because he was toying with the idea of marriage. There was a pocket of rebellion against the institution itself to overcome, but how else could he secure Amanda under his protection?

Amanda was dealing with resignation. At this moment it would be very easy to give up completely, to put everything, all her problems, all her fears, into Choice's hands. He was a confident, capable man. A man few people would challenge. He would deal with Wes Schuyler and the association. He would do something with the sheep. He would see to the Spencer cattle along with his own.

"What happened with Buck and Woody?" Choice questioned suddenly.

Amanda drew a shaky breath. "Lucy said some strange men showed up and talked to them. She saw them from the house. A little later, Buck and Woody came to the house and quit."

"And you decided Schuyler was behind it."

"Someone was."

Choice had never heard Amanda speak with so little emotion before.

"If you had seen the men, you might have recognized them," he said quietly.

"Yes, but I wasn't there." She'd been at Choice's place, kissing him, allowing him all sorts of intimacies. He not only wanted to take care of her, he wanted to make love to her. She could feel it now, that wanting, in the way his body molded to hers.

Choice felt it, too. He couldn't hold her this way without arousal. He cleared his throat.

"I went to Leavitt this morning and talked to Runnell." Choice relayed what the deputy had told him. "No one really knows who to believe at this point, but Runnell indicated that John has doubts about Lucy McMillan's story."

Another cloud of despair settled upon Amanda. Her body hurt, her heart was empty, her mind was sluggish with problems without solutions, and hearing that the sheriff wasn't satisfied with Lucy's story was a crowning blow.

Tears formed again, and she didn't even attempt to halt their flow. The sight of home in the distance seemed like a lifeline. She wanted to go in the house and lock the door against any more problems. She wanted a hot bath, a stiff shot of whiskey and her own bed.

They approached the barn. "Ginger's here," Choice said. "She looks all right."

Amanda's almost witless gaze found the mare in the corral. "Lucy must have unsaddled her."

Choice directed Bolo up to Amanda's back door, then he got down and held up his arms. She hesitated. Getting down was going to hurt like the very devil. Stiffness had settled into her joints. She leaned forward and put her hands on Choice's shoulders but couldn't hold back the low moan as he brought her down to the ground.

"You're hurt," he declared. "Where?" His hands moved over the sleeves of her jacket.

"Not there," she told him. "Where I landed." She turned to the door. "Thanks for the ride."

"Amanda?"

She glanced back. "What?"

"My men will bring in your cattle. Don't worry about roundup."

All she could manage was a very spiritless, ungrateful sounding, "Thanks."

Chapter Thirteen

Amanda found herself resenting Choice's attitude almost as much as she did Wes Schuyler's. She put in a restless night, with a sore behind and raw emotion keeping her eyes from closing for more than a few minutes at a time. She desperately wanted to best both men, to come out on top of this preposterous mess and prove to everyone that she wasn't some nitwit without a snowball's chance in Hades of successfully operating the Spencer ranch. She'd been doing just fine until the past few weeks, she assured herself.

She trusted that she would do just fine again, too, once the current roster of problems was taken care of. Despite Choice's opinion on the matter, Amanda couldn't force herself to believe that every rancher in the valley felt the same way Schuyler did. Surely someone understood what the word temporary meant, and anyone with even the rudiments of basic decency would be revolted by Schuyler's pressure tactics.

By sunup Amanda had decided to attend the association's meeting that evening. It would be a last effort, to be sure, and the thought of standing up in that hall in front of that group of hard-faced men was unnerving. But she had to take a public stand.

She told Lucy about her plans at breakfast. "If you'd like to come along to Leavitt, I'd be glad for your company,

Lucy. It would give you some time away from the ranch. The meeting is this evening. I'll have to rent a room at the hotel and return to the ranch tomorrow morning.''

Lucy's face seemed to pale before Amanda's eyes. ''Oh, I couldn't! No, I think not. I'll stay here, Amanda. You don't really mind, do you?''

Amanda became thoughtful. After Lucy's comment about the Speneer ranch being so far away from other people, she had been certain the woman would jump at the chance to go to town. There were facets to Lucy McMillan's personality that she didn't understand and had to wonder about, but regardless, she couldn't believe Lucy had lied to the sheriff.

But she also couldn't come right out and ask her about that night, either. Trust was important in a friendship, and Amanda still clung to the idea of Lucy opening up when the time was right.

''Are you sure? We could have supper in the hotel dining room, and the bedroom suites are quite pleasant.''

''The children . . . it would be a lot of trouble. Thank you for asking, but I think it best for me and the children to remain here.'' Lucy's expression grew concerned. ''Are you really up to going, Amanda? You have some bad bruises.''

Amanda took a swallow of coffee. ''Bad bruises'' was putting it mildly. Her entire behind was discolored, her left ankle was weak from a sprain—an injury she hadn't discovered until Lucy had helped her pull off her boots—and there was a dull ache in her back that she suspected would remind her of yesterday's incident for quite some time.

Aches, pains or what have you, she was not going to roll over and play dead because Wes Schuyler and Choice Brenton thought she should. Neither one was going to dictate the terms of how she lived her life. Tonight's event should get that point across—to the entire valley.

After breakfast was over, Amanda went through her wardrobe. Choice's disparaging remark about her dressing like a man had hit a nerve. She would not look anything like a man tonight. The members of the association would see a woman when she stood before them. She owned several pleasing gowns, even if there was little occasion to wear them, and tonight she would wear...

Which one? Tapping her cheek, Amanda studied the two prettiest dresses. One was a rainbow of pastel colors, the other a deep emerald gown. The pastel, an afternoon gown, had a demure neckline, while the green's neckline was lower, square-cut and suited best for evening. The thought of putting on a corset made her grimace. The restricting undergarment would also push up her bosom, exposing more of it than she liked but she couldn't get into either dress without one.

Still, she wanted to make an impact tonight, and the green dress would state in no uncertain terms that the body beneath it was female. It also had a rather elegant flair, appropriate for a mature woman, while the pastel made her think of youth.

That factor made the decision for Amanda. She would wear the green.

She carefully packed slippers, silk hosiery, the corset, her prettiest chemise and the dress in a trunk. She added her best evening wrap, a long black velvet cape and a pair of black silk gloves. Scented soap and lotion, her small cache of cosmetics, her hairbrush and combs and nightwear were all tucked into a small satchel.

Then she dressed in trousers, boots and a plain, everyday work shirt. She would primp and get ready for the meeting at the hotel. The long wagon trip to Leavitt would be conducted in comfort.

* * *

The hotel room was functional and even nicely decorated, but Amanda barely saw it. "Please have bath water brought up," she told the young man who had carried up her luggage. "I'll also require dinner in my room. Do you have a menu?"

"I'll have one sent up with the hot water, Mrs. Spencer."

Amanda passed the young man a silver dollar. "Thank you."

"Thank *you*, ma'am!" Jubilant with his generous tip, the young fellow dashed off. Amanda closed the door and took off her hat, which she tossed onto a table. The room was equipped with a large copper bathtub, but the water had to be carried up from the first floor.

During the next three hours she bathed, washed, dried and arranged her hair, ordered and ate a light meal and got dressed in her finery. The corset wasn't easy to manage on her own, but she did it, tightening its laces until she could barely breathe.

The dress really was beautiful, she thought while inspecting her image in the room's cheval mirror. She had forgotten how nice it felt to be dressed up, and she preened first to one side and then the other to view herself from all directions.

Amanda decided that she was not an unattractive woman, not tonight, at any rate. Her hair was full and lustrous, arranged on top of her head instead of at her nape, and her skin seemed to be glowing. She touched a straying wisp at her ear and smiled at herself in the mirror.

The smile faded quickly. Her stomach was tied in knots. Predicting the outcome of her bold venture this evening was impossible. Choice had said the members would either laugh at her plea or get mad. Maybe she was afraid of their anger and had dressed so femininely to appease it. Maybe... maybe...

Damn! She was scared to death and couldn't help it!

The hall was a barnlike structure with few amenities. A coal-burning iron stove stood just inside the front door, another at the far end of the long room. Mismatched tables and chairs seemed more strewn about than placed with any designation. The walls were wood paneling about halfway up from the floor, and an aged, smoke-dulled white paint from there to an equally dull ceiling. Lamps in wall brackets and two adjustable ceiling fixtures provided light. When Amanda slipped through the door, she saw that a man had lowered one of the ceiling fixtures and was igniting its circle of four lamps.

Three men stood in one group, two in a second. In another section of the large room, a man was pulling chairs up to a table. Everyone stopped what they were doing to look at Amanda.

Her lips formed a tentative smile as she scanned the room. Wes Schuyler was not there. She recognized several of the men present, but knew none of them very well.

The man at the table, Simon McHafee, glanced at the other men then walked up to Amanda. "Evenin', Mrs. Spencer."

"Good evening, Mr. McHafee." Her gaze swept the nearly vacant hall again. "There seems to be a poor turn-out tonight."

Simon McHafee wore a polite but distant expression. "Never much going on during roundup."

Amanda spotted the deck of cards on the table Simon had just left. A social evening was in progress, she realized with a sinking heart, not a regular meeting of the association.

She drew a deep, frustrated breath. Her long cape concealed her dress and she purposely kept it closed. "I anticipated a business meeting," she said quietly.

"Do you have some business with the association that needs discussion?"

"Yes. That's why I'm here."

McHafee looked away. He was one of the older members, a short, slight man with a balding head and spectacles. His ranch was small, only a few hundred acres, Amanda recalled. In fact, as she scrutinized the other men again, who all seemed ill at ease, she realized that no one present carried a whole lot of weight in the valley. She had visualized a packed hall, the way it had been the night Len had brought her to a meeting. She had thought Wes Schuyler would be here, and had hoped, even, for a public debate on the sheep issue.

No one was here except a handful of old men planning an evening of cards.

"You're a current member," McHafee stated bluntly. "We'll listen to what you have to say."

It was better than nothing, but just barely, Amanda thought with very little enthusiasm. If she had kept herself more aware of the association's routines, she would have known that few ranchers attended meetings during roundup.

And without Schuyler in the hall, she really had no one to confront.

McHafee turned to the other men, announcing, "Mrs. Spencer has something to say. I told her we'd listen."

Feet were shuffled, glances were exchanged. Amanda could see that her presence was an intrusion. She wondered if she shouldn't just excuse herself and leave. She was uncomfortable, and the men were even more so.

"Come along," McHafee told her, moving away from Amanda. She followed because she wasn't sure what else to do. The man stopped in the center of the room, where he rubbed his jaw and stated, "If we're gonna have a meeting, someone better take notes. John, how about you?"

"I'm putting everyone out," Amanda murmured. "That was not my intention, Mr. McHafee. I truly thought there would be a regular meeting this evening." She felt silly in her fine gown and velvet cape, and in the back of her mind was the unhappy thought that very little was working out for her these days.

"Meetings are scheduled for the third Wednesday of the month," McHafee stated gruffly. "You're a paid-up member and have a right to be heard. You're here and we'll listen. Now, John, you make a few notes so the absentee members will know what went on tonight. This meeting of the Leavitt chapter of the Wyoming Stock Growers Association is officially opened. Mrs. Spencer, you have the floor."

McHafee went to a chair and sat down; the other men sat down, also. Amanda looked at her scant audience, which looked back at her with steady, unblinking gazes. She cleared her throat. "I'm sure you're all aware of the herd of sheep on my land." No one moved a muscle. "I have a homeless family staying at my house, and the lady, Lucy McMillan, owns the sheep. She's a widow with two small children. Her husband was killed..." Amanda stopped speaking when one of the men got to his feet. She quickly searched her memory for his name. Isaac... Isaac...Isaacson! Yes, that was it, Peter Isaacson. "Yes, Mr. Isaacson?" she said.

"Is this about those sheep?"

"Yes, it is. You see—"

Isaacson interrupted. "Are you aware of the association's policy on sheep, Mrs. Spencer?"

Amanda nodded. "Yes, I am. Circumstances—"

"Mrs. Spencer, you pay your dues like everyone else here, which indicates to me—and probably everyone else—that you're a member of this group by choice."

"Of course."

"And yet you deliberately ignored one of the most important policies of the organization. If you're here looking for some sort of approval, Mrs. Spencer, I'm afraid you're in for a disappointment. No one wants sheep in this valley, whatever the circumstances."

A flush crept into Amanda's cheeks. "I don't disagree with policy, Mr. Isaacson. The sheep are in the valley on a temporary basis. That's what I wanted to explain. I've already talked to Wes Schuyler, several times, in fact, and—"

Another man spoke up, dryly. "I have a cousin who came to dinner one Sunday. That was twenty years ago and he's still got his feet under my table."

Laughter rippled among the men, but Amanda was hard pressed to drum up anything more than a weak smile. "I know what everyone is afraid of, that lenience on one herd of sheep will result in more coming in. Let me assure you—"

Isaacson was still standing. "Mrs. Spencer, I've heard recently that there are some outsiders who are very interested in this valley. Sheep people, Mrs. Spencer. Are you aware that the Lockwood ranch has been put up for sale?"

"No," Amanda replied in a very low, suddenly subdued voice.

"Do you see the problem?" Peter Isaacson pressed.

"I see what you're getting at, yes. If the association ignores the sheep on my land, the Lockwood ranch could be purchased by sheep owners, which would bring a great deal of dissension to the valley. Mr. Isaacson, my hands are virtually tied at this point. I have every intention of moving the sheep with all possible haste. Of selling them, so that Mrs. McMillan doesn't have to leave our valley penniless. But there are no sheep buyers around here. I've been planning a trip to Cheyenne, but . . ."

The men all began talking at once, and the gist of their many comments was that her intentions might have been good right from the outset, but she'd presumed much too much. Amanda wondered how candid she dare be. Somehow she sensed that as strongly as these men felt about the issue, none of them had made a trip to the Spencer ranch to talk her hired hands into quitting their jobs. Their outlook leaned toward idealistic—no sheep in the valley for any reason. Would any one of these men use force to inflict that ideology upon a neighbor?

She doubted it. One man was behind her own personal nightmare, Wes Schuyler. A chill prickled her spine. Schuyler was capable of violence. The bullet that had narrowly missed her and Ginger was proof of the man's temperament. Jed McMillan's death could be further proof. Yet her "proof" was almost laughable. She had nothing concrete, and she couldn't start hurling accusations based on instinct.

"I would like to relate a few facts," she said quietly. "First, there have been men watching my place. I've seen them myself, several times. They have kept their distance, so I had no opportunity to speak to them or recognize them. Secondly, while I was elsewhere the other day, some men came to the ranch and talked to my hands, Buck Connors and Woody Samuels. Both men quit their jobs shortly after."

She was receiving frankly appraising stares, but Amanda's gaze had moved beyond her small audience to the man who had walked into the hall during her little speech. Choice was leaning against the wall near the door, his arms folded, his hat a little too low on his forehead for her to make out his expression. She had thought he might be here, of course, but she had also thought Wes Schuyler and a dozen other ranchers would be present.

Peter Isaacson, whom Amanda now understood was the spokesman—self-appointed or not—of the present gathering, wore a deep frown. Sighing inwardly, Amanda ignored Choice's almost furtive arrival and turned her attention to Isaacson.

"Cowhands come and go," the man said matter-of-factly, as though he saw nothing out of the ordinary in her tale.

"I have no help for roundup, Mr. Isaacson. Also, no one has stopped at the ranch looking for temporary work. I think everyone here would agree that that's rather strange. In past years, at least a dozen men have come by hoping for a few weeks of work." Amanda saw that her audience was putting two and two together.

"You're saying no one's coming by because of the sheep?" Isaacson questioned.

"More precisely, Mr. Isaacson, no one's coming by because someone spread the word that it might be dangerous for a man to take a job at the Spencer ranch."

Tension was suddenly in the room. Isaacson's eyes had narrowed, and the other men stirred in their seats, their gazes moving to one another.

"Well, now," Isaacson said softly.

Choice tensed, too, but he stayed where he was. He was proud of Amanda. She'd behaved foolishly over that herd of sheep and he'd advised against her coming to the association. He'd been wrong on one point. The members were neither laughing nor angry. Actually, he thought now, it was too bad Schuyler and some of the other ranchers were missing this. The men present tonight didn't make the rules, although he knew for a fact that they agreed with them. And after Amanda left, they would probably rehash her comments for the rest of the evening, maybe even applaud her courage. But what Amanda still didn't grasp was that even if she raised some empathy for her situation, no one was going to relent on the association's policy.

Simon McHafee stood up. "Mrs. Spencer, I'm sure everyone here will back me up on this. The members of the association have never officially discussed the sheep on your land. It's common knowledge, make no mistake. I've heard about those sheep until I'm tired of the subject. I know Sheriff John Lawrence is involved because of the herder's death, and that, too, is another shopworn topic of gossip. Nevertheless, this body has taken no action. I want you to know that. I'm inclined at this point to lay your troubles on coincidence. All of us have lost good cowhands at one time or another, and with roundup underway, there are horsemen all over the valley and foothills. That's who you've probably spotted and interpreted as watching the activity on your ranch."

"And coincidence has kept every transient cowboy looking for work through roundup from knocking at my door, Mr. McHaffee?" Amanda asked quietly.

"It's possible, yes. Mrs. Spencer, you have to know that no one in this room nor any absentee member is going to side with you on the sheep. The decision to maintain this valley as strictly cattle country was made a long time ago and has proven to be sound and sensible. There are portions of the territory that welcome sheep and, as I understand, have prospered because of it. We have prospered because of cattle. We do not want sheep here, Mrs. Spencer, and temporary is a dangerous word."

McHafee sat down. Isaacson sat down. Amanda stood there and felt the meeting drawing to a close.

She lifted her chin. "I do not agree that coincidence has left me stranded at the most crucial time of year in the cattle business, gentlemen, but I thank you for hearing me out. Good evening."

As she walked to the door, she heard the men rising and moving around and the buzz of low conversation. Choice opened the door for her and followed her out. Amanda stopped to inhale the fresh, cold air, then shot him a sharp glance. "Well, you were right."

"Which gives me no pleasure."

"Some satisfaction, though, I have no doubt." She began walking to the hotel.

"Don't get mad at me just because the meeting wasn't to your liking. I didn't have anything to do with it."

"Oh, I think you did. You and every other male in the valley."

"Now you're mad because I'm male? You're not being very logical."

"I'm being..." Amanda stopped walking and pressed her gloved fingertips to the throbbing tension in her temples. "I wouldn't think that any honest person in this valley would dare label himself logical after the past few weeks. There's no logic in this mess, Choice, none that I can see."

"This is the first real threat to the association's policy against sheep, you know," he said softly. "There've been other herds, but none so dug in and menacing." He was breathing in Amanda's flowery scent, admiring her hair, noticing the long cape, which quite obviously covered a dress. "Are you staying in town tonight?"

"Yes," she replied absently, much too embroiled in the last few minutes to focus on anything else.

"Have supper with me. In the hotel dining room."

"What?" Amanda's eyes rose to Choice's, seeing at once that his thoughts had progressed beyond the meeting. "Oh, supper. I've already eaten, thank you."

"Dessert then, or a cup of coffee. Come with me while I eat."

She was so on edge, so uncertain of her next step, or if there even was a next step. It was too early to go to bed, especially when she was so keyed up. It came to her while looking at Choice and registering his clean-shaven jaw and good looks that he was probably her only real friend in the valley, even though he disapproved of everything she'd been doing and had no trouble saying so. And, she suspected, he had only come to tonight's meeting because he'd wondered if she might show up, as she had threatened to do yesterday.

"Yes, all right," she agreed.

They began the short walk to the hotel. "They didn't laugh or get mad, Amanda," Choice pointed out.

"No, but they're so irrevocably united. So positive," she replied grimly. "Nothing is ever going to sway their thinking. I had visualized a much different type of gathering, by the way."

"You thought Schuyler would be there?"

"And a lot more of the other ranchers."

"You didn't know attendance slacks off during roundup?"

"How would I know that? I attended only one meeting before tonight."

"I never thought of that, Amanda. So help me, if I had, I'd have mentioned it yesterday." God, he'd like to help her. More precisely, he'd like to gather her up and ward off any and all problems threatening her peace, to protect her, to take care of her in every way.

Just walking beside her was an honor. Opening the hotel's front door for her made him proud. Escorting her through the lobby to the dining room gave him intense pleasure, and helping her off with her cape brought him a physical awareness that seemed to constrict his chest. Her dress was beautiful; *she* was beautiful.

They were led to a table by a sprightly young woman. "Good evening, Mr. Brenton."

"Good evening, Mrs. Lorry. Amanda, do you know Judith Lorry?"

Amanda smiled at the woman. "We've never met. Hello, Mrs. Lorry."

"Very nice meeting you." Mrs. Lorry laid down menus. "May I get you something from the bar?"

"Amanda?" Choice questioned.

"No...yes! A glass of wine, please. Red."

"Mr. Brenton?"

"I'll have a whiskey, Mrs. Lorry. A double."

Amanda sat back and looked around as Mrs. Lorry departed. There were only a few other diners, as they were past the prevailing dinner hour. It felt strange to be here with Choice. Across the candlelit table his eyes looked darker than usual, with that mysterious, brooding quality that never failed to affect her even more pronounced.

Choice wanted to tell her how beautiful she looked tonight. Her throat was bare. The neckline of her dress exposed a creamy expanse of skin and just a hint of cleavage. Her hair was becoming. Her cheeks and lips were pinker than normal, evidencing a light dusting of cosmetics. She had taken special pains with her appearance, obviously wanting to make the best possible impression at the meeting tonight.

Perhaps it had worked. The members in attendance had treated her with respect, and he'd been sincere in his opinion that they wouldn't. Not because of Amanda, but because the issue at stake was so important.

Mrs. Lorry appeared with two glasses, and she placed the wine before Amanda and the whiskey in front of Choice. "Are you ready to order?"

"Nothing for me, thank you," Amanda replied. "I've already had dinner."

"I'll have a steak," Choice stated. "Whatever comes with it is fine."

"Thank you." Smiling, Mrs. Lorry again left the table.

Amanda sipped her wine then sighed. "I'm afraid I'm not going to be very good company."

"You couldn't be anything else."

Her eyes went to his, and a strong urge to just let go and talk freely was nearly overwhelming. But candor with Choice would make everything worse than it already was. That gunshot, for example. And her sleepless nights, her growing sense of helplessness, of hopelessness. He wouldn't understand. And he certainly wouldn't listen and then do nothing.

There were other factors influencing her hesitancy. He had hurt her yesterday. He had come to her rescue then turned on her, and her feelings were still raw from his insensitivity. Actually, she'd been wondering if he even liked her. He wanted her, yes, but she'd always known that a man could want a woman's body without feeling the slightest trace of genuine affection for her.

Choice was her friend, but she mustn't forget why. If she were a man and had been doing the things she had, he would more than likely be as cold and nasty as Wes Schuyler. Maybe worse, because she was an immediate neighbor to Brenton land.

Amanda took another sip of wine. She would be careful tonight. Choice wasn't above pressing any advantage, and her staying in a rented room had to seem like an opportunity for intimacy. Unquestionably she had let him assume that Lucy's presence in her home had been the primary deterrent to their making love. And the way she'd behaved in his house had no doubt bolstered his confidence.

She searched her mind for a neutral topic. "When are you going to begin roundup?"

"Tomorrow. The men and I will get started in the morning."

"I appreciate your help, more than I can say."

"I know you do."

"Choice, I've been thinking about something. You know I've been planning to go to Cheyenne to sell the sheep. But time keeps slipping away." Amanda met his eyes across the table. "Maybe driving the sheep to the railhead along with the cattle makes sense. What do you think?"

The warmth left his eyes. He didn't like having anything to do with those sheep, and not only because of association policy. The amount of trouble they were causing Amanda—and indirectly, himself—made leniency toward that herd of dumb animals damned near impossible.

"Well, that's one way of getting them out of the valley," he remarked dryly.

"You don't want to be bothered."

"I'll think about it." Dammit, he didn't want to sit here and talk about sheep with Amanda. Or any other phase of ranching. Not the weather or Wes Schuyler or the association. He'd planned to go back home tonight. His men were preparing for roundup, loading up the cook wagon, packing equipment for an extended stay in the hills.

But he'd gladly put everything on hold for a night with Amanda. She was within reach tonight, beautiful, totally feminine, a longtime dream come true.

He picked up his glass of whiskey and took a swallow, his eyes on Amanda. "Let's forget those sheep for tonight. This could be a very special evening. I'd like to make the most of it."

He'd never been more honest with her, Amanda realized with a sinking sensation. What he hoped for from the evening was written all over his usually inscrutable face.

She was in no mood for romance, or whatever one called the heated expression in his eyes. He might be able to dismiss the sheep and her complete failure at the meeting tonight, but she could not.

"The sheep are what's on my mind," she said with some coolness. "I told you I wouldn't be good company. Perhaps I should leave you to enjoy your dinner in peace." When he stared at her with a strangely disbelieving air, she set down her wine glass. "I've disappointed you and I'm sorry."

"Sit down," he said evenly when she started to get up. "Finish your wine. I'll be leaving right after I eat." Amanda slowly settled into her chair. Choice watched her toy with her wineglass, her eyes on it rather than him. He was beginning to grasp why men gave up their freedom and independence for one particular woman, something that had totally eluded him before.

He had a powerful lot of feeling for Amanda, although her sense of independence was daunting. How did a man— a husband, if you will—deal with a wife who consistently told him to mind his own business? He thought of the other day when he had bared her breasts and kissed her lips. When she had *let* him bare her breasts and most definitely kissed him back.

She was receptive to no such advances this evening. Her mind, as she had just stated so bluntly, was on those stinking sheep. Choice felt his tension mounting. The damned animals were roaming everywhere. He'd shooed some of them away from the foothills, but he didn't have the time nor the inclination to play nursemaid to two hundred sheep.

He finished off the last of the whiskey in his glass just as Mrs. Lorry arrived at the table with a large plate of food. "Here you are, Mr. Brenton."

"Thanks." He looked at the food. He was hungry, but not only for steak and potatoes. His dark, brooding gaze rose to Amanda. She still wasn't looking at him.

He picked up his fork.

Chapter Fourteen

"I'll walk you to your room," Choice stated gruffly when he'd finished eating.

"That's not..." Amanda's voice faltered. "...necessary," she finished lamely. Her nerves were on edge, even more so than before dinner. Understanding Choice's sour mood didn't reduce Amanda's resentment of it. He had no right to assume she would behave indiscreetly just because she was staying in a hotel. His ego was tremendous, she was beginning to sense, and tonight, apparently, she had damaged it in some unfathomable way.

She hadn't done so intentionally, she reasoned as they left the dining room. Choice carried her cape and his jacket and hat. The hotel was already settling down for the night. No one was in the lobby when they passed through, nor on the stairs as they made their way to the second floor.

Amanda had her key ready before they reached the door to her room. She turned then, feeling pressed to give him an apology. "I'm sorry, Choice."

His rigid posture conceded nothing. "Are you?"

She searched for words to express the unexplainable. "We just don't get along very well."

"We could."

His reply had been too quick, too positive for Amanda. "We don't think alike."

Choice spoke with some bitterness. "No, and we don't look alike, either. We're opposites, Amanda." His gaze dropped to her bosom. "You're as female as they come, and I've sure never been accused of being anything but a man. Why would you and I think alike about anything?"

"You're oversimplifying. Our differences are a little more complex than gender."

"Well, maybe I'm not a complex man. I know one thing, I'm a damned frustrated man. I pick up things from you, Amanda. I didn't imagine you kissing me back the other day, or a couple of times before that, either. You want to know what I think? I think you're holding out for a marriage proposal."

"A *what?*"

"Don't look so shocked, and don't expect me to believe you haven't thought about it. Well, I've been thinking about it, too. Maybe that is the answer. I guess we could get married, if that's what you really want."

Amanda was speechless. Not only had her throat closed, her brain had ceased to function.

"So... what d'ya say?"

Inexplicably, she felt like crying. Her body slumped against the framework of the door. He wore the most peculiar expression, boyish almost, and cocky, as though a decision of this magnitude was all his to make. As though her answer would merely be a formality.

"You're not serious," she whispered.

Choice's confidence wavered. Amanda looked stunned. He'd never proposed marriage to a woman before, and maybe Amanda's reaction was what every man faced who did. Marriage proposals were one topic that men didn't talk about among themselves. Women, yes. Women were a favored subject, as a matter of fact, although not in the context of proposals of wedlock. Choice remembered one friend who'd told him, "I asked her and she said yes." But nothing had been said about how he'd asked, or how the lady had accepted.

Amanda's weak and rather numb expression was nothing to get alarmed about, he told himself. She was so pretty in that dress. The color did something special to her eyes, deepening them, intensifying their unique hue. The creamy skin of her throat and upper chest invited and incited. He would like to place his mouth on it, to test its smoothness, to taste, to savor.

He moistened his lips, forcing himself to remain calm when what he wanted to do was toss aside his load of coats, pull Amanda into his arms and kiss her senseless.

"I am serious," he told her, aware of the huskiness of his voice and wondering if she realized what a monumental step he had just taken.

Amanda was still finding speech difficult. Her mind was spinning with a deluge of objections. He'd said nothing about love, hadn't even hinted at his feelings.

"Why?" she finally managed.

"Why?" he repeated, frowning.

She could see that he truly didn't grasp the implication of the question. "What do we have in common? We just agreed that we're nothing alike."

He studied her. "Is that important?"

Her eyes rose to the ceiling in a gesture of helplessness. There wasn't a romantic bone in Choice Brenton's body. No tact, no subtlety, no sensitivity. He'd thought about marriage, which in itself was stunning, and had concluded that because she wasn't falling into bed with him every time he suggested it, she must be restraining her desire for him out of a sense of propriety.

Had he no sense at all of what brought a man and woman to the point of wedding one another? No understanding of commitment or emotional love?

Her eyes dropped from the ceiling but still avoided his. "My answer is no. I'll say good-night now." Turning, Amanda attempted to fit the key into the lock. Her hand was shaking, making the normally trivial task a chore. Her insides were a tumult. She liked nothing about her life at the present. Her concern for the McMillan family had isolated her from everyone else in the valley, except for Choice, who wanted her to sleep with him badly enough to suggest marriage.

Disbelief struck Choice hard and fast. He stood there, watching her fumble with the key. "You said no?"

She sent him a glance over her shoulder and saw his incredulity, realizing with a little incredulity of her own that it had never occurred to him that she might refuse. Oh, yes, he really did have an enormous ego. Had no one never said no to him before?

"Choice, you must understand..." she began.

"Just tell me why," he demanded, his mood evolving from disbelief to defensiveness.

Amanda began feeling defensive, too. Had she invited anything from him tonight? Had she ever, for that matter? Yes, there was something personal going on with the two of them. She couldn't deny the excitement of his kisses, nor her own curiosity about what they could lead to. But she was in no frame of mind to pursue intimacy now, which a man with any sensitivity at all would understand.

Her voice became noticeably cooler. "First of all, I never once thought of marriage between us. Your assumption that I'm holding out for a wedding ring is insulting and points out our differences in attitudes to an alarming degree. Secondly, if I ever do marry again, it will be for only one reason. Love, Choice. Do you know about love at all? Are you aware that it exists? I'm not talking about physical expression. Frankly, I'm not all that positive that love and sex are even related."

He looked as if she had just slapped him. Amanda's heart instantly softened in empathy and she spoke more gently. "Choice, no woman would be moved by such a dispassionate, cold-blooded declaration of intent."

Choice felt the unnatural heat of embarrassment start in his midsection and radiate upward. He'd made a fool of himself, although exactly how he'd accomplished it escaped him. He could feel the muscles of his body stiffening. Embarrassment wasn't an emotion he was accustomed to dealing with.

"Well, I guess that's plain enough," he said flatly, which was a lie because it wasn't plain at all.

He was regressing to his former distant and guarded self right before Amanda's eyes. She felt like crying again. He had demanded an explanation and she had given him the one that was most distinct in her heart, but there were so many nuances to the situation that she couldn't begin to explain.

Her hand rose to his arm. "We just don't . . . think alike, Choice."

"Nope, I guess we don't."

His don't-give-a-damn tone surprised Amanda. She dropped her hand from his arm.

Choice was angrier than he knew was healthy. If a man had made him this angry, something bad would happen. With Amanda, he could only bury it and get the hell away from her until he cooled off. He held out her cape, which she took with a barely perceptible thank-you.

"I'll be in the foothills for the next three or four days," he declared coldly. He slapped his hat onto his head. "I'll see you when I get back."

Dumbfounded, Amanda watched him walking away. "Choice!"

He stopped and turned. "What?"

She had nothing to say, certainly nothing that would undo the damage of the past few minutes. "Uh...I'd like to help with roundup. Can you give me an idea of where you and your men will be working?"

His dark, unflinching gaze bore into Amanda. "Stay close to home and take care of that herd of sheep. There's no one else to do it."

"Wait!" she cried when he started down the corridor. His expression was impatient when he stopped again. "Choice, I'm sorry."

He looked at her for a tense few moments, then strode back to her. His eyes were narrowed, conveying barely contained fury. "What the hell do you want from me?"

Tears clogged her throat. "I...don't want your anger."

"That's a good answer, Amanda. Right on the money. You know what you don't want, but you don't have one single idea of what you *do* want."

"I've never pretended anything else with you. I've never given you any reason..."

"You send out signals," he interrupted, harshly. "You always have, whether you can admit it or not."

A man came out of a room. Choice turned his back to the stranger, who passed by them with a curious glance.

"We can't stand out here and argue," she said in a low voice.

Choice smirked. "And you're sure as hell not going to invite me into your room. You want to know why you won't? It's because you're afraid of what might happen. For some reason, you've made up your mind to keep me at arm's length. That's a lonely decision, honey, and one of these days you're going to figure it all out."

He put on his jacket. "I've got to get going. It's a long ride home."

A thought arose in Amanda's befuddled brain. She could do exactly what he had just taunted her about, invite him into her room. Her gaze moved down his lean body, and she remembered how it had appeared without a shirt. He had, at least, succeeded in drawing her mind away from the evening's futile meeting at the association hall.

Give him every freedom, an urgent voice in her head advised. Do it, open the door, ask him in. He would do it in a minute, in a heartbeat. You would have made love with him already if he hadn't stopped things at his house that day.

Choice couldn't begin to decipher the strange expression on Amanda's face. He straightened the collar of his jacket. "See you in a few days."

Amanda stood there at her door and let him walk away. When he was gone, she went into her room and closed the door. There was no light, and she didn't go immediately to the dresser for the lamp. Instead, she made her way through the dark to the window, where she folded back the lace curtain to look down at the street.

There were a few people around, not many. Leavitt's residents retired early, except for those who availed themselves of the pleasures of Foxy's Saloon. Amanda craned her neck to see the rowdy tavern, but the position of her room limited her view.

Choice came out and started down the street. Amanda's heart sank when she saw which direction he was heading. As if the lace had suddenly grown searingly hot, she dropped the curtain, telling herself that it was no concern of hers if Choice went to Foxy's Saloon.

But Foxy's had women who. . .

Tears scalded her eyes. She had no right to be jealous.

He had proposed to her. She hadn't reacted to it at all well, but he'd taken her by surprise. Yes, it had been dispassionate. Overbearing, for that matter. But it was astonishing to know that he'd been thinking along those lines. There was something very vital between them, she was past denying that. But marriage?

For a moment, Amanda's mind wandered. Where would they live, his ranch or hers? What kind of marriage would they have? Her curiosity took her imagination into the bedroom, and a flush warmed her skin.

She may have ruined everything. Choice had left with deeply wounded pride. He was not a forgiving man. The breach between them suddenly seemed insurmountable, and it gave Amanda a feeling of helplessness to know she had caused it. A tactful refusal would have kept the door open.

Her thoughts reversed. Dammit, she *had* tried to be tactful! He hadn't accepted tact, he'd insisted on an explanation.

A wave of utter misery hit Amanda. Neither she or Choice had the diplomacy of a gnat. There was no meeting of the minds between them, not on any subject. Probably because neither of them ever truly let down his or her guard.

Amanda covered her face with her hands. Her solitude felt deadly. Without Choice caring about her, which was probably the case now, things *were* worse, just as he'd said they would be.

And he was probably in Foxy's right this minute, probably climbing the stairs to the women's rooms. Was there one he liked more than the others? To her knowledge, there were four women selling their favors.

Dear God, what was so special about *her* favors that she thought they should be guarded like something precious?

Men were men in these parts, crude, realistic, down to earth. And reticent. Even Len hadn't come right out and said I love you very often. Not once they were married.

Amanda's hands came down. She would not permit this to happen. The next time she saw Choice, she would apologize again and, somehow, she would make him understand how much she meant it.

Chapter Fifteen

Nights later, Amanda opened her eyes and listened for whatever it was that had awakened her. Her room was dimly lit by moonlight and heavily shadowed. She slid to the edge of the bed, pushed the blankets back and sat up, putting her feet on the floor.

Remembering the shawl she had left on a chair, she reached for it and draped it around her shoulders. Her feet slid into the slippers beside the bed.

She stood up and heard the sound more distinctly. Riders. The hooves of many horses were more felt than heard, an awareness that seemed to come up through the soles of Amanda's feet.

Her heart began thudding fearfully, and she sped to the high shelf above a bureau that contained her rifle. She quickly yanked back the bolt and checked to see if the weapon was loaded, then, carrying it, raced through the house.

She was about to jerk the back door open when Lucy rushed in. "Don't, Amanda! Don't go outside!"

"Do you hear them?"

"Yes...yes..."

Lucy's frantic fear penetrated Amanda's outrage. She hesitated for a moment, then went to the kitchen window and peered into the darkness. She winced at the *pop, pop,*

pop of distant gunshots. "They're after the sheep," she said angrily. Lucy was weeping. "If they come near the house, I'll shoot them!"

"Yes, but stay inside. Please!"

The urge to confront the scum that would prowl in the night and frighten people gripped Amanda like a clenched fist, but there was little one rifle could do against what had to be at least a dozen. She couldn't see much through the window, perceiving only ill-defined movement beyond the barn.

Emotion choked Amanda. She had never felt anything but secure on the ranch, and even that comfort was disappearing. Could she take much more?

No one came near the house. The noise died out. Amanda drew a long, unsteady breath. "They're gone."

Lucy was still weeping. "Oh, Amanda, I've caused you so much trouble."

Amanda put down the rifle and went to Lucy, putting her arms around the forlorn woman. "Prejudice has caused me trouble, Lucy. I'm not blaming you." Her eyes blazed. "Cowards, that's what they are. How noble they must feel to have frightened two women in the middle of the night."

Turning away, Amanda located the lamp on the table and lit it. "You go back to bed, Lucy. I'm going to stay up." The house was cold, and Amanda began building a fire in the cookstove. Lucy stood by for a moment, then, sniffling, left the kitchen.

Amanda prepared a pot of coffee and set it on the stove. She hugged the shawl around herself with grim thoughts. Choice had been busy with roundup, but probably he wouldn't have come around even if he'd had time on his hands. She had driven him away that night in the hotel.

The herds—both Choice's and hers—should be getting very close after three days. She would find Choice tomorrow. She would start out very early and look for him until she did find him.

She would apologize for her hasty, unkind reply to his proposal and tell him how much she valued his friendship.

Amanda moved a chair close to the stove and sat down. Friendship was not all she wanted from him. Facing her own need for a more fulfilling relationship had not been a simple matter, and she had wrestled with it for three days now.

He would probably never speak of marriage to her again. He was not a man to turn the other cheek when the first one had been soundly slapped.

But maybe that was best. They were very different people. They each had a ranch to run. There were other relationships besides marriage between a man and a woman. Choice had been trying to tell her that all along.

The past few weeks had finally shocked every remnant of girlishness out of her system. If she wanted Choice Brenton, it was time to stand up and say so. He had said he would see her when he got back, but she could no longer just sit back and wait for him to return.

She didn't like sitting back in any case. Someone else was doing her work. Brenton hands were seeing to Spencer cattle.

Amanda stared at the flames she could see through a crack around the door of the stove's firebox. With each additional chapter of the mess she was in, she kept thinking that each incident was the final blow. Somehow, she would survive the present desolation in her life, the bitter threat to the contentment she had known on the ranch. But she would never be so naive again.

Her thoughts returned to Choice. His marriage proposal seemed to repeat in her brain with the pulsing of her own heart. Perhaps he had presented it so offhandedly because he had been uncertain of her response. She had looked at it in so many different ways, wondering belatedly what had really been in his mind at that moment. She had been much too judgmental, and she must make him see how sorry she was.

She would find him and make the attempt tomorrow.

Nearly two thousand cattle on the move raised a lot of dust. Choice rode with a bandanna around his nose and mouth, as did most of the other men. He should have had more help, but he hadn't put on extra men because he didn't anticipate rounding up the Spencer cattle with his own. The Brenton cowhands had each been doing the work of two, enduring long hours in the saddle with few breaks.

Cattle bawled, cowhands shouted and whistled, hooves beat the earth. Everyone was concentrating on keeping the herd moving in the right direction as the noisy, dusty procession of men, horses and cattle wound through the foothills, heading for lower ground.

Choice rode Bolo onto a rocky knoll to get out of the dust for a breather. He lowered the bandanna from his nose and mouth and let it droop just below his chin. They were almost down. One more day would put the immense, slow-moving herd on Brenton range. He was tired, his men were tired. Everyone would be glad to get home.

He had a tremendous view of the valley from this hillside, and Choice's keen eyesight spotted a far-off horse and rider. The rider, whoever he was, couldn't possibly miss the herd up here, and he seemed to be heading right for it. He squinted at the distant silhouette until he recognized who was coming. Amanda.

His insides seemed to compact into a tightly knit mass. Amanda Spencer was out of his life, except as a neighbor. He would get her cattle to the railroad—maybe even those damned sheep—but after that, there would be little reason for him and Amanda to see each other. It was what she wanted and what made good sense to him now.

He'd made a total fool out of himself with that marriage proposal, and he didn't much care for feeling like a fool. It wouldn't happen again.

"Ross?" Choice yelled at the nearest man as he rode down from the knoll. "I'm riding ahead. Keep everything going, okay?"

The man gave him a sign, and Choice directed Bolo through the commotion of men and cattle until he'd reached the point of the herd. He rode up next to another man. "I'm riding ahead, Pete. Shouldn't be gone long."

"Sure thing, boss. See ya later."

Choice was about twenty yards away when he turned back. "Bed 'em down in Immigrant Canyon if I'm not back before dark."

While he rode away again, Choice wondered why he'd said that. He and Amanda didn't have that much to say to one another. She'd come out of curiosity about her herd, most likely, and it would take him but a few minutes to recite details.

He beat some of the dust from his clothing as he rode, a granitelike determination to feel nothing building within him. At moments, it seemed impossible that he had even mentioned marriage. In retrospect, he could not remember one single time when she had given him any indication that she would consider marrying him. The whole absurd idea had been his alone, and the humiliation of exposing such a foolish hope would never be forgotten. Nor repeated.

They got closer to one another. Without emotion he registered Amanda's trousers, jacket and slouch hat. The day was overcast and chilly. The earth had a taupe tone to it, the color of fall in this high, grassy country.

One small bit of color stood out, Choice saw, the bright pink scarf at Amanda's throat. He'd never seen her wear pink with her work clothes, and the touch of femininity to her otherwise masculine garb struck a note deep within him.

They drew abreast. "Hello, Choice."

"Amanda."

Ginger and Bolo stopped with simultaneous directions from their riders. Amanda took in the whisker stubble on Choice's face, the dust on his dark clothing, the red bandanna draping just below his chin. Then she looked into his eyes and saw nothing but polite recognition. He'd told her they couldn't be only neighbors again, but that was obviously how he felt now.

"I need to talk to you," she said, denying the sudden, fearful sense of futility deep within her.

"Go ahead."

She looked away. Talking here would hinder rather than help any discussion. She focused on the distant cattle. "The herd's almost down."

"Be on Brenton range tomorrow."

"And then?"

"We'll cut and sort. You'll have to tell us which of your cattle are to go to market."

"Yes, of course." Her gaze returned to Choice. "Thank you for doing this for me."

He nodded, a curt acknowledgment of her gratitude. There wasn't anything further to talk about that he could think of, but Amanda didn't seem inclined to leave. "Anything else?"

Amanda took a breath. "Something happened on my place last night. I can't handle it alone."

It was the very first time Choice had ever heard her admit anything but complete control, even when he'd known full well she'd been in over her head. "What happened?"

"Some men shot about a dozen sheep. Their carcasses must be disposed of."

It took a few seconds for Choice to control the hot flash of fury in his system. "Do you know who did it?"

"It was dark. No one came near the house." She could see his barely contained rage, and she swallowed an impulse to plead with him to squelch his anger, sensing that he wouldn't take kindly to admonitions right now, particularly from her.

"Choice, do you think any of your men would agree to burying the sheep? I'll pay them. Twenty dollars a man."

The cowhands worked for thirty-five dollars a month. Most of them would do almost anything for an extra twenty bucks, even lose their aversion to getting near sheep.

"I'll go back and ask 'em," Choice said, his eyes narrowed and hard. He wasn't over how those sheep had been killed yet. Not that he'd give a damn if the whole herd should suddenly drop dead. But men with guns going on Spencer land and very near to Amanda's house made his blood boil. "Do you wanna wait here?"

Amanda kept her gaze very steady. "I'd rather wait at your house. It's not that far from here, is it?"

Something hot and electrifying bolted through Choice. He took a ragged breath. "Why would you want to do that?"

"I need to talk to you."

"About more than the sheep?"

"Yes."

There was something in her green eyes that set his skin to humming. Yet he was afraid to trust his instincts. "I don't know what we have to talk about, Amanda."

How stubborn he sounded. How distant. Apologies were not going to be easy. "I guess I'm asking for another favor," she said quietly.

"You've never asked for many."

"I've tried not to."

"But this is important."

"It is to me. Maybe it will be to you, too."

Don't surmise, he told himself. Don't try to figure it out. You'd be wrong, no matter what you came up with.

"I should stay with the herd," he said aloud.

"Please," she said softly.

It was her completely female tone of voice that infiltrated his determination. "All right. I'll go back and talk to the men. If some of them are interested in your offer, they can bed the herd down early and head for your place. I'll get to the house as soon as I can. Just go in and make yourself to home."

"I'll do that. Thank you."

He cleared his throat. "You're welcome."

They rode off in opposite directions, neither looking back at the other.

Amanda got busy the minute she arrived at the Brenton ranch house. First she checked Choice's root cellar, made a quick decision and carried a nice piece of ham and an armload of vegetables into the house. She built a fire in the cookstove and located a large pot in the pantry. Into it she put about two quarts of water and the ham, and set the pot on the stove.

Next she filled the reservoir of the stove with water to heat, and went on from there to clean the carrots, onions and potatoes she had brought in from the root cellar.

Another search of the pantry provided flour, lard and the other ingredients she would need to mix up a batch of biscuits. When the mixture was ready, except for the liquid, she set it aside and looked around the kitchen. It was relatively neat considering only men lived on the place. But she had to stay busy, so she found the broom and swept the floor.

She checked the pot on the stove and saw that the water was bubbling around the ham. Poking the fire, she fed it a few more sticks of wood, then sliced the vegetables.

All the while, dashing from one chore to the next, her mind was trying to hone her plan. She had managed the worst hurdle, she told herself, but deep down she knew that wasn't true. The worst hurdle would be when Choice got home. He would expect an immediate explanation, and she must be ready to give him one.

You are ready.

Yes, but can I really make him understand?

You have to.

Yes, she had to. Seeing him today had brought that home very clearly. The future looked unbearably bleak without Choice in it. But once the cattle drive was over and winter set in, opportunities to see one another would have to be created, not merely hoped for.

Visualizing the long winter ahead with Choice staying on his land and her staying on Spencer ground weakened Amanda's knees. People without families in this vast country endured winter and prayed for spring. She remembered last year's seclusion vividly, and if Choice hadn't intruded on her personal life this summer, she would have no doubt gone into the upcoming winter armed with books, satisfied to have a full larder.

It wasn't enough anymore. Once the sheep were sold, Lucy and the children would leave for Pennsylvania. The house would be empty and silent again.

And Choice Brenton had proposed marriage. He had deep feelings for her, or marriage would never have occurred to him. Her feelings for him were not distinct, beyond an almost desperate need, but she could not go back to utter and complete aloneness.

The cooking was progressing nicely. Amanda began pulling the pins from her hair.

Chapter Sixteen

Choice walked into his own kitchen and stopped dead in his tracks. His eyes went to the pot on the stove, from which arose a fragrant, mouth-watering steam, then to Amanda.

He saw the dark blue skirt and white blouse she was wearing, the pink scarf still at her throat, her unbound hair, the flushed rosiness of her cheeks. Something unusual was going on, but what?

He closed the door. "Smells good in here."

"I thought you might be hungry."

"Ravenous is more like it."

Amanda moved to the stove and with a pad lifted the lid of the reservoir. "There's hot water, if you'd like to wash up."

"Thanks." This was too much for Choice to digest quickly. Amanda must have had the skirt and blouse in her saddlebags. She'd taken her hair down. The hot meal and bathwater could merely be thanks for his help with her cattle, but she wasn't wearing her hair down and a skirt out of gratitude.

Choice wasn't green, but neither was he an authority on women's whims. Perplexed, he took off his hat and hung it on a hook by the door. He shrugged out of his jacket and hung it on another hook. Then, slowly, he unbuckled his gun belt.

Amanda watched his hands and felt a wave of warmth. Nervous suddenly, she turned away and stirred the biscuit mix. Her change of clothing and free-flowing hair were an invitation, and she had never once knowingly and deliberately issued an invitation to a man.

Choice filled a large basin with hot water from the reservoir and left the room, but he returned almost at once to gather up his shaving gear, which resided on a shelf between a mirror on the wall and a small cupboard.

When he was gone again, Amanda released a long-held breath, placed her hands upon the counter and let her head fall forward. She had feared that he would walk in and immediately demand an explanation.

Choice returned some twenty minutes later, shaved and combed and wearing clean clothing. Amanda briskly whisked the pan of browned biscuits out of the oven and brought it to the table. The pot of ham and vegetable stew waited in the center of the table with the handle of a ladle protruding between cover and pan. Amanda poured coffee. "It's all ready. Please sit down."

There was a napkin beside Choice's plate—where in heck had she dug up napkins?—and he sat down and picked up the piece of blue linen. When Amanda shook hers out and placed it on her lap, he did the same.

"Please," she urged. "Help yourself."

"After you."

He was polite but stringently reserved, showing nothing of what he might be thinking or feeling. He was the Choice she remembered from before Len's passing, not the man she had seen in the past few weeks.

She ladled out vegetables, ham and broth onto her plate. "I hope you like this dish."

"I like anything." Choice filled his plate with the steaming concoction and reached for a biscuit. He hadn't exaggerated his hunger when he'd labeled himself ravenous. Trail food was filling enough, but his last meal had been a long time ago. He dove in with genuine relish.

Amanda slowly mashed a piece of carrot into the broth on her plate with her fork. "Did any of your men take my offer?"

Choice glanced up. "Three of them. The others had to stay with the herd."

Again Amanda felt an enormous relief. "I'll pay them tomorrow."

"Fine."

He was eating like he might never get enough, and there was something immutably satisfying about watching a man so obviously enjoying food she had prepared. She remembered that feeling with Len and acknowledged missing it since his death. Losing the little things was sometimes the hardest sorrow to bear. Sitting at the table with another person. Awakening in the night and feeling his presence. Knowing during long daytime hours of solitude that suppertime would bring that person home again.

She put Choice in that picture and felt a quickening of breath and pulse. If she had thought beyond his attempts at physical persuasion before his proposal, she would not have reacted so negatively.

Choice's hunger was relenting. He took a swallow of coffee and regarded Amanda across his table. "You're a good cook."

"Thank you."

"But I knew that before." He reached for another biscuit.

Amanda sighed and took a sip of coffee.

His full stomach and the warmth generated by the kitchen stove were lulling Choice. He pushed his plate back, cautioning himself not to get too relaxed. As pleasant as coming home to a hot meal and a pretty woman was, he might not like the reason Amanda had put herself to so much trouble.

She got up and refilled their coffee cups. He stole the moment her back was turned to give her a brooding, speculative look. She sat down again.

"I don't like men coming to your place at night," he announced brusquely.

She didn't like it, either. She'd been scared, frustrated and angry last night, and it was easy to dredge up and relive those feelings while she'd strained to see out the window into the dark night.

But there was nothing to add to the story she'd already told Choice, not unless she started reciting suspicions that felt like certainties but couldn't be proved.

"It's over," she replied. "When the sheep are gone, there'll no longer be a reason for strife." Her eyes rose to Choice's. "Have you made a decision about including the sheep in the cattle drive to the railroad?"

He hadn't. The idea had churned in the background of the long, tiring days in the hills. His men would object, and he objected, too. But someone had to move that herd out of the valley. "I'll take 'em along," he said grimly.

Amanda drew a deep breath. "If there's ever a way to repay you, please . . ."

"I don't want payment."

How cold he sounded. How cold he *was!* He might listen to her apology, but would he ever really forgive and forget?

Disheartened, Amanda got up and began to clear the table. Choice got up, too, and walked outside. Through the kitchen window, she saw him stop and roll a cigarette. The sun was waning, the late afternoon light shadowing his tall form with dark dips and angles.

She washed the dishes quickly, wanting them out of the way when he came back. The fire in the kitchen stove was fueled against the chill of an encroaching evening, the pot of ham stew carried out to the root cellar to preserve it for a future meal. In the descending twilight, she saw Choice walking back from the barn.

Without haste, although her heart was pounding, she returned to the house.

Choice strode in. "It's nearly dark."

His inference was that she should be home at this time of day. Amanda nodded. "I know. There's more coffee. Would you like some?"

He narrowed his eyes on her. "What's this all about, Amanda?"

She lifted her chin. "An apology. An explanation. I owe—"

"You owe me nothing."

"I don't? Well, in that case, let's just say that I want to explain and apologize. Will you listen?"

Choice looked at her for the longest time. She hadn't had to put on a skirt to explain. She was not a bold woman.

"I'll listen," he said softly.

His tone of voice chilled her. Its softness was deceiving, for he always spoke softly when deeply agitated about something. She knew that much about him now.

She inhaled a long breath. "I'm sorry about the way I refused your...marriage proposal. I wasn't very nice and...I'm sorry."

He didn't move or speak, and the silence stretched. Finally, he nodded. "All right."

"You took me by surprise."

His response was a rather cynical half smile. "I took myself by surprise."

"I value your friendship. I wanted you to know that."

The room was darkening. Choice glanced to the unlit lamp on the table. "It's getting late."

"Yes...but I thought...I might...stay here tonight."

His eyes flashed to her face, and he saw its unnaturally high color, the price she was paying for saying what she had. She was offering herself to him, and his first reaction was a rush of heat through his body.

His second was appraisal, conjecture. "To what end?"

She stepped closer. "Do I have to spell it out?"

"Maybe."

Her voice was low and husky. "Do you still want me?"

Choice sucked in a tortured breath. "Do you want me?"

"I . . . think so."

"You're not sure."

"I'm not sure of anything anymore. I've made a lot of mistakes. The worst one was with you."

"And you're here . . . for what, Amanda? What do you want from me now?" He would not offer marriage again, not quickly, at least. Whatever she intended having from him tonight would be her doing, not his.

Amanda moved closer to him. Her right hand lifted, hesitated a moment, then laid flat upon his chest. "I want to share your bed," she whispered. Through her palm, she felt the increased pace of his heartbeat. His eyes were dark and staring into hers, probing hers. She held her gaze steady and let him have his look.

"You've changed," he said then.

"Yes, I've changed."

"There's no way I could say no to you. Not about this," he said, his voice hoarse and slightly ragged. "Be certain. A man reaches a point where there's no turning back."

It was a fair warning and Amanda took it as Choice had intended her to. She could back off now; a little later he might not give her that freedom.

The thought of such uncontrollable passion fired her senses. She dampened her lips. "Do . . . what you want."

He shook his head. "Not me. You."

Her eyes widened. "Me? But . . ."

"Do it slowly, whatever you want."

Amanda's heart was suddenly in her throat. "I hadn't thought..."

"You thought I'd do it all? Did you also think I would do it quickly?"

Her cheeks flamed. No one had ever said the kinds of things to her that Choice did. Why was he so different than Len had been? How could he talk about things so openly when Len had never even hinted at such topics?

Maybe Choice lacked respect for her, she thought, and then realized that she only felt honesty from him, not disrespect. The sort of honesty she had always considered admirable.

But applied to the subject at hand, such brutal honesty was embarrassing. She couldn't pretend otherwise.

"It's up to you," Choice declared flatly.

She had never heard a more ominous ultimatum. Seduce him or leave him alone. He would not assume responsibility for tonight in any way. It was her decision, her turmoil.

The light was almost gone. The features of his face were blurred, barely discernible. The darkness, at least, provided cover for the stinging heat in her own face.

But once started, he would assume control, she felt, despite his warning to the contrary. All she had to do was kiss him; he would do the rest.

She swallowed and inched closer to his dark bulk, aware instantly of a bandlike sensation tightening the muscles of her rib cage. She could smell the soap he had bathed with, the leather of his belt and boots, the spicy scent she had noticed before.

Both her hands splayed on the front of his shirt, mostly to support herself on tiptoes. He stood there, neither helping nor hindering, and wondered where in God's name she was finding courage when it was so obvious she was scared stiff.

Their relationship could not be one of a common variety, he thought wryly. No two other people could possibly be as wary with one another as he and Amanda had been since their first meeting. He understood her better now than he had before the past few weeks, but better didn't mean completely. There were layers to her personality he could only guess at, and she had told him straight out that she didn't know him.

If this progressed to his bedroom, she would know him very well by morning.

He held his breath as her face neared his. This battle of wills was going to pain him a lot more than it did her, but he'd barged in and been rebuffed enough. He'd kissed her without asking, touched her without permission, positive that because he felt so much himself and thought he detected response from her, all barriers could be broken down. He'd learned how wrong he had been the night he'd proposed marriage.

Her lips touched his, softly, briefly, and Amanda felt a great weakness settle upon her limbs. She couldn't let herself think or she would dash away from him, from his house, and maybe never recoup the nerve to seek him out again.

"I know I hurt you," she whispered, her breath caressing his lips. "I'm sorry." Now he would take her in his arms, she thought, and she reeled slightly when he didn't. How much bolder could she be?

With enormous effort, Choice's hands remained at his sides. "I'm sorry for some things, too," he mumbled thickly. "I rushed you."

"Yes. I wasn't . . . ready."

"But you're ready now?"

It seemed to Amanda that they had talked about her readiness before, and God help her, the mere word was confusing. How could she know if she was ready, when she had only memories of one man to judge this one by?

"I'm . . . ready," she quavered.

"Fine." He stood there stoically, without a dram of co-operation.

He was not going to help her past this very awkward moment, Amanda realized frantically. What should she do next, kiss him again? Perhaps with more . . . fervor? If only her heart and head weren't pounding so.

She raised up on tiptoe again. He was very tall, and to reach his lips with hers when he was so unyieldingly straight required her to stretch her body, to lift her chin. She lost her balance and dug her fingers into his shirt to steady herself.

Choice's jaw clenched. "Put your arms around my neck."

"All right." She did it slowly, sliding her hands up his chest. But to clasp her hands behind his head required contact, her body to his, and the strangest shudder rippled through her when her breasts met the solid wall of his chest.

"That's it," he whispered, bringing his hands up to rest on her back, closing his eyes at the delicious waves of desire washing over him.

He felt wonderful to Amanda. Exciting. Her breasts were aching, puckering. Her temperature was rising, as though the kitchen cookstove had mysteriously become twice, three times as potent as normal.

Heat pooled in her lower body. She laid her cheek on his shirt and listened to his loud, strong heartbeat. Her fingers twined with one another behind his head, locking together.

As once before when he had held her, Amanda thought how secure she felt up against him. She was suddenly deluged with longing, a yearning to know, a need to experience. If she felt so protected during the onset of lovemaking with this man, what would she feel from the next step? And the one after that?

"Teach me," she whispered. "Show me."

Choice tipped her chin and looked into her eyes, which he could barely make out in the murky light. "You teach me. You show me."

"Choice . . ." She said it helplessly.

"Touch me, kiss me. You know what to do."

She did know, only she had never initiated passion.

"Undress me," he whispered.

Oh, dear Lord. Amanda's senses went flying. Undress him?

"Unbutton my shirt. Kiss me. Think of nothing else but what you're feeling."

His voice dropped, becoming lower, deeper. "Your breasts feel good against my chest." He could have continued—her entire body felt like warm plush satin—but he was realizing something. He'd never been bashful about doing, but he sure as hell had never said much during lovemaking. Maybe she *would* teach him. One thing was certain. The tiredness he'd arrived home with seemed a million miles away.

The days of wanting her stacked up to months, to years, in his mind. He stood there and held her and wondered what she would do next, and why she had changed and was doing it at all.

"Bring your head down," she whispered, and when he did, she pressed her lips to his.

Choice nearly lost control. His arms tightened around her without any direction from his brain. Her mouth moved on his, seeking the perfect fit. He angled his head and parted his lips, groaning deep in his chest when her tongue probed for his.

Her mouth lifted to whisper, "I like your mustache," and returned for another kiss.

His hunger expanded until his head was spinning. His eyes squeezed tightly closed, and his arms tightened around her again and lifted her off the floor. He could take her here.

He could sit her on the table and lift her skirt. He could carry her to the bed. He could . . .

He raised his head and gritted his teeth and slowly brought her down so her feet were on the floor. She was breathing in short, shallow puffs. It seemed to him that there wasn't enough air in the entire kitchen to fill his heaving lungs.

Her hands unlocked behind his head and slid around to his face, her fingertips caressing, smoothing, touching, his jaw, his mustache and mouth, his throat. He let her explore, restraining his own urge to do so with her. Something was happening to Amanda, and the desire to see where it would lead was overpowering.

"That's good," he whispered.

Her fingers slid down his throat to the top button of his shirt and slowly worked it open. She concentrated on her task, moving to the second button. The hair on his chest invited a kiss, and she pressed her lips to it and closed her eyes. Each opened button revealed more of the man within the shirt. Her fingers trembled as they neared his belt, and she avoided the buckle and slid her hands upward again to bunch the panels of his shirt to either side of his chest. She could hear his ragged breathing, feel his heat.

His hands moved on her back, dropping slowly to her hips, drawing her forward, pressing her into the configuration of his thighs. Her mind suddenly seemed to be focused below his belt, to that mysterious maleness pressed into her abdomen. She had experienced only one man's body, and she had never felt such a dizzying desire to see it, to touch it, as she did now with Choice.

Her hands slid downward with exquisite dalliance. She strained to see into the dark eyes looking down at her, but it was too dark. Choice was there, looming tall and decidedly masculine, allowing and encouraging every freedom, but what he was thinking was impossible to detect.

She touched the buckle of his belt, examining its design with her fingertip. It was cool to the touch.

When she hesitated, Choice hoarsely whispered, "Don't stop now." She was standing where he had placed her, her hips fitted to his, her upper body angled from his to make room for her hands.

"I don't plan to stop," she whispered back, as she undid the buckle. There were several buttons on his fly, and she started undoing them one by one.

Choice closed his eyes and gritted his teeth. He was almost to the point he had mentioned a few minutes ago, the one where there would be no turning back.

And yet, none of his past experiences with women had been so provocative, so simultaneously satisfying and disruptive. Persistent, unalterable feelings for Amanda were involved in this encounter, and he'd never had anything but need of a woman's body to deal with before.

And then, without further fanfare, she had him out of his pants. The groan in his throat came out like a growl. Her hands on his aching manhood were like nothing he'd ever felt before. Skyrockets went off in his head as she touched and explored.

"You're beautiful," she whispered, holding him with both hands.

He grabbed her then, unable to stand there for another second without participation. His embrace was rough, his kiss hot and demanding. She'd driven him over the edge, and he could think of nothing but being inside her. His tongue plunged into her mouth while his hand found a breast.

Amanda couldn't breathe and didn't care. Even air was secondary to the wild, fomenting need gripping her. She strained toward him, groping as heedlessly as he was doing. Her skirt was lifted, and his hand beneath her underdrawers caused her to shudder. "Not here," she managed to gasp out.

He scooped her up and strode from the kitchen and Amanda buried her face in the angle of his throat and shoulder.

He set her on her feet beside his bed and moved away. While he lit a lamp, she began to undress. The flare of the match, then the glow of the lamplight softly illuminated the room.

As Choice turned toward her, Amanda dropped her blouse on a chair, then her skirt. He stepped closer. "Let me do that." His hands rose to the ribbons on her chemise.

She watched his face intently, breathing shallowly. There was something dangerous in his eyes. Nothing she could say or do now would stop him.

A feverish shudder rippled her skin. The ribbons gave way, and he pushed the panels of her chemise aside. She let the garment slide down her arms to the floor. His hands took her breasts, one in each, and his touch was surprisingly gentle.

He bent over then, bringing his face down. She inhaled deeply and lifted her hands to his hair. He kissed and nuzzled, and she closed her eyes, swamped with sensation.

Choice straightened up and began removing the rest of his clothing. Weak-kneed, Amanda moved to the bed and clung to a foot post.

"Turn down the blankets," he told her while shedding his shirt.

"Yes." She was so breathless, the word was barely understandable. Turning her back to him, she took great care in folding back the blankets. She wanted to peek at him, to see all of him, but she kept her gaze on the blankets.

He came up behind her, and the sense of his total nudity hit Amanda in a sweltering wave. His arms wrapped around her, and her head fell against his chest. Her heart was beating furiously, filling her ears with its rhythmic sound. He lowered his head and kissed the side of her neck while his hands stroked and fondled and his fingers teased her.

He unbuttoned the waist of her drawers and pushed them down. Her face burned, whether he could see it or not. She had been married for more than a year, and Len had never insisted on total nudity.

Nor had she offered it, nor suggested it from him.

"Tell me if anything I do displeases you," Choice whispered, and slowly brought his hand down her stomach. His hand moved lower, going into the moist curls at the base of her belly.

Pleasure curled in her body like lazily drifting smoke. Of her own accord, she parted her thighs and gave him more room to explore. His touch remained gentle, but her system began demanding more. She couldn't stay still any longer. It wasn't possible to enjoy such intimacy and remain passive.

Nor did he want her to, she remembered. She twisted suddenly, bringing them face to face, and when she began to touch him again, he moved quickly and brought them both down to the bed.

He wanted to explain his haste, but the words got caught in his throat. He wasn't accustomed to explaining much of anything to women.

He covered her body with his, separated her thighs, kissed her mouth and slid into the heat and moisture between her legs. His thrusts, deep and powerful, began at once.

Amanda wasn't worrying about his lack of control, not when her own was totally gone. She was beneath him, and he was possessing her body in a heart-stopping way that had her in a tailspin of ragged emotions. He was masterful, domineering, breathing loud enough to wake the dead, shaking and rocking the bed. Her cries were as rhythmic as his thrusts. Her hands moved over the straining muscles in his back and down to his buttocks.

Nothing in her life had prepared her for the near savagery of Choice's lovemaking, nor for her own response. The spasms of intense pleasure began almost at once, low in her body, spiraling and radiating from a central core of almost blinding ecstasy.

She wept and clung and marveled that she didn't pass out.

And she marveled again when movement had stopped and Choice lay upon her, breathing raggedly, his skin slick and sweaty, his face buried in her hair on the pillow. In her wildest dreams, she couldn't have imagined what she had just felt—no woman could.

Chapter Seventeen

Amanda awoke to a hand on her breast. The room was dark. She remembered going to sleep with Choice curled around her, her back to his chest, his arm across her waist. She had awakened in the same position.

She smiled and almost spoke, then stopped herself when she realized that Choice might be seeking intimacy again, but he was doing so in his sleep. Lying there with him, so closely joined, she smiled again. His hand was moving so gently, and she had never, ever thought of him as a gentle man.

But there was more than just gentleness in his touch, there was a lovely leisure, as though time was standing still for them tonight. His palm slowly chafed a nipple, sending waves of pleasure through her system.

Wondering if he was faking sleep, she raised her head slightly from the pillow, listening to his shallow breathing. No, he seemed to be truly asleep.

But he was so magnificently aroused. The hand that was languorously roaming her bare skin had to be the result of a dream. It was a curious hand, skimming down her stomach and hips and thighs to her kneecaps and up to her breasts again, unhurried, warm, quite the most delicious hand Amanda had ever felt upon her person.

She would like to do the same with him, she realized, just lie there and lazily explore his body. Could she turn over without awakening him? She moved tentatively, cautiously, and he did nothing except sigh in his sleep. Gradually she eased onto her back then to her other side. Choice's hand seemed to float with her movements, to adjust to her different position without protest.

Her heart had begun a harder beat. She lifted a hand to his chest and sampled the opposing textures of hair and skin. She liked his chest, she thought, with its rigid muscles and pattern of hair, dense in some spots, sparse in others.

His arms and shoulders were marvels of symmetry, and his belly was flat, and firm.

She gingerly traced her forefinger down his torso to his thighs, bristly with hair, conveying power even in repose.

He had to be as perfectly proportioned as any man could be, Amanda decided, moving her hand higher again.

"Amanda," Choice mumbled.

"Oh, are you awake?" she asked, startled.

"I'm awake. Are you awake?"

"Yes . . . I'm awake," she whispered. She started to move her hand away, but his pressed against it, urging it to stay where it was.

"Don't stop just because I'm awake," he groaned. "It's great to be woken up like this. It feels like heaven must."

"I . . . was just . . . curious."

"Are you still curious?"

Her voice was low, husky. "Yes."

"I'm curious, too. You go first."

She took a breath. "Go first?"

"Yeah. Check me out. That's what you were doing, isn't it?"

"I've never done this before."

A low growl escaped his throat. He threw the blankets back. Amanda sat up so she could bend over and kiss his chest. Her lips lingered on the bud of his nipple, which surprised her by getting as hard as a tiny pebble.

"Do you like that?" she questioned.

"I like anything you do."

"But . . . do you feel something when I kiss your nipple?"

He laughed, softly again. "Do you feel something when I kiss yours?"

"Yes, of course, but I didn't know men did."

"Honey, anything you should happen to kiss on me would respond."

Her long hair caressed his skin as she trailed kisses down his belly. "Here, too?"

"Oh, yeah, there, too." He groaned. "Anywhere."

"Your throat?" she asked, twisting around to invade the curve of his throat. She began dropping soft kisses right below his chin. "Your shoulders?" Her tongue flicked against the rigid muscles of his right shoulder.

Choice growled, flipping her over onto her back in one smooth movement that put him on top of her. His hands smoothed her hair from her face. "I can barely see you."

"But the dark is very exciting."

"You like making love in the dark?"

"I'm beginning to think I might like anything with you."

"I always suspected you would." His mouth made contact with her forehead, then slowly slid down her cheek.

He was lying between her sprawled thighs. He kissed her lips, softly, briefly, again and again, and then her throat, just as she had done to him. Her shoulders were next in line for gentle, nipping kisses, then he surprised her by sliding down, his whole body moving.

"Choice?"

"I'm tasting you," he murmured as he took a nipple into his mouth.

Sighing, she closed her eyes to savor the smoky sensations drifting through her body. Her mind seemed to be floating. Choice lifted her to yet another plateau of life, she thought then, a higher plane than she had existed upon for twenty-three years.

His tongue swirled and created sparks in its wake. "Oh," she whispered, and wove her fingers into his hair. "Why do I respond so strongly to you?"

"Chemistry," he murmured, giving attention to the ripe, puckered crest of her other breast. "Some people have it, some don't."

Chemistry. An interesting theory that seemed as logical as any other explanation she could think of. Still...

"That would suggest that people have very little control over who they make love with."

"Sounds about right," Choice replied agreeably.

"But in that case..."

Choice lifted his head. "Didn't you consciously try to prevent this from happening with me?"

"Well, yes, but..."

"But here we are. Chemistry, Amanda, yours and mine. It's more powerful than good intentions, honey." Burrowing his hands beneath her waist, he began kissing her abdomen. "Your skin is as soft and smooth as a flower petal."

He was again lower in the bed, his face level with her waistline. She took in a long, slow breath, completely mesmerized by his passionate dedication to detail. Every inch of her skin was being kissed, each in its own turn, but slowly, without any trace of haste. Each kiss left another patch of warmth and created a desire for more. Gradually but unquestionably she was being drawn into an almost dreamlike yearning. Choice was not unaffected, either. His voice sounded gravelly, his breathing erratic.

Vaguely she registered Choice moving up in the bed, lying over her again. His mouth sought hers, and her mind went spinning in a burst of energy that brought strength to her arms. She crushed him to herself, moaning deep in her throat, squeezing his body to hers.

He entered her in one long slide, going deep, and the rapturous spasms began at once, shocking her senses.

"You're perfect," he whispered raggedly. "We're right, Amanda, you and me. I always suspected . . . *knew* it would be this way for us."

In the back of her mind danced stunning thoughts of their early acquaintanceship, those days when she had uneasily recognized his magnetism and known instinctively that he was a dangerous man. All that time, while she had been going out of her way to avoid him, he had been thinking of this.

Overlying those discomfiting images, however, was the reality of their lovemaking. She was wholly and completely Choice's. No man could ever possess more of her than he did now. She recognized a degree of vulnerability in herself that made every unstable moment of her past seem like child's play.

Knowledge and understanding of her own condition did not increase her emotional strength. She could no more resist what Choice made her feel than she could fly to the moon.

She moaned with each thrust of her body, opened and malleable to his every demand. And every few minutes, another rise of heat and excruciating pleasure would send her spinning. Each time she thought would be the last, but in seconds he had her writhing beneath him again.

Everything was becoming softer and dimmer. Even his body seemed softer, like an extension of her own flowing emotions. Which were his legs, his arms? Which were hers?

Her bosom heaved against his chest. She was perspiring despite the coolness of the room. Choice's skin was as slick as drenched satin.

His hands went beneath her hips, lifting them higher. His head was beside hers on the pillow, and his breaths fell on her right ear, moistening the tangled hair covering it. The choked words from his lips were indecipherable, and she only understood the almost savage passion behind them.

Then she heard, quite clearly, "Amanda. *Amanda!*" And he stiffened upon her, every muscle rigid and straining.

She was too weak to do more than close her eyes. Her heart was like a drum in her chest, beating with a cadence that slowed only gradually. He was heavy and lifeless for a long time, but she was too strengthless to even let him know that she felt his weight.

She made no attempt to focus her mind on anything. Rather, she lay there in a state of euphoria that would have been totally incomprehensible only a few hours earlier.

Choice's head came up slowly and Amanda felt a tender kiss on her lips. In the darkness he was all shadow and bulk. His hands skimmed down her sweaty body. "You'll get cold." He drew the blankets over them and curled around her, bringing her head to his shoulder.

"Are you all right?" he whispered with a gentle kiss to her forehead.

"Weak."

He laughed softly. "That will pass."

"I'll never have need of you again." She sighed.

He laughed again. "You will. Sooner than seems possible right now."

"Impossible."

"You're a passionate woman."

"I never was before. You must have cast a spell over me."

Everything was warm and snuggly under the blankets. Despite the notable disparity in their sizes, they fit together with remarkable ease. Where she curved out, he seemed to curve in. His hand rested on her waist, and its possessive warmth gave her a surprising tingle. She sighed and let her drowsy eyelids drift shut. She might never be content to sleep alone again, she thought dreamily. Choice's touch carried no intent to inflame. Rather, it relayed closeness, togetherness, sensations that were every bit as special as the more heated emotions.

She fell asleep in a soft, pink cloud of utter contentment.

The room was still dark when she awoke.

Choice's breath heated the side of her neck. "You awake?"

"Yes."

"I may never get enough of you. I hope you know that."

"You'll be tired tomorrow."

"A small price to pay for a night like this. No one's ever given me the joy you do, no one."

Amanda swallowed. His words, all whispery and smacking of secret confidences in the dark night, made her quiver with something brand new. It took a moment to figure out what was pricking her soul, for she'd never had cause to experience jealousy before.

He had done all this with other women, she realized weakly; he could not be so informed and confident without a great deal of practice. A parade of faceless females filing through her mind brought tears to her eyes. It wasn't the physical side to his making love to other women that gnawed at her. But to discover that the emotional plane she'd felt herself on with Choice was not only theirs was a terrible blow.

Amanda stiffened, and Choice sensed something immediately. He raised his head. "What happened?"

She couldn't tell him. Making love with him did not give her any control over his life. If she wanted him, she had to take him as he was, which she'd known all along. Perhaps he was capable of going from her arms to another woman's without a moment's hesitation.

It didn't matter. If she had to share him with other women, it would be better than not having him at all. Her arms moved around his neck, and her lips parted, waiting for his kiss.

He left her breathless, needing more. "Everything's okay now?" he whispered.

"Yes. Make love to me. I will never get enough of you, either."

"That's good to hear. We have something very special."

"Yes, special." Some emotions could not be mingled with lovemaking, Amanda thought with a touch of sadness. There was no room in this bed for jealousy, and she had no right to jealousy. He was not her possession, no more than she was his.

The trade was not comforting, even in its wisdom—if he was free to seek other women, she was equally free to seek other men.

But the thought of other men left her cold. It had taken her twenty-three years to find Choice, and she would waste no time looking for an impossible replacement.

They made love for a very long time, kissing, touching, working themselves up to the very edge of the final rapture then retreating to start anew. He commanded her senses with soft words, her body with heated hands and lips.

When they finally settled down to sleep again, Amanda nearly passed out from exhaustion.

Her last thought was that one of them would awaken the other at least once more before dawn. Their hunger for each other was not appeased by repetition, apparently, nor suppressed by sleep.

Chapter Eighteen

Amanda stirred and saw the gray light of dawn in the room. Choice was up and getting dressed. Through her eyelashes, she watched him moving around, attempting silence. He dragged on his pants and buttoned them, then reached for his shirt. His physical beauty filled her soul, and she thought of the long night and the passion that had seared her again and again. A warmth stole over her skin, but it was a blush of pleasure, not embarrassment.

She sat up and bunched the blankets at her breasts. Her hair was wildly disarrayed, a tangle of curls and snarls that she knew would take forever to brush through. There were very noticeable aches in her body but it didn't seem to matter very much, not when she became overheated and tingly again just from looking at her wonderful lover.

Holding his shirt, Choice saw that she had awakened and moved to sit on the bed. "I tried to be quiet so you could sleep."

"You didn't waken me." She looked into his eyes and saw the warmth of genuine approval.

"You look beautiful even without a lot of sleep."

"So do you."

He smiled, laid his shirt down and brushed a lock of hair from her cheek. "You don't have to get up yet. Go back to sleep."

"Thanks, but I have to go home."

Taking her hand, he brought it to his lips. "It was an incredible night, Amanda."

"Yes, it was."

His eyes held hers. "You're not disappointed."

"I think you know I'm not. I couldn't be. No woman could be."

"Will you meet me again?"

"Yes."

"It won't be as simple as last night. The herd will be down by tonight. My men will be all over the place. You have Lucy at yours."

"Once the sheep are sold, Lucy will go to Pennsylvania. You'll be able to come to my house whenever you want."

"Often," he said softly.

"I hope so. I can't bear the thought of winter without you."

She had already told him that. During one conversation in the night, she had confessed that her dread of the impending winter months was what had really infused her with such uncharacteristic boldness. Choice had accepted the explanation with the logic of one who had put in some bad winters himself. They had become close last night, closer than either could have visualized.

Yet, throughout the night, neither had hinted at love or anything permanent between them. There was a long list of problems to solve before they advanced beyond what they found last night. For the present Amanda was exceedingly happy, happier than she'd ever been. Discovering the power of sex and her capacity for enjoying it was like being handed a brand-new lease on life.

She knew that not just any man would do for her, no matter how many other women Choice might bed. Her desire was aimed directly and strictly at Choice Brenton. The night had been glorious, awe-inspiring. Again and again he'd taken her to the stars. There was no part of her body he hadn't kissed, no part of his she hadn't kissed.

She loved making love with him, but with the dawn, priorities were clear again. They each had a ranch to run. She had a house she loved. Choice's house was bigger, but not nearly so pretty. It could be pretty, of course. At present it was very obviously neglected, aside from Choice's personal preference for cleanliness.

Not that it sparkled, as hers did. But the floors were reasonably clean, as was the linen on his bed. There was no mess or clutter in any of the rooms. He apparently picked up after himself and washed the dishes he used.

Their houses were not a hurdle, but they were one aspect of the general situation that would take a sensible and mature point of view to reconcile, should they ever decide to take their relationship further.

Choice leaned forward and pressed his lips to hers. She released her hold on the blanket and hooked her arms around his neck. He raised his head, grinning. "You're a fast learner."

"I had a good teacher."

"If I didn't have two thousand cattle waiting, I'd climb back in this bed and teach you a few other tricks."

She arched an eyebrow. "There are more?"

"A few."

"How did you get so smart about women?" she whispered. Her eyes closed for a moment in a wave of surprisingly sharp anguish. "Forget I asked that. I really don't want to know."

He laughed softly. "There's nothing for you to worry about, Amanda. Every woman I ever knew pales by comparison, believe me."

Her eyelashes lifted. "Is that true?"

The expression on his face sobered. "On my honor." At her peculiar expression, his eyes narrowed. "You didn't sense what last night meant to me?"

In spite of their many hours of intimacy, Amanda's cheeks got warm. "I sensed that you . . . enjoyed it."

He pushed her against the pillow and kissed her soundly, finally lifting his head to murmur, "You're very sweet. Don't ever forget how to blush, okay?"

She touched his face. "With your candor, I couldn't possibly."

"Amanda . . ."

Her breath caught. He was rationalizing, she realized, weighing the waiting cattle against making love again. The animals were losing the battle, she saw in the darkening of his eyes. He stood up abruptly and shed his pants, giving her a look of pure sass. "Once more before I go."

"Well, you're certainly prepared for it," she drawled. Laughing deep in his chest, he lifted the blankets and crawled in beside her.

His arms wrapped around her, bringing her body in close contact with his. He rubbed his face in her hair. "Your scent intoxicates me," he whispered.

"I like that word. That's what you do to me, too."

"I intoxicate you?"

"Definitely."

He chuckled. "We intoxicate each other."

"We'll have an exciting winter, Choice," she murmured, thinking dreamily of long, bitterly cold nights with the two of them snuggling in bed together. Thanksgiving this year would be lovely, Christmas even better. She would make and buy gifts for him, all sorts of things. She would put up a tree, plan an extra-special dinner.

He wasn't thinking of Christmas right now, she decided wryly when his hands began wandering beneath the blankets. He had one thing on his mind, and one thing only.

Even so, when he probably should be hurrying so he could join his men in the foothills, he didn't seem to be in any haste whatsoever. His fingers were gentle and lazy on her breasts, caressing with great patience, when she knew very well that he wasn't normally a patient man. In bed he was caring, delicious and as patient as Job.

He was, in a word, irresistible.

Sighing with deep satisfaction, Amanda began her own exploration. She would never tire of touching him. Her hands skimmed over his chest, his belly and downward. His mouth sought hers and claimed it in a long, drugging kiss that sent her mind reeling.

Perhaps he *was* a trifle impatient this morning, she amended when he laid her back and mounted her with a low growl of possession. "Look at me," he whispered raggedly.

Her eyes opened. Making love by feeble lamplight and in the dark had not prepared her for the expression in his eyes in daylight. There was something fierce there, something totally male. Possessiveness, yes. Ownership, perhaps. Domination, without question.

Oddly, she realized, she liked the feeling of being dominated. It was a strange sensation for a woman who had striven all her life for independence and self-sufficiency, but it was much too strong to deny or ignore. She quite simply liked it, and she stared into his eyes to absorb the feeling while he labored over her and reached for the highest pinnacle attainable by lovers.

This time, every step of the way, she watched his feelings on his face. Nothing she'd felt in her life, last night included, moved her the way seeing passion on Choice's face did. As her fever mounted, tears misted her vision. She felt choked on emotion, both hers and his, and finally she could take no more. She pulled his head down to kiss his lips for the final rush to ecstasy.

When it was over, Choice brushed at the tears on her face and asked softly, "What's this?"

Her trembling lips formed a small smile. "Emotion, I guess."

"Amanda..."

For the first time in their relationship his expression was completely readable, and she wasn't ready to cope with another marriage proposal. Not even after the most earth-shattering experience of her life. Quickly she laid a finger on his lips. "Not now. Please."

"Why not?"

"Things...aren't quite right yet."

"Meaning they will be right at some unknown point in the future?"

She wiped her eyes. "Please. Let's not rush into anything."

"I think we already did that, don't you? Is an affair all you want from me?" He grimaced. "God, I hate that word. It cheapens what we have."

She couldn't disagree, but neither could she consider marriage just yet. Maybe after all of the present disorder and chaos of her life had settled down she would feel differently. In all probability, she would feel *very* differently. But things were in such an awful mess right now.

"Don't be angry," she whispered.

"I'm not angry, but I sure don't get it. You're not a woman to bed a man and..."

"You're not just any man. I've never done this before and I'll probably never do it again. Except with you," she added in a husky, unsteady voice.

His eyes got very hard. "I'd kill any man who touched you."

"None are going to. Please believe that."

He looked at her, studied her, then heaved a sigh and rolled off her. "You're a puzzle, Amanda, too damned much for a poor old country boy like me to comprehend."

She smiled at his tone because it was boyishly petulant, and she'd never heard him use it before. He had his moments of confusion, the same as she did, apparently, which made him seem a little more endearing.

He finally sat up. "I've got to get going." Instead of doing so, however, he leaned down and kissed her. "You're in my blood, Amanda Spencer."

Her fingertips rose to caress his cheek, which was rough from his nighttime growth of whiskers. "You're in mine, too, Choice. Don't doubt it."

He was silent a moment, but eventually nodded. "Good. Let's keep it like that." Getting off the bed, he snagged his pants from the floor. "It'll take about three days to sort out the Spencer brand. You should plan on riding over about then."

"I will." Her eyes followed him as he dressed. She would get up after he left and bathe before she donned her clothing.

Choice was ready but seemed reluctant to go. "I wish there was somewhere to meet before the sheep are sold."

"I do, too."

He stood at the door. "Well, see ya."

She smiled. "Soon." He was almost through the door. "Choice? What about the Spencers' old soddy? It's probably horribly dusty, but I could ride out and pick it up a bit. We could bring blankets and build a fire. It has a good fireplace."

Choice hurried across the room to kiss her again. "When?"

"Tomorrow night?"

"Perfect. I'll see you there tomorrow night. Around eight?"

"Perfect," she echoed. As he was leaving, she added, "I'll bring the money I promised to pay your men along with me. You can pass it on to them."

Riding home later, Amanda gloried in the satisfaction within herself. She wasn't only physically satisfied in a way she'd never before experienced, but her emotions had settled down so much she could hardly believe it. The trials and tribulations of the past few weeks seemed unimportant today, when rationally she knew they were anything but.

Still, things were falling into place. Once the sheep were gone, she shouldn't have any trouble in locating new ranch hands. She would take Jess on again, she realized, but not Woody and Buck. Jess had been straightforward and honest with her, while the other two had slunk away like thieves in the night. Even though she had been away from the ranch that day, they could have waited and talked to her before walking off the job.

As for Wes Schuyler and his attempts to coerce her, there was little she could do beyond ignoring the man's existence. A formal, explicit complaint to the association would garner little aid from her neighbors, and one to the sheriff even less.

She was relieved that she hadn't told Choice about the bullet that had narrowly missed her. The thought of Choice involved in hostility of any form was unbelievably frightening. It was entirely possible that she was in love with him, Amanda pondered, although that, too, seemed rather unimportant. She had what she wanted, maybe what she had always wanted, complete freedom, an independence that could only grow stronger, and enough maturity to deal with a strong-willed lover. She was an extremely fortunate woman.

From the same knobby knoll he had watched Amanda from yesterday, Choice sat on Bolo and squinted at the speck of movement on the range below, which he knew was her and Ginger going home.

He couldn't see her, even indistinctly, without reliving last night and this morning. He'd nearly blurted out another marriage proposal, damn his impulsiveness! And after vowing repeatedly to steer clear of the subject, too.

She had stopped him in time, apparently sensing his intention. She was beautiful and sensual and exciting beyond his own vivid imagination, but she withheld part of herself. Who had taught whom last night was not precisely clear; Amanda might have learned of her own capacity for physical adventure, but he, too, had learned a few things. For one, she was not anywhere close to wanting a second marriage.

The knowledge, so clear and undoubtable in his mind, created a surprising discomfort. A man knew when a woman was maneuvering the conversation around to a certain subject, like marriage, for instance, and she hadn't. Not once. If she had so much as hinted at something lasting between them, something beyond murmured references to clandestine meetings to make love, he probably would have forgotten every vow and begged her to marry him.

Probably? Choice shook his head in self-disgust. Hell, he'd nearly brought it up *without* a hint this morning. Last night he'd been so dizzy-headed, it was a wonder he'd known which end was up.

Choice frowned. Maybe he hadn't known which end was up. Maybe he still didn't.

The truth was, Amanda had him going in emotional circles. He knew he would do just about anything for her. Like he'd told her, she was in his blood.

When Amanda and Ginger were no longer in sight, Choice turned Bolo's head toward the herd of cattle. He had work to do, and he would live through it with the thought of seeing Amanda tomorrow night. He wasn't a thousand percent satisfied with things as they stood right now with her, but he wasn't unhappy about them, either. Who knew what the future might bring?

Amanda tended to Ginger, then walked to the house. Lucy opened the door for her. "You stayed at the Brenton ranch all night?"

"I told you I might." Amanda smiled contentedly. "Choice and I have . . . an understanding now."

"Did he agree to include the sheep in the drive to the railroad?"

They went into the house and Lucy closed the door. "Yes, he agreed. It will take about a week before everything's ready for the trek."

Lucy sat down. "Oh, Amanda, I'm so relieved."

"I am, too, Lucy. Where's Tad?"

"Napping. He slept restlessly last night."

Amanda became alarmed. "You didn't have any trouble, did you?"

"No, everything was quiet. Amanda, I've been thinking about something. When the sheep are sold, I want to give you half the money."

"Half! Whatever for?"

"For everything you've done for me and the children. What would have happened to us without you? No one else cared that we had nothing."

Amanda walked over to her friend. "Lucy, almost anyone in the valley would have given you shelter. I'm not close to my neighbors, but most of them are very decent people. There are just some lines they won't cross, and a herd of sheep is one of them."

"You're very fair-minded. I'm not sure I could ever be that generous."

"That's your right. You've had a harrowing experience and . . ." Frowning slightly, Amanda took the nearest chair.

She had ignored Lucy's silence the best she could for as long as she could. Now she felt the subject welling, demanding discussion. "Lucy, I've tried to curb my curiosity for your sake, but I have so many questions about that night."

The woman's gaze slid away from Amanda's. "It was horrible."

"I'm sure it was. Will you tell me about it? Please?"

Lucy got up and went to the window, standing with her back to Amanda. "I...don't remember much. I was struck and knocked unconscious. When I came to..." Her voice dropped to a whisper. "I don't like thinking about it."

Amanda sighed. She wanted to hear Lucy's story from her own lips in the worst way, but forcing it out of her would require more selfishness than Amanda possessed, especially today. "I'm sorry, Lucy. You don't have to talk about it. I shouldn't have asked."

Lucy turned and Amanda could see the telltale moisture in the woman's pale blue eyes. "You're the nicest person I've ever known, Amanda, and I want you to have part of the money from the sale of the sheep."

Rising, Amanda went over to Lucy and put her arms around her. "No, Lucy. That money will give you and Tad and Elizabeth a new start. I don't need it and I will not take it."

"We're eating your food."

"The little you and Tad eat will never be missed. Don't even think about repayment."

That afternoon, Amanda saddled Ginger, loaded another horse with blankets, a feather bed, cleaning supplies and some firewood, and rode toward the old soddy. The Spencers had chosen a different location for their second house, and the soddy was nearly a mile away from the present homesite.

Thinking about tomorrow night made Amanda's heart beat faster. She would clean the soddy, lay a fire in the fireplace and prepare a comfortable bed for her and Choice. They would meet there until after the sheep and cattle were sold, then, when Lucy and the children had departed for Pennsylvania, Choice could come to the house. All during the long, mostly idle months of winter, he would share her bed, her table. They would make love with blizzards battering the house and snuggle beneath warm blankets during the dark stormy nights.

Last night was like a beautiful dream. No, not a dream, not when it was the most real thing that had ever happened to her. She had come alive last night, and little that went on between men and women would ever have the power to shock her again. Choice functioned on a completely primal level, without shame or modesty, and he'd drawn the same propensity from her.

Amanda realized that she was happier than she had ever been. Her system was buzzing with elation, with eagerness for tomorrow night. She saw a rosy, exciting future, and startled herself by laughing out of pure joy. Ginger pricked up her ears at the sound, and Amanda leaned forward and petted the horse's neck. "It's only me, Ginger. Me, being happy, my good and faithful friend."

Chapter Nineteen

That night the Spencer household settled down early. Cleaning the soddy had sapped Amanda's strength, which already had been depleted by her nearly sleepless night in Choice's bed.

Lying in her bed after the lamp had been extinguished, Amanda listened to the wind beyond the walls of the house and thought about tomorrow night. The soddy was as ready for the tryst as was possible, considering its state of decay. Weathered and eroded boards covered the two windows of the structure, as the glass panes had long ago been removed for use in the Spencers' second home. There were no furnishings, and the soddy's well, dug so many years ago, had caved in during one violent spring storm.

But...one match would start the tinder-dry brush and wood Amanda had arranged in the cavity of the fieldstone fireplace. The walls and floor had been swept clean of cobwebs and dust, and the feather bed and blankets had been spread out very near the hearth.

Tomorrow night she would feel Choice's hands and mouth on her skin again. She would see the splendor of his body again, feel the exquisite torture of his touch. He was a fever in her blood, raising her temperature by memory, creating a yearning for the hours until tomorrow night to fly. She would bathe and wash her hair and soften her skin with lilac-scented lotion. She would tell Lucy not to expect her home until the next morning, and she would not worry about what Lucy or anyone else might think of a woman who stayed out all night with a man.

Amanda's eyes drifted shut, but opened almost at once when baby Elizabeth whimpered in the next room. With the now familiar sound came a thought—a baby. Yes, it was entirely possible. She hadn't become pregnant during her marriage, but such uninhibited behavior with Choice could result in a child, particularly when she hoped for their physical relationship to go on and on.

A child born out of wedlock was no trivial matter, even in this enlightened age. As isolated as the ranch was, word would get around. Wes Schuyler had been accurate on one point—news seemed to travel on the wind.

Amanda stared into the dark with an increased heartbeat. She could never be unhappy about a child, whatever the circumstances. A baby of her own, to love and bathe and care for, as she did with Elizabeth when Lucy was otherwise occupied. No, a child would never bring her unhappiness or regret.

But what about Choice? How would he feel about parenthood? Did he even like children? Did he privately harbor a hope to have a child of his own someday?

Perhaps tomorrow night she would broach the subject. Cautiously, of course. Subtly. Just to hear how he felt about children in general.

The wind howled with a strange mournfulness. It was a cold wind, rife with reminders of the snow already in the mountains. This was going to be a hard winter, Amanda felt. The animals' coats were becoming unusually thick. The brush and trees on the ranch seemed to shiver as their leaves fell away in the path of the blustering wind. The weather had changed quickly, which was not abnormal, but it seemed earlier than usual.

She would dress warmly for the ride to the soddy tomorrow night, and plan her arrival for seven rather than eight so she could ignite the fire. When Choice got there, he would be greeted by the glowing warmth and light of the fireplace. And with kisses, and with all the intimacy he could ever want.

Amanda's eyes closed, and she drifted off to sleep with her thoughts a mile away in a deserted one-room sod house, with a fireplace awaiting a match and a feather bed awaiting lovers.

It was a lovely dream. Amanda was kneeling before a fireplace seemingly golden in color, holding a match. Her clothing felt soft and ethereal. Her hair was a cloud around her face. She was unutterably happy, smiling...

But she hadn't lit the fire yet and she could smell smoke.

Her eyes opened as the dream faded to reality. *Smoke!* "Oh, my God!" she cried, and leaped out of bed. Frantically, she ran from her bedroom. The house was filled with smoke! "Lucy! Wake up! There's a fire!"

But where? She could see no flames. Amanda dashed to the kitchen, found only smoke, then to the parlor door, which she yanked open. The heat and fumes of an angry blaze drove her back. Terror filled her heart, and she slammed the door shut and ran to Lucy's room. "Lucy, wake up! Hurry! We must get the children out!"

Everything was dark. The smoke was burning Amanda's eyes. Lucy coughed and struggled out of bed. "Wrap them in blankets! It's cold out," Amanda instructed, then added, "hurry, Lucy, hurry!"

Lucy grabbed a blanket off the bed and wrapped it around Tad. Amanda did the same with Elizabeth. "Through the kitchen, Lucy. Follow me. Stay close."

The two women stumbled through the house. They were barefoot and in nightclothes, and the freezing wind struck without mercy as they ran outside. "To the barn," Amanda shouted, realizing that the fire was noisy in its consumption of her precious home. "Here, take Elizabeth. Tad must walk, Lucy. I have to go back inside."

Lucy's face was wild with fear. "Amanda...please...you shouldn't go back."

"Go! To the barn, Lucy. There's no time to argue!" She shoved Elizabeth at her mother. "Stay with the children! Keep them safe!"

Spinning, Amanda entered the house. The smoke was thicker, and she could hear the crackling of flames. She ran to her bedroom and shoved her icy feet into slippers, then hurriedly yanked the window open. Through it, she tossed blankets, shoes, dresses, trousers, anything she could reach quickly, including her rifle and money box, as far from the house as she could throw them.

Then she raced to Lucy's room and opened the window. Baby clothes went sailing through it, Tad's things, Lucy's few garments. Amanda's eyes were tearing, stinging from the smoke. What else? she thought frantically. What else should she try to save?

Flames broke through the bedroom wall in a mad rush, hissing and spewing. There was no more time. She had to get out.

Feeling her way, Amanda made it to the kitchen door and lunged through it. Wheezing and gasping for air, she started around the burning building to where she had thrown out the items. Quickly she gathered things and carried them away from the fire.

Then, quite suddenly, there was nothing left for her to do except watch the flames. She stood back, away from the searing heat of the inferno, her eyes dull and vacant, her heart feeling like a stone in her body.

Her beautiful house, burning. Why? How had it happened? They hadn't been using the parlor, and she had kept the door closed to avoid heating the room.

The sound of hooves barely penetrated Amanda's lethargy. Without warning, seemingly out of nowhere, two riders bore down on the scene. Amanda turned just as the horses sped past her, and she saw a face she thought she recognized—Rocky, the man who had been with Wes the day she visited the Schuyler ranch.

Belatedly, but with too much adrenaline overwhelming her system to stand there and do nothing, Amanda ran for her rifle. She cocked it and fired into the night, once, twice, three times.

Lucy shrieked from the barn. "Amanda! Amanda!"

"I'm all right! Stay with the children!" Amanda shouted, then sank to her knees, tears of defeat coursing down her sooty cheeks. The wind was whipping the flames, which, despite the enormous draft, were starting to slow down. The house was about gone, and the sheds were too far away to be in danger. Amanda's eyes rose to a burning cottonwood, another hapless victim of Schuyler's treachery.

Amanda wept bitterly, her head down, her face covered by her hands. She sensed movement behind her and looked up to see Lucy huddling beneath a blanket. "Are the children all right?"

"They're safe." Lucy's eyes were on the dying fire. The roof of the house and most of the walls were gone. It would take time for every last piece of wood to be consumed, but nothing would be saved. "What were you shooting at?"

"Two men," Amanda replied dully.

"Oh, dear Lord! Then the fire was deliberately set?"

"Yes." She heard a rush of great choking sobs from Lucy. Wearily, Amanda got to her feet. "I managed to throw out a few things. Come, Lucy, help me carry them to the barn."

Together the two women toted what Amanda had saved down to the barn. Lucy was relieved to see her shoes and some of the children's clothing. She wept as she worked, but Amanda did not. Amanda felt as if there was ice in her veins instead of blood.

In the barn, she saw that Tad was lying beside his baby sister in a pile of hay. Lucy had located a lantern and matches to light it with. The children were very quiet. Elizabeth had stayed asleep and Tad was barely awake, his eyes heavy and drowsy.

They were both safe and warm in their blankets, which put one small spark of gladness in Amanda's ravaged soul. She began rummaging through the clothing she had saved and found a pair of trousers and a shirt. "Get dressed, Lucy. We have enough blankets to keep warm for the rest of the night, but clothing will help." Lucy couldn't seem to stop crying, and Amanda had no words of comfort to offer her. She turned away and pulled the pants and shirt on over her nightgown.

Then, with a blanket around her shoulders, she went to the door of the barn and looked at the house. Gone. It didn't seem possible. She didn't seem able to think clearly. Her body felt numb. *The piano!* For some reason her mind focused on the spinet. Len's mother had played, he'd told her proudly. Amanda sometimes picked out tunes with one finger. It wasn't her musical ability that made the loss of the piano so painful, it was the beautiful instrument itself, sitting in the parlor, polished and cared for with so much pride.

The Spencer family photo album. Letters. The ranch's financial records. A large and valuable set of Spode china. Her gold wedding band. Len's gold pocket watch, which had been his father's. Clothing, dishes, furniture, books. So many books. Her collection had included a complete set of Shakespeare and an old and precious Bible.

All gone, everything gone, melted and seared and...gone.

The enormity of it settled upon Amanda like a weight. Clutching the blanket, she stood at the barn door and watched the fire. Flames shot here and there, but they were smaller, less potent, their appetite curbed by the growing lack of fresh fuel.

Behind her Lucy continued to sob, even after she had fallen into an exhausted sleep with her arms around her children.

Nothing remained of the house except some charred, slowly burning timbers. Embers glowed in the dark, eerie and sparking from the wind. An occasional finger of flame shot up, only to die down again.

Amanda couldn't think about morning, let alone next week, next month, the winter ahead. She couldn't ask herself what she would do now. Her mind was centered on the ghostly remains of her house. Her will to survive had seemingly been destroyed with her home.

Gradually a sound penetrated her despondency—the distant beating of hooves. Quite calmly, Amanda picked up the rifle, and when the sound got closer, she raised the weapon to her shoulder.

Voices reached her ears, ringing of fearful speculation. The horses were being ridden hard, blowing and heaving. One voice, deep and gruff, was familiar. *"Amanda!"*

She lowered the rifle as the horses galloped into her line of vision. Leaning the gun against the wall, she stepped through the barn door. "I'm here, Choice."

The riders pulled their horses up, and the animals milled and stamped and blew. Choice hit the ground running and grabbed Amanda into a fierce embrace. "We saw the flames clear over to my place."

"It's gone, Choice. My house is gone."

He held her and stroked her hair. "I know, honey, I know. Are you all right? Are you hurt?"

"I'm not . . . hurt." It was such an inane statement, when she was hurting so bad, she wanted to die.

"What about the McMillans?"

"They're all right, too." Amanda could see Choice's men walking to the fire. They were talking in hushed tones, the way people spoke to one another at funerals.

That's what it felt like to Amanda, like death and grief and anguish. She clung to Choice and suffered the scorching heat of bitter tears again. For a few torturous moments she wasn't able to speak, but there was hatred in her heart, and it finally came spewing out.

"I saw one of the men who did this," she said with acrid resentment.

Choice stiffened, then took her shoulders and held her away from him to see her face. "Are you saying the fire wasn't an accident?"

"That's exactly what I'm saying. There were two men. They rode right past me. I recognized one of them. His name is Rocky, and he works for Wes Schuyler. I saw him the day I went to Schuyler's ranch." She could feel Choice's steely response, the way his body was tightening. But she couldn't stop herself from spilling it all.

"Someone took a shot at me, too, when I was riding home that day. Ginger didn't just throw me without good cause. A bullet barely missed us."

"Are you certain, Amanda?"

"I'm deadly certain."

Choice let go of her abruptly and walked away. His mind was seething. He would pay Wes Schuyler a visit. But he couldn't leave two women and two babies huddling in a cold barn while he did what he should have done weeks ago.

Amanda was beginning to comprehend what was going through Choice's mind. The rigid set of his shoulders conveyed a fury just barely contained. She put a hand to her mouth in horror while fear gathered like a fist in her stomach. "No...Choice...I didn't tell you everything because I want revenge!"

His voice fell like shards of ice. "Get Lucy and the children. You're all coming to my place. I'll hitch up the wagon." He strode toward the shed that housed Amanda's wagon.

She stumbled after him. "Wait! Choice, I don't want you going after Schuyler!"

He turned sharply, holding up a hand as if to warn her. "Save your breath. I'm taking you to my house, then I'm going to see Schuyler. This goddamn mess has gone far enough. Now go and get ready, if there's any gettin' ready to do."

Stunned, Amanda stood and watched his purposeful stride to the wagon shed. She'd caused this, her willfulness, her pride, her stupid damned determination to function independently! Being right wasn't enough when dealing with people of Wes Schuyler's caliber.

Her knees were suddenly shaking. "I don't want you hurt," she whispered as Choice disappeared through the small door of the shed. In seconds, the much larger wagon door was dragged open. Some of Choice's men ran to help him, and she could hear Choice telling them that he was planning to take Amanda and the McMillan family to his house.

Amanda turned away and started for the barn on instinct alone. Her mind was dazed, with too many images and disjointed thoughts darting every which way to make sense of any one of them.

Lucy was standing at the barn door. "I heard," she said in a choked, tear-clogged voice. "Shall we bring the things you saved?"

"Yes," Amanda said wearily. "We'll bundle Tad and Elizabeth in the blankets. It's getting colder out."

* * *

Choice drove the wagon. Lucy and the children were in the back, but Amanda rode on the seat beside Choice. The Brenton ranch hands trailed behind, alert to possible trouble.

The caravan passed sheep, cattle and property lines. "Do you know what time it is?" Amanda asked.

"Around midnight."

"How did you happen to see the fire?"

"One of the men spotted it."

"Choice, it won't do any good to confront Schuyler."

"Maybe, maybe not."

"I don't want you to do it."

"You're entitled."

"I'm entitled to disagree, but you're going to do it anyway."

"That's right."

They were speaking quietly, trying to keep their conversation private. "Even if I begged you not to, you would do it."

"Yes, I would. I did what you asked and stayed out of it, ever since this thing started. It was a bad mistake."

That soft, deadly tone was in his voice, and Amanda closed her eyes with a wave of fearful nausea. She could easily be sick, she realized, and wished there was a hole to crawl into so she wouldn't have to face one more calamity. She had no more courage left, if she even dared to label her previous stubbornness so generously. Why had she thought she could buck a man like Wes Schuyler? She'd brought disaster on her own head, and before tonight was over, her obstinate refusal to heed Choice's many warnings could result in disaster for him, too.

"I want to talk to you when we get to the house," Choice said in an undertone. "When we're alone."

"What about?"

"Us."

Amanda's spirit crumbled, suspecting that he was going to tell her that he wanted nothing more to do with her. The worst part of that speculation was that she couldn't fault him for it. Why would any man want a woman who constantly caused him to worry and fret about her well-being? He probably doubted her good sense, probably wondered if she even had any. Just because he had made love to her all of last night didn't guarantee anything. Suspecting that he had almost proposed marriage this morning guaranteed nothing, either. She could have been wrong, or Choice could have changed his mind.

God, if only she could just disappear. How could a person feel so miserable and still remain upright? Choice's renunciation would be the final straw. She simply could not take any more.

Or could she? Oddly, that progression of thought put a little starch in Amanda's spine. She had thought every speck of her normal pride had been crushed out of her, but she still had enough left to lift her chin and pretend that she didn't care if he dropped her like a hot potato.

Everything became bustling activity when they reached the Brenton homestead. The men carried Amanda's and Lucy's things into the house. The women carried in the sleeping children. Choice assigned bedrooms, then drew his men off in a corner to speak in voices too low for her to hear.

After the men left the house and Lucy was busy settling Tad and Elizabeth into bed, Choice crooked a finger at Amanda, beckoning her into his room. She entered with her head high when what she wanted to do was sink into some dark corner and cry until she passed out.

Choice closed the bedroom door. "I'll be leaving in a few minutes. I want to tell you something first."

"Fine, go right ahead."

"It came to me, clear as a bell, while I was riding hell-bent for leather for your place, thinking you might have been caught in that fire. I've thought about it before, wondered about it. But I don't need to wonder anymore. I love you, Amanda. I never thought I'd ever say that to anyone. No one's ever said it to me, but that's the way it is. I love you. You might not want to hear it, but I wanted you to know."

He took her face between his hands and kissed her mouth. "Get some sleep. I'll see you sometime tomorrow."

Amanda stood there, seemingly frozen, while he walked out of the room. Nothing seemed to be working, not her legs, not her brain. Her hands slowly rose to her temples, and she massaged the tension there with trembling fingertips.

Then, in a burst of life, she raced through the house after Choice, calling his name. "Wait! Please wait!" The rooms were empty, and she sped through the Brenton kitchen to the back door.

She was too late. Choice was mounted, as were his men, and riding away. Frantic, disoriented, Amanda ran inside, and then out again. There were horses in the corral. Unfamiliar with the Brenton place, she wasn't sure where she might find a saddle.

But she could ride bareback, if necessary. She had to go after Choice, make him see the danger he could be riding toward. Wes Schuyler was no fool, and if his directive had caused the fire, he might be expecting some sort of retribution. A gun battle was entirely possible. Choice and his men could be riding into a trap!

Amanda dashed back into the house to where her rifle had been piled with her other meager possessions. Her panicked gaze probed the nooks and crannies of the room. Somewhere Choice had to have extra bullets. She ran from room to room, and finally located some cartridges that would fit her rifle in a small drawer of a bureau. Grabbing a handful, she filled her pockets.

"Amanda?"

Glancing over her shoulder, Amanda saw Lucy in the doorway. "I'm going after Choice."

"Amanda..."

Amanda started from the room. "Go to bed, Lucy. You look ready to drop. Get some sleep. The children will need you in the morning." She was going to walk past Lucy, but the woman looked ready to keel over. Her face was blotchy and swollen from weeping, and tears were still dripping down her cheeks. "Oh, Lucy," she sighed, enfolding the woman in her arms.

She hugged her then stepped back quickly. "I've got to go. We'll talk tomorrow."

"Amanda, I...I have to tell you something."

"Not tonight, Lucy, please. Choice..."

Lucy grabbed her arm. "You must listen!"

The strange, almost feral gleam in Lucy's pale blue eyes alarmed Amanda. But Choice was getting farther away with every tick of the clock.

Amanda slumped against the wall. She wouldn't be able to catch up with Choice in the dark, not even if she was positive which route he had taken to the Schuyler ranch. He was more than likely riding into a trap, and dear God, she loved him. Loved him madly. She'd known before this, but perhaps she hadn't really faced it. He, too, had been reluctant to mention love. But he did love her, he'd said so, and for a moment, a dizzying joy ricocheted through her system.

She closed her eyes, blocking out Lucy's nearly hysterical face. Whatever was troubling Lucy couldn't possibly be as bad as Amanda's worry about Choice and Wes Schuyler going head to head.

Lucy's rhythmic sobs reached Amanda's subconscious, and wearily, she opened her eyes and pushed away from the wall. "All right. What is it?"

"I...I have to tell you something."

"Yes, I understand. I'm listening."

"It's about..." Lucy reeled, on the verge of collapse, Amanda saw. Quickly she put an arm around the distraught woman and led her to a chair.

"Lucy, you must calm yourself," she said soothingly, wondering where she was finding the strength to face one more problem.

"Calm myself? After all I've put you through? I'll never forgive myself, Amanda, never!" Lucy fell back against the chair, sobbing wildly again.

Amanda kneeled beside the chair. "You're blaming yourself for the fire, aren't you? What can I say to make you feel better? Lucy, Choice warned me repeatedly and still I wouldn't believe that anyone could be so full of hate for sheep that they would go out of their way to harm me. That's not your fault. I should have heeded Choice's warnings. I could have done differently than I did. For one thing, when I still had three men to help me, I should have immediately driven your sheep out of the valley and protected them elsewhere instead of moving them in closer. Then—"

"No! I will not let you take any of the blame! You've been kind and generous and...trusting. Oh, Amanda." Fresh tears flooded Lucy's eyes. "I have misled you so horribly."

A chill prickled Amanda's spine. "About what, Lucy? How have you misled me?"

Lucy dropped her head forward and looked at her tightly clasped hands. "I let...encouraged you to...believe that the men who hazed the sheep also killed..."

Dry-mouthed, Amanda waited. Choice had intimated something like this, and she had wondered about Lucy's reluctance to talk about her husband's death.

Oh, Lord, yesterday seemed ten years off. She'd been so happy riding home, so excited about preparing the soddy.

A sudden rush of hope surprised her. She would be happy again. With Choice beside her and loving her...

Amanda choked on a prayer and turned her thoughts to Lucy. "The men didn't kill Jed, did they?"

Lucy hesitated then gave her head a small shake. She was still looking down, as though unable to face Amanda.

"Tell me about it," Amanda said gently.

"Jed was a...violent man," Lucy whispered. "He had a fierce temper and often took it out on...me. I was accustomed to..."

"He gave you that bruise on your face."

"Yes. We were all sleeping and were awakened by shouts and laughter and the sounds of the sheep running. It was obvious what was happening, that some men on horseback were chasing and scattering the animals. Then there were some gunshots. Jed grabbed his rifle and ran outside. I could hear him yelling curses and shooting. Amanda, I think he shot the horse himself. By accident. It was so dark, and there was a lot of dust. I opened the door a crack and tried to see out. The men were riding off and Jed was shooting at them. The horse had panicked and was bucking and running in circles, and then it just fell over.

"Jed screamed obscenities and shook his fist at the riders, but they were already too far away to even see anymore. I closed the door. The babies were crying. The wagon was pitch-black, and I lit a lantern to tend to the children.

"Jed came in, shouting vile words, so enraged he kicked everything that got in his way. There was little room to move in the wagon. I was trying to comfort the babies. Elizabeth was bawling, little Tad was up and clinging to my nightgown. I was holding Elizabeth and trying to stay out of Jed's way, but he was roaring around and it was impossible. He...struck me...very hard...and I fell back on the bed. For a minute I went black. Elizabeth rolled out of my arms to the bed, and Tad was crying and trying to climb up on it.

"It all happened so quickly then. I saw Tad slip and fall. Jed grabbed him by the arm and cursed him and called him a mama's boy, a sissy, and then he kicked him.

"I didn't think about anything but protecting Tad. A knife lay within reach, and I grabbed it and went after Jed. I could take any amount of punishment myself, but Tad never deserved the kind of treatment he got from his father."

Lucy drew a long, forlorn breath. "I don't think I meant to kill him. I only knew I had to stop him from hurting Tad. Jed's face was almost purple with rage. His eyes looked insane. Mine probably did, too. His concentration was on Tad, and I raised the knife and..."

Lucy put her elbow on the arm of the chair and held her forehead with one hand. "When he fell, he knocked over the lantern. The flames spread quickly. I grabbed up Tad and Elizabeth and brought them outside. Then I went back in and dragged Jed out. I didn't know he was dead until he was on the ground."

Her eyes rose to Amanda's. "I was glad, Amanda. Glad he could never hurt any of us again. I felt no remorse that I had been the one to..." Her voice trailed off. "That's the story. I still have no remorse about protecting Tad—I'd do it again in a heartbeat—but I feel like dying for what I've put you through. Tonight...your house..." Lucy began to sob again. "They burned your beautiful house, just because you were kind to me. How cruel! How horrible!"

"Not because I was kind to you, Lucy. Because I didn't obey orders. Because I did what I thought I had every right to do. This is an old battle, Lucy. Sheepherders and cattlemen have gone at each other for years around here. I thought I understood it, but I didn't, not really." Amanda rose tiredly.

"Do...do you hate me?" Lucy whispered.

"Of course I don't hate you. If I had babies, I'd do anything to protect them, just as you did."

"But I lied to you."

"Maybe you had to. Don't fret anymore. Go to bed. I'm going to wait up for Choice."

Lucy slowly got to her feet. "You love him, don't you?"

Amanda nodded. "Yes, I love him."

"I want your happiness more than my own," Lucy said softly. "No one deserves happiness more than you do." She stepped closer and put her arms around Amanda. "Is he kind to you?" she whispered.

Amanda swallowed. "I think he tries to be. He cares about me, and worries." She sighed and stepped back. "Lucy, I'm almost positive that I recognized one of the men at the fire tonight. He works for Wes Schuyler. I was upset when Choice showed up tonight, and I told him about it."

Lucy's hand went to her throat. "And that's where Choice went, to confront the man?"

"I'm so frightened," Amanda said huskily.

"Don't be," Lucy said. "Choice Brenton doesn't seem to me like the sort of man who would barge into danger without caution. He wears that gun like he knows how to use it, and I'd be willing to bet anything that he knows what he's doing with it. Trust him, Amanda. If he's a good man and you love him, trust him."

Chapter Twenty

During the long night Amanda built a fire in Choice's cook-stove and heated water for a bath. Her skin and hair were sooty and smelled of smoke. She had no underwear, she discovered when she went through the pile of clothing she'd tossed out the window. After washing her hair and bathing, she put on a dress.

With a pot of coffee, she sat down to wait for Choice's return. Oddly, she was no longer despondent. The loss of her home was a shock she wouldn't easily get over, but she knew now that nothing that had happened to her in the past few weeks was as important as what she had found with Choice. The love she felt for him was like no other emotion of her life. Yes, she had loved Len, but not like this. Not with every fiber of her being, not with passion and desire and what felt like a rising fever every time Choice's image appeared in her mind. This was a complete love, she realized, a mature and eternal kind of love.

And he loved her, too. In saying those words to her, he had set some part of herself free, some bit of private restraint that she hadn't even been aware of guarding. Her last vestiges of youthful naïveté fell away while she sat in that silent house and faced her emotional growth. Choice loved her. Was it possible that he always had? With a man who didn't show his feelings easily, it was difficult to know.

His offhand marriage proposal made more sense now. Perhaps he hadn't yet faced his own feelings. She certainly hadn't, and he was much more reticent than she was.

When he returned—and he *would* return, Amanda thought fiercely—she would tell him what he meant to her, how much she loved him. Never again would she be anything but totally honest with Choice. If explanations came hard, she would somehow stammer through them. If exposing her every feeling felt like nakedness, she would overcome that lifelong reluctance, too. She needed Choice in so many ways, and there was no shame in one person needing another.

If he didn't mention marriage again, she would.

Throughout the long, bleak night, Amanda waited.

Dawn was just beginning to lighten the eastern horizon when Choice and his men pulled their horses to a halt within sight of the buildings on the Schuyler ranch. Choice issued some orders in a low, tense voice, and the group split up, with Choice going in one direction and the men going in another.

Some distance from the house, Choice dismounted and tethered Bolo to a small bush. Off to his right, he saw his men doing the same near the bunkhouse. No one spoke. Everyone knew his role. Choice moved a little closer to the house and waited until his men had reached the bunkhouse. When they went inside, he silently stole to Schuyler's house, climbed the stairs and crossed the front porch. He tried the door and found it unlocked. Locked doors were rare things in these parts, and a barricaded door might have indicated Schuyler's participation in tonight's havoc.

But nothing was guarded, not the grounds, not the house. Choice had thought it through during the long ride. Setting fire to someone's house was damned serious business. If Wes had been involved, he surely would have put some men on watch just in case Amanda sent someone to the Schuyler ranch to return the favor.

The truth was, Choice wasn't completely convinced that Schuyler had done it. If it weren't for the gunshot spooking Ginger immediately after Amanda's visit to the Schuyler ranch, Choice wouldn't know what to think right now. Someone had deliberately set the fire; Amanda seeing those two men afterward was proof of that. But here he was, standing on Wes Schuyler's front porch, and Brenton men were in Schuyler's own bunkhouse. Such total unconcern on Schuyler's part looked like innocence.

Choice's jaw tightened. Maybe that's what Schuyler wanted to portray, innocence. A little conversation wouldn't hurt anyone, and it was time everyone around learned that Amanda Spencer had better be left alone. No matter what she did in the future, anyone bothering her would answer to Choice. Choice was prepared to do whatever needed doing this morning; it all hinged on Schuyler.

Choice stepped across the threshold, glanced around and listened for any noise. There was none. The household had not yet awakened. He'd been in Schuyler's house before and he remembered its layout. Moving quietly, he headed for the bedroom wing, which was the one area of the large house he wasn't familiar with.

He cautiously turned the knob on a door, opened it a crack and saw that the room was empty. A second door revealed a sleeping woman, Schuyler's sister. A third door opened onto Schuyler's room, and Choice narrowed his eyes at the snoring figure in the bed. Wes was sound asleep, as though he hadn't a care in the world. Again Choice felt some doubt.

But he was here, and he and Schuyler were going to have that little talk. It was something he should have taken care of weeks ago. Letting a problem fester rather than going at it headfirst was a mistake he wouldn't make again.

Choice slipped into the room, quietly closed the door, drew his gun and walked over to the bed.

He prodded Schuyler's bulk with the end of his pistol. "Wake up, Schuyler!"

The man turned over. "Wha . . . what? Who's there?"

"Choice Brenton."

"Choice! What the hell are you doing here?" Wes struggled to a sitting position, then saw the gun. His attitude instantly changed from belligerent to cautious. "What's going on?"

Choice pulled a chair over to the bed and sat down. "That's what I'm here to find out," he drawled, lifting one boot to his other knee and resting the gun on his thigh.

"At gunpoint?"

"Just keeping ya honest, Wes."

"My men . . ."

"Are being kept honest, too. By *my* men. This little chat won't hurt a bit."

"I don't get it. What have we got to talk about at such an ungodly hour."

Choice leaned forward slightly. "How about fires?"

"Fires!"

"Yeah, fires. You got a man named Rocky working for you?"

"Rocky Gannet? Sure, Rocky works for me. He's not here, though. Been off in the hills with a crew for three days now. You must be roundin' up your cattle, too."

"All done. So Rocky hasn't been around for three days, huh?"

"That's right. Why?"

"He was seen earlier tonight at the scene of a very nasty fire. I don't like fires, Schuyler, especially when they're deliberately set. *Especially* when they destroy the house of the woman I love."

"What woman? What the hell are you talkin' about?"

Choice sat back. "You're a fine actor, Wes. Maybe you missed your calling."

"Dammit, I'm not acting!" Schuyler threw back the blankets. He settled down again, gingerly, when the barrel of Choice's pistol raised menacingly. "You don't intend to use that thing, do you?"

"I'm deciding." Schuyler was beginning to sweat. The room was taking on a little light from the breaking dawn and Choice could see a gray film on the man's skin. "Maybe you should tell me, Wes. What kind of punishment should a man receive for torching a woman's house? Isn't that just about the lowest thing you've ever heard of?"

"Jesus, Choice."

"Are you scared, Wes? I hope so. I hope you're feeling just half the fear that Amanda must have felt when she awakened to flames." Choice's voice got lower, softer. "You son of a bitch. I could shoot you easier than I could a loco bear in the woods. At least an animal runs strictly on instinct, but a man like you functions on greed and power."

"I never meant... I never told anyone to torch her house. I swear it, Choice."

"No? What *did* you tell your men to do? Shoot at her, try to scare her? Just enough to bring her into line?"

Wes wiped his sweating brow. "I never told 'em to torch her house."

"If you were twenty years younger, I'd beat the living hell out of you. Let's get something real straight, okay? If anyone, *anyone,* bothers Amanda Spencer again, I'll shoot first and ask questions later. Got it?"

"She can't keep sheep, Choice," Wes said weakly.

"She can keep any damned thing she wants!" Choice got to his feet. "You know something, Schuyler? I've been thinking about getting a few sheep of my own."

"You wouldn't."

Choice smiled at his own lie. He didn't want anything to do with sheep, but the thought of Schuyler worrying about it was exhilarating. His smile faded. "Let's just say that if I ever do, it'll be my decision and I'll face you on it anytime you want. Do we understand one another?"

"Yeah, we understand one another."

"Good. I thought we might." Choice backed to the door.

"I didn't know you and Amanda were so . . . close."

"It's not a subject that's open to discussion. By the way, if Amanda wants her house rebuilt, I'm sure I can count on you for some materials and your men for labor, right?"

Schuyler gave a feeble nod. "That's what neighbors do around here. Did . . . did she lose everything?"

"Everything in the house."

"Then maybe we should take up a little collection, for furniture and things."

"Great idea! I'll tell her. Probably cheer her up no end." Choice holstered his weapon. "So long, Wes. Don't do something to make me come back. The next visit wouldn't be nearly so pleasant. And tell Mr. Gannet, the next time you see him, that I'd like to have a little talk with him, too."

"I'll pass it on, but he wasn't at that fire, Choice."

"Can you swear to that?"

The man looked ill. "No, I guess I can't."

"Anyone here know Rocky Gannet?" Choice asked his men when they regrouped for the ride home.

"I do," one guy replied.

"Was he in the bunkhouse?"

"Nope. There were only four men, Choice. Almost everyone's off in the hills taking care of roundup." The man chuckled. "Caught 'em off guard, didn't we?"

"That was the general idea," Choice drawled dryly.

The ride back across the valley was conducted mostly in silence. The men were tired and a few of them dozed while they rode, so inured to the saddle that they could catch a nap and still stay upright. Choice was tired, too, but had too much on his mind to shut it down completely. He thought about the conversation with Schuyler and realized that he still wasn't positive about the man's role in the night's episode. Unquestionably, Schuyler had issued a few nefarious orders to bring Amanda Spencer to her knees, but he seemed genuinely stunned to hear about the fire.

It was possible that Amanda had made a mistake in identification last night. The darkness, the shock of the fire—Amanda could have been dazed and confused. But, Choice thought, it was also possible that Gannet had gone one step further than his boss had suggested.

Whatever, it was over. Schuyler had the message now. Choice wasn't one bit worried that the man would overstep his bounds again where Amanda was concerned. A woman alone was fair game; Choice in the picture made a big difference. It might not be right, but that's the way the world functioned. It was what he'd been trying to get across to Amanda for weeks now. He shouldn't have let her objections sway him. He should have paid Schuyler a call long before this.

Thinking about Amanda brought Choice a tide of discomfiting sensations. He'd had just about enough of pussyfooting around any and every subject with Amanda. That probably was his own fault. He'd never been much of a talker, much preferring action to words.

Well, he'd had action, two very distinctly different kinds, this morning with Schuyler and with Amanda the other night. Schuyler he could forget about; Amanda was another story.

Her house was gone. Yes, it could be rebuilt. But why put time and money into another house on Spencer land when she should be sharing his as his wife?

Yes, by God, as his wife! He loved her, and a woman didn't respond to a man the way Amanda had the other night unless she had some powerful feelings for him. The minute, the *second* he got home, he was going to awaken her and tell her how he felt. Enough was enough. It was time to resolve that problem, too.

Amanda went to the kitchen window at the first sign of the approaching horses. She spotted Choice at once and admitted that she had died a thousand deaths since he'd ridden away. She had forced herself to trust, as Lucy had advised, but beneath the trust had been fear, all the same.

Her heartbeat was suddenly fast and excited. She watched Choice dismount, pass the reins of his horse to one of the men and start for the house. Dampening her lips with the tip of her tongue, she smoothed her hair.

She waited by the door. Choice came in, and she put her finger to her lips, whispering, "Lucy and the children are still sleeping."

A small, pleased grin tugged at his lips. Nodding, he took off his hat and jacket and hung them on their customary hooks. Then he clasped Amanda's hand and led her through the house to his bedroom, closing the door so carefully there wasn't even the tiniest sound.

With his dark eyes on her, he unbuckled his gun belt and placed it on the bureau. Almost holding her breath, Amanda stood by. How she loved him! Why had it taken her so long to see that, to admit it? When he opened his arms to her, she fell into them. "Oh, Choice," she whispered.

"You're all right?" His kisses were landing everywhere, on her forehead, her eyes, her mouth. His hands roamed her body, greedily, possessively. She felt warm, exquisitely female. He adored her.

"I'm fine. Hold me. Love me."

They were attempting silence so as not to awaken the McMillans. Clutching one another, they fell to the bed. As they kissed and groped wildly, the skirt of Amanda's dress was soon past her hips. Choice raised his head at the sensation of bare skin beneath his hands.

"I have no underwear," she whispered.

The pupils of his eyes seemed to contract. "Good. I like you this way." He parted her legs and began to stroke the moist female flesh between. Amanda's eyes glazed over and her breathing altered. His mouth covered hers, with his tongue seeking the velvet heat of hers. Amanda struggled to undo his belt buckle and the buttons below it.

They coupled almost savagely, dizzy with need, driven by emotion. Choice stopped long enough to unbutton the bodice of her dress, to free her breasts. Half-clothed, they strained to touch and caress. Hoarsely, raggedly, their words came in breathless phrases.

"Do that again," came rasping out of Choice. "I love you."

"I love you, too."

"Do you?"

"Yes . . . yes."

The bed was rocking. "Lucy will hear."

Amanda's head moved back and forth. Her face was flushed, her skin dewy. "I don't care who hears. Don't stop."

"I couldn't stop if I wanted to." He was moving hard and fast, feeling like the whole world was about to disintegrate into a million rapturous pieces. "Tell me you love me again."

"I love you. I love you more than life."

"And you'll marry me?"

"Yes . . . yes. I was going to ask you if you didn't ask me again."

"I'm asking."

She brought his head down for an open-mouthed kiss as completion left them both weak and trembling.

Choice lay on her, breathing hard, unable to move a muscle. Amanda's eyes were closed; it seemed to take her forever to cool down. Never had she experienced anything so forceful as Choice's lovemaking.

He finally raised his head. Her hand rose to his face. "You look tired," she whispered.

"So do you."

"It was a long night."

"You meant what you said? About loving and marrying me?"

Her fingertips softly brushed his mustache. "I meant it."

He kissed her fingers and her mouth, then separated their bodies by rolling onto his back. Amanda raised up on an elbow and looked at Choice, loving the closeness and familiarity between them.

"I fell in love with you the first time I saw you," he said softly.

Amanda's breath caught. "Choice..."

"Don't stop me from saying it. I've lived with terrible guilt, Amanda, but that doesn't make it any less true. If Len had lived, I would never have let you know how I felt. But he didn't live, and I waited a year. I thought about calling on you, but I knew you needed time to grieve. I heard that a few other men had tried to court you, and that you'd sent them packing."

There were tears in Amanda's eyes, and she attempted to smile through them. "I tried to send you packing, too, but you wouldn't listen. You're a stubborn man, thank goodness."

Choice's hand rose to her hair. "I love your hair. I used to look at it and want to touch it so bad that I ached." His eyes met hers. "You said you were afraid of me."

"Afraid of what you made me feel, I think. No man's ever reached me the way you do."

"You noticed it right away, too, didn't you? You can say it, Amanda. It's not a sin to want someone. I know you loved Len, and I know you would never have been unfaithful to him."

"I wouldn't have," she whispered. "And I did love Len, Choice. Very much. But not in the same way I love you. Maybe the good Lord designed us that way. Maybe every love is different from every other."

"I've only felt it once, Amanda. With you."

"You've really never said it to anyone else?"

"Nor heard it from anyone else. Not even from my dad. I don't remember my mother. Maybe she said it, but I was too young when she died to remember it."

"My mother is dead, too. I don't know about my dad."

Choice remembered Len telling him about Amanda's father being a miner and having deserted his daughter when she was around fifteen. "Do you want to know about him?"

Sighing, Amanda lay back. "I don't know. I think about him sometimes. He didn't love me, and sometimes that's almost impossible to accept, even after all this time."

Choice rolled over and sat up so he could see her face. "How do you know he didn't love you? Because he didn't say so?"

"A parent who loves his child doesn't just go off and forget her, Choice. He drank a lot. He probably went off in a drunken stupor and forgot I was even in the same town."

"Why don't you find out for sure?"

"How? I have no idea where he might have gone after he left Alma."

"Hire a detective."

Amanda regarded him for a moment. "Do you really think that might work?"

"It's worth a try."

"Choice, would you...love your child?"

"Are you pregnant?"

She laughed. "If I am, it's too soon to tell." Her laughter vanished. "I hope I am. I want a child very much. But..."

He took her hand and brought it to his lips. "No buts. If you want babies, then I want babies. Anything you want, Amanda, if it's in my power to give it to you, you'll have it."

"Giving me a baby is certainly within your power," she said softly.

His eyes darkened. "Yeah, it is." He lowered his face and nuzzled her breasts. "I love you so much it hurts." His head came up. "Why didn't you tell me about that gunshot the day it happened?"

"Because I didn't want you going after Schuyler."

"You don't have to worry about him anymore."

"What happened at his place?"

"Nothing much. Just some conversation. I'll be honest with you. If Schuyler had tried something, it wouldn't only have been conversation. But he took it like a gentleman."

"Did he admit...?"

"He admitted nothing."

"He's a clever man. A dangerous man."

"Not anymore. You won't be bothered again." Choice had a feeling that Rocky Gannet would quietly vanish from the scene. Schuyler probably wouldn't want the man around anymore, whether he'd torched Amanda's house or not. The fire was a terrible climax to the weeks of strife, but Choice truly felt a clearing of the air, as though everyone had settled back to normal. They might not ever know who had been at the Spencer ranch last night, but it never would have happened without Wes Schuyler causing trouble.

Choice knew his own reputation very well, and so did Schuyler. The wind had been neatly knocked out of the man's sails this morning; he'd leave Amanda alone from now on.

Amanda sighed. "I...we have one more problem, Choice. After you left last night, Lucy told me everything about the night Jed was killed."

"She did it, didn't she?"

"You knew?"

"I suspected. I think John Lawrence suspects the same thing. What did she tell you?"

Amanda relayed Lucy's story. "I believe her, Choice. Little Tad had a bad bruise on his behind when he came to my house, and Lucy's face had taken an awful blow."

"Yeah, I know. We can't just ignore it, though. She's going to have to talk to the sheriff."

"Oh, Choice."

"It can't be helped, Amanda. Lucy is going to have to stand up and tell the truth. If she was protecting her children, I'm sure the law will be lenient."

"I'll go with her. I saw those bruises and will testify in court, if necessary."

"Would you like me to go to the sheriff with you?"

"Oh, would you? Choice, it would mean so much to have you with us."

"Then it's all settled. You can tell Lucy that she's got both you and me behind her. We'll all go to Leavitt and speak to John, you, me, Lucy and the babies."

Amanda threw her arms around his neck. "Oh, I do love you. Why did I fight you so hard?"

He grinned. "Because you're an independent, stubborn lady."

"I love it when you smile. It makes you incredibly handsome."

He deliberately glowered. "You're teasing me again."

"I wasn't teasing. You are very handsome. I adore you."

He didn't laugh, and while Amanda looked into his eyes, she saw them fill with love and a suspect moisture. His head came down slowly, and his lips pressed to hers in the most tender kiss Amanda had ever received from him. From anyone. Her eyes teared, and she hugged him as hard as she could.

They looked long and deeply into one another's eyes. "We're going to be happy, Amanda."

"Yes."

"Forever and ever."

An unmistakable cry from the next room made Amanda smile. "I think Elizabeth is awake. Forever and ever might have to wait for a while."

"We'll have our own babies, Amanda."

"Yes, my love. Oh, yes!"

Epilogue

The winter had been cruel. Whole herds of cattle had perished in the prolonged subzero temperatures and fierce blizzards, and some ranchers lost everything they had worked all their lives to gain. Several people had died in the bitter cold. In one way or another, the abnormally harsh winter had tried the spirit of every rancher, homesteader and town dweller in the territory.

The Brenton and Spencer herds had not survived unscathed. Amanda was more fortunate than most, as she had sold a good portion of her stock at roundup, having made the decision to decrease her ranching responsibilities the day she and Choice were married. As it was, she still lost several hundred animals to the weather.

But the long, horrible winter was over. Spring had finally arrived, and with warm weather and the scent of plants and trees and grass coming to life, Amanda was spending a great deal of time outdoors. There were new calves and foals to inspect and a garden to plant. She moved unhurriedly these days, taking her time because of the additional bulk she was carrying. She was pregnant, with the baby due in mid-July.

For her, the winter had been a time of nesting. She had decorated a bedroom for a nursery. She had sewn curtains and ordered special items for the house from catalogues. By the last snowfall, the Brentons' home was as sparkling and as charming as the Spencer house had been.

Everything had turned out well, Amanda mused while taking a late afternoon stroll one lovely June day. Lucy had been exonerated of any crime, due to circumstances, and had gone to her sister in Pennsylvania. Choice had sold her sheep without a speck of difficulty. The buyers had been as eager to snap up good mutton as beef, apparently, which made Amanda shake her head every time she thought about it. So much trouble over a handful of sheep. When would people ever learn to live in harmony?

Actually, there was more harmony in the valley than last year, Amanda had to admit. For one thing, there was a certain amount of justice in Wes Schuyler facing bankruptcy. He had sold only a very small percentage of his herd in the fall, and his winter losses had been astronomical. Try as she might, Amanda could not drum up much sympathy for the man.

Other rumors were flying. The unusually severe winter had changed the entire face of the valley. The Lockwood ranch had been purchased by a large, brawny family that raised cattle, horses and...sheep. Every time Amanda thought about it, something giggled within her. The other ranchers were scrambling to save their own necks, Schuyler included, and were not worried about much else, least of all another herd of sheep invading their sacred ground.

Amanda expected to hear of barbed wire fences next, and the anticipation brought a smile to her lips whenever it came to mind.

Letters arrived from Lucy with pleasing regularity. She was happy in Pennsylvania and being courted by a kindhearted widower with two young sons. Tad was doing well, coming out of his shell, responding to the affections of a truly warm and considerate man. Elizabeth was growing like a weed, walking and starting to talk.

But the letter that really lightened Amanda's heart had been written by Richard Shell, the detective she had hired to uncover information about her father.

Dear Mrs. Brenton:

As you suggested, I started in Alma, Nevada and tracked your father, Hardin P. Dolan, from there. I have news of a varied nature, Mrs. Brenton. First, I'm saddened to write that Mr. Dolan died in a mining accident about a year and a half ago. But it was his own mine, as he had located and filed on a silver claim of some value. I am enclosing a copy of his Last Will and Testament, and you can see from the document that you are his only beneficiary.

You were candid in your initial correspondence, Mrs. Brenton, relating that your primary objective in locating Mr. Dolan was to uncover your father's true feelings for you, his only child. Let me say this: I have personally conversed with several of Mr. Dolan's friends, and they assured me that he spoke of you often. He had stopped drinking some years ago, and lived since with Christian charity and piety.

In summation, it appears that Mr. Dolan cared a great deal about you. I would rely on that opinion, Mrs. Brenton. People who have forgotten or have no fondness for a member of their family do not leave what they have spent their life accumulating to that person.

I took the liberty of passing on your address to James W. Boswell, the attorney who is handling your father's estate. I am sure you will be hearing from him in the very near future.

Your friend and servant,
Richard G. Shell

Although Amanda was saddened by the news of her father's death, the letter contained enough solace to give her peace. The size of her father's estate was unimportant, but the fact that he had remembered her filled her with a quiet joy. He had not had it easy, either, she remembered. He had been shattered by her mother's death. His life had been mining and mines and little else, and whiskey had probably eradicated any hope he might have once had for a better existence.

All the loose ends of her life were tied up, Amanda thought as she spotted Choice coming out of the barn. There were no longer any private points of dissension within her, no unfulfilled hopes, no uncomforted sorrows.

She waved and saw Choice wave back. They walked toward one another, the same way they had been doing every day since the weather turned decent enough for Amanda to leave the house.

A memory—strong and swift—slowed her steps. The day Choice and she had met. She could see him so clearly in her mind's eye, riding Bolo, visible in the distance then becoming more distinct. At Len's urging, she had left the porch and gone out to shake hands with the man in black. She had looked into his guarded gray eyes and held his hand and felt like she had just received a burn.

Choice believed that he had fallen in love with her at that precise moment. She had felt something, too, but her heart and mind had been full of Len, and whatever new feelings had attempted life that day had been efficiently channeled into wariness.

Amanda smiled as she waddled toward her husband. She had led Choice a merry chase. Not in the way of coy, flirtatious women, but because she had truly been put off by Choice's somber eyes and brooding personality. It was unfortunate, too, that their first personal interaction had evolved from a troublesome issue. He had laid down barely disguised orders and conveyed his disgust because she wouldn't obey, and she had rebelled at what she perceived as an encroachment on her independence.

Now she saw it for what it had really been, a dance of courtship, a series of advancements and retreats while they became more familiar with one another. While they uncovered and discovered their own feelings, while they sorted out those feelings and decided ultimately that neither of them wanted a future without the other.

Amanda knew her husband very well now. His unsmiling, serious countenance and aura of danger were who he was and not a facade. He approached responsibilities and people with complete seriousness and absolute control. His one soft spot was her, and she knew without question that he was the kind of man to give his heart only once in his lifetime.

With her he was sweet and kind and even funny at times. And so loving, so touchingly, beautifully loving. She often recalled, with gratitude, how he had taunted her into making love with him, gradually breaking down her defensive inhibitions, getting her past her own exaggerated sense of what was proper and acceptable and what was not.

Her love for Choice expanded daily. He awaited the birth of their baby with an eagerness that challenged her own. She would never forget her two years at the Spencer homestead, nor Len, but this was her home now. This was contentment, peace, security and the most profound happiness of her life.

Smiling softly, Amanda walked into her husband's waiting arms. They kissed once, twice, a third time, then, arm in arm, they strolled to the house.

* * * * *

presents
MARCH MADNESS!

Come March, we're lining up four wonderful stories by four daz-
zling newcomers—and we guarantee you won't be disappointed!
From the stark beauty of Medieval Wales to marauding *bandidos* in
Chihuahua, Mexico, return to the days of enchantment and high
adventure with characters who will touch your heart.

LOOK FOR
    STEAL THE STARS (HH #115) by *Miranda Jarrett*
    THE BANDIT'S BRIDE (HH #116) by *Ana Seymour*
    ARABESQUE (HH #117) by *Kit Gardner*
    A WARRIOR'S HEART (HH #118) by *Margaret Moore*

So rev up for spring with a bit of March Madness . . . only from
        Harlequin Historicals!

my VALENTINE 1992

Celebrate the most romantic day of the year with
MY VALENTINE 1992—a sexy new collection of four
romantic stories written by our famous Temptation
authors:

GINA WILKINS
KRISTINE ROLOFSON
JOANN ROSS
VICKI LEWIS THOMPSON

My Valentine 1992—an exquisite escape into a romantic
and sensuous world.

 Harlequin Books ®

VAL-92-R